# WRATH AND RECKONING

## A MAX KENWORTH SUSPENSE THRILLER, BOOK 3

# PATRICK PARKER

# BOOKS BY PATRICK PARKER

# CHAPTER 1

Thursday, November 17, 2016
Arlington National Cemetery
Arlington, Virginia

T HE GRAVESIDE SERVICE for Deputy Secretary of Defense Wes Brock was attended—as you would expect—by family members, politicians, members of the senior executive service, and dignitaries. Among those dignitaries were Stew and Jenny Gareth.

The afternoon sky was overcast with intermittent drizzle, making the cool day an even more solemn occasion. This was Jenny's first public outing since her failed presidential bid two weeks ago. Jenny—supported by security men holding umbrellas on either side of her—wore a raincoat. Sunglasses hid the bags under her bloodshot eyes and swollen eyelids.

Stew—the driving force behind Jenny's campaign and head of the Gareth Foundation—wore a raincoat over his black Brioni suit and held an umbrella. As the eulogy was given—emphasizing Brock's patriotism, selfless service, and accomplishments fighting terrorism—Stew's eyes studied those present and landed on Deputy Secretary of State Aaron Fitzgerald—selected to be Jenny's secretary of state—who was also more interested in the people than the ceremony. Stew followed Aaron's gaze to Acting CIA Director Jonathan Wellington—selected to be Jenny's CIA director—who, like the other two, was studying the people. Stew made eye contact with Jonathan and lifted his chin.

Wes Brock was to become the secretary of defense after Jenny's election. He had had knee surgery the month before and was progressing well toward recovery. Then, a week ago, without warning, he died. His wife found him unresponsive, and the EMTs were unable to revive him.

They noted that he exhibited signs of fentanyl overdose. His distraught wife knew he was prescribed OxyContin for pain management and denied any knowledge of him having a prescription for fentanyl.

Fentanyl-related overdose deaths had spiked in the Washington metropolitan area. Pharmaceutical fentanyl—a synthetic opioid—is similar to morphine but fifty to 100 times more potent and must be prescribed by a doctor for severe pain management, cancer, and palliative care. Most cases of fentanyl-related overdoses were from the illegal manufacture of the drug. Because of its extreme strength, it was cheaper on the streets. Heroin with the same potency as fentanyl would cost about fifty times more than fentanyl. In most overdose cases, the user was unaware that their drug of choice had been cut with fentanyl. The drug was also made into pills to look like prescription opioids like OxyContin.

Since the Brock residence was in the DC city limits, the Metropolitan Police were notified. Captain Hadley interviewed the widow and took the prescription bottle for examination.

The toxicology report at the time of his death confirmed the paramedic's suspicion and showed a high level of fentanyl. Brock's death—as one might imagine—caused the FBI, Secret Service, Defense Intelligence Agency (DIA), and DC Metropolitan Police to get involved and claim responsibility for the investigation. Even Homeland Security injected its interest so as not to be outshined by the other agencies. This was as much about politics as it was about Brock's death. The current administration was ending in about two months, and the outgoing heads of agencies were determined to cross the finish line as winners. Like the old saying: *Too many chefs spoil the stew.* But in this case, that didn't matter—the glowing marks on their reports did. The investigation surrounding Brock's death was ongoing.

As people began leaving the service, Stew stepped to one of the security men supporting Jenny and said in a low voice, "Take her back to the limousine, and I will be along in a few minutes."

Jenny didn't utter a word—it would have been incoherent if she had.

The man nodded and guided Jenny to the vehicle.

Stew turned to make eye contact with Fitzgerald and Wellington, then nodded for them to join him. Both men excused themselves from their spouses and security, then stepped toward Stew. The three moved farther away and out of eavesdropping distance.

"Jonathan," Stew said as he stopped and turned toward the two. "What do we have on Nassar and Madison?"

Anticipating what was coming, Jonathan planted his feet, took a deep breath, and said, "Both have gone to ground. We believe Nassar is in Turkey, and Madison—well, he is suspected to be in Central America somewhere."

Suppressing his anger, Stew said through gritted teeth, "Damn it, man! It's been three months, and you don't know where these two guys are? You're heading up the CIA. What the hell's wrong with your people? Madison almost blew up Manhattan with me in it. You were told to take him and Nassar out. Light a fire under your people's ass!"

Jonathan hesitated before he replied, "Yes, I know, but we're getting into the holiday season, and things are slowing down…"

Stew's face flushed as he said, "I don't give a shit if it's Christmas Day! Get those *sonsabitches.*"

Stew turned to Aaron and said, "Work with Jonathan and find that missing item before Madison tries to use it. We may not be so lucky the next time." Stew paused and stuck an unlit cigar in his mouth.

Bart Madison had led an attack on Incirlik Air Base in Turkey, and he had stolen six B61 thermonuclear bombs. Four were recovered, and Madison used one—which turned out to be a dirty bomb—in Manhattan. Stew Gareth had contracted with the terrorists for one of the nukes to be brought into the US and detonated when and where he specified. His plan was for the bomb to eliminate Jenny's opponent, which Stew believed would ensure her election. But when Madison learned that Gareth was going to set him up, he double-crossed him and attempted to detonate it in Manhattan close enough to his residence to eliminate both Gareths. Although Madison was shot in an exchange of gunfire, he managed to escape. His accomplice, a local thug, was apprehended at a bakery in Manhattan. Under interrogation, he claimed he didn't know anything about Madison, other than this guy contacted him and paid him in cash for that one job. He didn't know anything about a backup in the alley either—that was his story, and he never deviated from it.

The sixth and final nuke was believed to be under the control of the Muslim Brotherhood somewhere in the Middle East. For more than three months there had been no communications or internet traffic from the terrorists relating to the missing nuke.

"We're going to start working on Jenny's new campaign right after the new year," Stew continued, "and I want your recommendations for a replacement for Archie. I don't need another fat slob of a senator like Archie Chapman."

Aaron nodded, glanced at Jonathan, and said, "Will do."

Stew focused his attention on Jonathan and said, "Is it true that Wes died of a fentanyl overdose? Did your people do it?"

"No," Jonathan replied emphatically. "All I know is that the toxicology report shows it was fentanyl."

"I didn't know he was into drugs," Stew said with a serious look, more of a question than a statement. "If I had, I wouldn't have brought him onto the team."

"I don't believe he was," Jonathan replied. "We don't have anything to make us think otherwise. Perhaps he just needed something stronger for the pain after his surgery and got it off the street so it wouldn't be in his medical records."

Stew nodded at the answer, then said, "He was a fit guy. I didn't picture him as one to do that."

"Neither did we," Jonathan said. "It was quite a surprise. DC Police took his prescription bottle of OxyContin to have it analyzed. I talked to Captain Hadley at DC, who is working the investigation, and he said the pharmacy where Wes got the prescription filled checks out. All of the pills have been accounted for. That's all the police are saying."

"Both of you, keep me informed," Stew said. "If you find out anything else about Wes's death, get with me. Make it a priority to find Nassar and Madison. Keep everything locked down about those two and the item. If someone gets to them first, we have a big problem. As soon as you locate that one item, get with me right away. I have an idea. We'll discuss it then."

———— ·✦· ————

Friday, November 18, 2016
Headquarters, US Special Operations Command
MacDill Air Force Base, Florida

Max Kenworth, Lieutenant Colonel Andy Johnston, FBI Special Agent Gail Summers, and DIA Analyst David Elsworth sat around the walnut conference table in their work area. Mossad Intelligence Officer Danya Mayer was with them on a secure VTC (video teleconference). She had returned to Panama when all the intelligence dried up after the bombing in New York so she would be closer to her contacts there. The team suspected that since Madison had spent a lot of time there and worked for the FARC (Revolutionary Armed Forces of Colombia), he might have returned there to recover from his wounds.

Danya and Max were married on Saint Lucia Island in August and honeymooned there for ten days. Although it was their holiday and a special time for them, Madison and the missing nuke were never far from their minds. They received regular updates from the team at MacDill, and with each report, they were ready to return to Florida on a moment's notice.

Max, head of SOCOM's Nuclear Weapons Planning and Counterproliferation of Weapons of Mass Destruction, had led the discussion with the others for almost thirty minutes, bringing them up-to-date on the latest information that might lead them to the nuke or Madison. But nothing provided a clue. As the meeting was winding down, David, a senior DIA analyst, slid a copy of a newspaper article in front of Andy and said as he tapped the paper, "Did you see this? Deputy SecDef Wes Brock's funeral was yesterday."

Lieutenant Colonel Andy Johnston, DIA, slid the article closer and began reading it. He looked up and said, "Max, did you see this article on Brock's funeral?"

Max paused, then said, "No. What about it? I knew he died but haven't seen anything else."

"In the article it says he died as a result of an accidental fentanyl overdose after knee surgery," Andy said. He paused, then continued, "That seems odd to me."

"Why's that?" FBI Special Agent Gail Summers asked. "Although, it does raise the question as to why he was prescribed fentanyl and not a safer pain drug."

"That's a good question," Max replied. "Life has been a little better around here without him breathing down the SOCOM commander's neck. He was just a little too involved."

"He was to be Jenny Gareth's SecDef," Gail said. "He was probably trying to look good going out of the old administration. You know, the glowing accolades and all that shit."

With a serious expression, Max said, "Possibly...but it is odd. Gail, you thought Gareth might have had something to do with Senator Chapman's death. Do you think Brock knew too much and Gareth had him killed when Jenny lost the election?"

"I must be rubbing off on you," Gail replied with a smirk. "I wouldn't put anything past Gareth. Hell, we have a list of who not to trust inside the 495, and he's at the top."

Max looked to David and said, "Get back with NSA and see if they might have missed a transmission between Gareth and Madison or Gareth and Nassar. Have them search back to 15 July."

David scribbled on his notepad, then said, "Yes, sir. Do you want me to search around DIA and see if there's anything else on Brock's death?"

"That's not a bad idea," Max said. "No telling what you might turn up. Be discreet. Also, see if your contacts can come up with anything on Nassar." His eyes shot to Andy, and he said, "See if the CIA has put anything out on Brock. This may be a wild goose chase, but we should check. Is the CIA still blocking info out of Turkey? Contact George again, the CIA agent in Turkey, and see what he has to say."

"The CIA is still a black hole," Andy replied.

Gail laid her glasses on the table and said, "The FBI has released a condolence for Brock, but I'll dig a little deeper."

Max focused on Gail for a moment, then said, "Get with your contacts on the border and see if they'll give you an update on the cartels. Specifically, if the cartels have changed tactics or any mention of new initiatives. Even new equipment. Anything that may be a signal that Madison is working with them. Give Captain Mackenzie a call and see if the thug that was captured in Manhattan has deviated from his story. It might be worth a trip back to Manhattan to question him again."

"Marion is still pissed at me, but I'll give him a call."

David snickered when Gail referred to Captain Mackenzie as Marion.

Gail shot a stern look at David, then continued, "I'll make the rounds with my contacts again. It's worth the effort at this point." She wrote on her notepad.

Danya gave her update on Panama. She told them she had been in touch with her contacts, and they hadn't heard anything about Madison. She went on to tell them that the agreed-upon ceasefire between FARC and the Colombian government was defeated by the Colombians last month. The government negotiated a new agreement and was supposed to go before the parliament on November 30. "This could be in our favor," she said. "If they know anything about Madison, they may provide us some information as a good-faith gesture. I am not all that optimistic, though."

"It's worth a try," Max replied. "Be careful. They probably have several hardliners that don't want to go along with the peace deal and may warn Madison. They'll want something."

"I'm sure they will," Danya replied. "Both sides want an agreement, so it depends on which way the wind is blowing."

Max sat back in his chair and said, "I know you all are working hard on this. But it just seems odd to me that all intelligence has dried up. It's uncharacteristic that the terrorists are not boasting about the nuke. It is worrisome that nothing is popping up on Nassar, Madison, or the nuke. Dig deeper and turn over every rock and see what crawls out. Use your imagination and look at everything, no matter how trivial it seems. Somebody knows something; we need to find that somebody."

# CHAPTER 2

Monday, November 21, 2016
Molos Restaurant
Weehawken, New Jersey

A GENT GAIL SUMMERS had arranged, with persuasion, to meet with Captain M. Taner Mackenzie, NYPD, on neutral ground. He was still angry at her over the Manhattan incident, in which she didn't inform him in advance of the terrorist attack. She didn't want to risk a confrontation with his chief, either. She knew how to finesse Mackenzie to get him back on her side—not her customary approach, but a necessary one.

She chose Molos Restaurant for a dinner meeting, as it was located along the Hudson River with a charming view of the New York skyline through floor-to-ceiling windows. It was a well-known Mediterranean seafood restaurant with excellent reviews. She had reserved a table by the window. The tall blonde opted not to wear her usual black slacks, white shirt, and black FBI jacket, choosing gray wool trousers and a black cashmere turtleneck instead. Gail had arrived a few minutes before her reservation and was escorted to the table without delay. She wanted to be seated when Mackenzie arrived and opted to give him the full-on view of the city.

Within a few minutes, Captain Mackenzie was shown to the table. He wore slacks and a crisp shirt beneath his jacket. The broad-shouldered captain was six feet tall with reddish-blond hair cut short—an attractive man. He approached the table with determination, but his demeanor signaled his mood. He stopped at the table, and before he sat, he said, "Hello, Summers. Wanna drink?" Without waiting for her reply, he faced the waiter and said, "Bring me a bourbon."

The waiter nodded and said, "And for the lady?" He shot a look at Gail.

She replied with a smile, "Sauvignon Blanc."

Mackenzie sat, folded his arms on the table, and said, "OK, Summers, your meeting. "Whatta ya got?"

"Hello, Marion," Gail replied. Her sarcasm was thick. "How was your day?"

Mackenzie paused and took a deep breath. "Hello, Gail. You look nice."

"Thank you," she replied. "That didn't hurt, did it?"

He didn't reply, but it was obvious he wanted to.

"Could we just enjoy the view and our drinks before business?" she asked. "I've had a long day, and apparently you have too."

He checked his watch, then looked to the skyline. "Nice view."

"I thought so."

The waiter returned, set the drinks in front of them, and said, "Are you ready to order?"

"In a few minutes, please," Gail replied.

Gail struggled to engage Mackenzie in small talk to ease the tension, but she managed. At times the table fell silent. Soon she was able to extract a smile from him. She watched him empty his glass, then she said, "Are you ready to order?"

Without responding, he motioned for the waiter. They both glanced over the menu.

"Would you like to share the red snapper?" Gail asked.

"Sure," Mackenzie replied. "And the roasted lemon potatoes with wild thyme."

When the waiter arrived, Mackenzie ordered for them both and added a bottle of Sauvignon Blanc. "You would like more wine, right?" He smiled.

"Yes, thank you," she replied.

Mackenzie paused, looked her in the eyes, and said, "The mayor was all over the chief, and the chief made it clear to me how unhappy he was with you as a result of the bombing…"

"Marion," Gail said, "We'll talk business after we eat. This is a peace offering, and I don't want to spoil it."

"Ok, Gail," he replied. "Can you, *please,* call me Taner, Captain Mackenzie, or just plain Mac?"

"I can, but I like Marion much better than Taner or *Just Plain Mac. Just Plain Mac* doesn't suit you. But if you insist."

"I do."

Their conversation continued and meandered through numerous topics. As their dinner was served, Mackenzie was relaxed, and he smiled several times. She had even gotten a chuckle out of him. All the tables were filled, and the patrons were involved in their own little worlds, enjoying the ambience and fabulous food. No one paid any attention to Gail and Mackenzie. Although they both occasionally, out of habit, scanned the expanse of the dining room, they observed only a normal routine. Their main course finished, Gail made eye contact with Mackenzie as he leaned back, and she said, "*Just Plain Mac,* split a baklava with me?"

"OK, Gail," he replied and rolled his eyes. "Marion is fine."

The waiter brought the dessert and two plates. The pastry was topped with strawberries, raspberries, and a drizzle of chocolate. Gail divided the dessert, serving him first, then herself. She took a small bite and said, "Madison's accomplice at the bakery, has he provided any other information or changed his story at all? Can I interview him?"

"No, he hasn't changed anything. He's out on bail."

"Out on bail? The DA was charging him with terrorism."

"I know. The DA's politics and letting him out on bail are making our job a lot harder. We're watching him. Do you have anything on Madison?"

"Nothing new. We believe he's in Central America and we're looking for him. I need your help."

"Whatta ya need?"

"There is still a missing nuke out there. We believe it's under the control of the Muslim Brotherhood in the Middle East. Madison was, or is, out for revenge. He wants to take out the Gareths. I need you to keep your ear to the ground and see if you can turn up anything in the Muslim community. He may make another attempt at Gareth. Keep this low-key for now. Send me anything you can turn up, no matter what."

"Low-key? As in don't tell anyone unless absolutely necessary?"

"Yes, then no more than you need to. But don't say anything about the other nuke unless you call me first. Remember, there are a lot of people we don't trust."

"I don't like it. You are asking a lot."

"I know I am. We want to find the nuke and Madison outside the US, if at all possible. Are you still keeping an eye on Gareth?"

"I hope you do find him outside the US. Yes, we're still watching Gareth but can't stay on him full-time. He has others do his dirty work and doesn't leave his fingerprints on very many things."

"Can you arrange to bring in Madison's accomplice so I can interview him?"

"I doubt it, but I'll try. It'll take a couple of days. His attorney is gonna raise holy hell and accuse us of harassing him. I'll let you know."

"I appreciate your help."

"This was your treat, right?"

"Yes, Marion. I'll get the tab."

———— ✦ ————

Monday, November 22, 2016
DC Metropolitan Police
Washington, DC

Gail had taken the early flight to DC to talk to Captain Hadley, DC Police, and—since she was there—she would check in with the FBI field station. She had had many dealings with Hadley over the years and knew him to be a smart cop. He was dedicated, and obnoxious. Since he was involved in the investigation of Deputy Secretary of Defense Wes Brock's death, she believed she might be able to get some information out of him.

She marched down the hall to his office. She paused at his door and took a deep breath—she would rather eat worms than meet with Hadley. She stepped in, and his office looked unchanged—cluttered. Same as the last time she was there, but she couldn't remember when that was. Papers were strewn about his desk, the inbox overflowed, and the trash can was full—overflowing with Styrofoam coffee cups and wrappers from vending machine snacks.

Hadley looked up as she entered, leaned back in his chair, and said with a smirk, "To what honor do I attribute the presence of the FBI gracing our halls?"

"Hello, Hadley," she replied. "I need…"

"Me, right?"

"Hadley, knock it off," she replied, already wanting to smack him. "You're working on the Brock case and…"

"That's a touchy subject, doll. Yeah, I'm working it, but I'm supposed to get clearance before I release any information. The feds are jockeying for the lead, and who's in charge changes daily. I'm supposed to be in charge, but if you ask any of the agencies—take your pick—they say they are."

"I'm not here for information on Brock's death, but what I'm working on may touch on Brock. You know about the bombing in Manhattan back in July, right?"

"Yeah, that was some bad shit. I did hear you were working on that. Some special task force, right?"

"Something like that. The mercenary I was after three years ago is the same guy responsible for Manhattan. He escaped the city and dropped out of sight. We believe he is out for revenge. I'm just checking into every possibility and wanted to touch base with you to see if there could be a connection."

"Maybe we should discuss this over dinner tonight," he said as his eyes traveled up from her shoes.

"Hadley!"

"OK, sweetheart. Whatta ya want?"

"Brock's death is listed as possible fentanyl overdose."

"Well…if you ask the Secret Service or Homeland why Brock died, that would be the answer they would give you. And fentanyl overdose is certainly a possibility."

"And…you're not telling me something. Out with it, Hadley."

"Off-the-record, and I didn't tell you…" He paused, then stood, stepped to his door, and closed it. He turned back to Summers and continued. "I can't picture Brock as the kind of guy to take fentanyl, although the toxicology report confirmed it. We couldn't find evidence of the drug anywhere in the house. The only place that showed any traces of fentanyl was in his OxyContin prescription bottle. It doesn't make sense for him to mix the two. However, the drug dealers are making fentanyl look just like OxyContin pills. The pharmacy where the prescription was filled checks out. Sometime between when it was filled and when his wife found him, a tablet with fentanyl was put in there. Only his and his wife's prints were on the bottle."

"So, you don't think it was accidental?"

"I didn't say that. I did say it is possible, but my gut says something ain't right."

"What about his wife? Could she have put the pill in there?" Summers asked.

"I thought about that, and we questioned her. I even asked her if she saw one of his pills on the dresser or counter and put it back in the bottle. She denied it. No, I don't think so," he said.

"Housekeeper, landscapers, maintenance workers?"

He paused, then replied, "This is not to be released, and you didn't hear it from me. We've been interviewing them too. Nothing there." He winked. "The housekeeper has been on vacation, and we'll question her when she gets back—FBI's instructions."

"Where's she vacationing?" Summers asked.

"I know where you are going," Hadley said. "Mexico, and she *was* illegal. According to Brock's wife, she left on vacation a week before he died. The landscapers are illegal as well. Brock's wife said they haven't been inside the house and no maintenance workers have been in the house for over a month. I think it's the illegal aliens working for a government executive is why the feds are trying to keep it quiet and close the file as accidental."

"Embarrassment to the government," she said with a nod, then continued. "So, you're not going to interview her until she returns. Why not?"

"The feds. Their instructions." Hadley's eyebrows raised as his eyes rolled, signaling his disagreement.

"Give me her name and where she went. I'll check her out and get back with you, personally," Summers said.

"Hmm. That's asking a lot. The feds'll pitch a fit if they find out I gave you her information."

"Hadley," she said as she looked him in the eyes, "I just want to find out if she has any connection to Madison. I'll owe you."

He paused, fixing his eyes on hers for a moment. He then stepped to his desk, opened a folder, and scribbled on a piece of paper. He turned, handed it to her, and said, "My retirement is in your hands."

"Don't worry, Hadley. I'll take care of you."

"Right! Now, let's talk about our date."

"Hadley, *please*," she replied, her brow furrowed and the corner of her mouth wrinkled up. "If you hear anything about the mercenary, Bart Madison, or possible assassinations, let me know. Pay particular attention to what you may hear from the Muslims and cartel folks you pick up. Regardless of how small, please let me know right away."

———— • • • ————

Monday, November 22, 2016
FBI Field Office
Washington, DC

From Captain Hadley's office, Agent Summers drove to the FBI field office. There, she met with Special Agent Felix Sherard of the Counterterrorism Division—she dreaded meeting with him almost as much as with Hadley. He had worked counterterrorism for eighteen years at various offices around the country. Summers knew to be careful around him, as he had become political and was jockeying for the deputy director position at headquarters.

She endured the first five minutes of their meeting as he berated her for not notifying the New York field office or the FBI headquarters about the bombing in New York. When he finally paused, she told him she was under orders not to divulge anything on their classified operation in advance and that she wasn't sure where the terrorist planned to strike until a few days before it occurred. "This is all in my report," she said.

He puffed up and said, "Why are you here?"

"As you know, the terrorist in Manhattan got away…"

"He wouldn't have if you would've notified the Bureau."

"I'm checking out leads to see if there could be any connection between the terrorist attack and Brock's death," she replied.

"There isn't any," he said. "Brock's death was an accidental fentanyl overdose—unless you are not telling me something."

"No, I've told you everything," she replied. "We believe the terrorist, Bart Madison, is out for revenge. Since Brock was working with the Gareths and would have been the SecDef in the Gareth administration if she had won, he could have been one of Madison's targets."

"That's a big stretch, Summers."

"Possibly," she replied. "Did any of their hired help know anything?"

"No, they all check out. Stay away from this. Brock died of an accidental overdose. We believe he purchased the fentanyl on the street—for his post-op knee pain—so it wouldn't be in his records. Dumb, I know, but it looks like that's what happened. We don't need you stirring the pot and prolonging the investigation."

"Madison is on the loose and still has one nuke," she said. "If you should hear anything, no matter how small, in connection with Brock or Madison, please let me know."

"Thank you for stopping by, Summers." He picked up a piece of paper and began reading it, signaling the meeting was over.

Summers stood and walked out of his office. *Asshole*, she thought. *Protect the administration. Don't embarrass them with exposing one of their own employing illegal immigrants. No help here, no matter the cost.*

# CHAPTER 3

Wednesday, November 23, 2016
InterContinental Costa Rica at Multiplaza Mall
San José, Costa Rica

THE MUSLIM BROTHERHOOD representative, Nassar, had arranged to meet with Bart Madison in Costa Rica—at Madison's insistence. He knew that Gareth, SOCOM, the FBI, and no telling who else would be looking for him or trying to collect the reward that had been posted on him. He was aware that his estate in Venezuela was being watched, as that was where Mossad snatched his former lover, Maurine Rowen.

Madison also believed they would be watching Panama, as he had worked for the FARC for a time—an all-too-familiar place for him and the place where several meetings with Senator Chapman had been conducted. Even meeting with Nassar posed a risk for Madison, but it was one he tried to mitigate. For the past four months, Madison had fed the rumor mill that he had died as a result of gunshot wounds. More and more people began to believe the rumor, since he had not been seen. He altered his appearance by allowing his beard and hair to grow, wearing glasses, adding a wedge in his shoe to give him a limp, and sporting a variety of hats to hinder recognition. But Nassar represented a well-paying client, and this meeting was business.

The two met in Madison's suite; Nassar sat on the sofa and Madison sat on the matching upholstered wingback chair across from his guest. An ice bucket, two glasses, and a bottle of Crown Royal Reserve were on the coffee table between them. They had been talking for over a half hour when Madison leaned forward, picked up two cubes from the bucket, dropped them in one of the glasses, and poured in two fingers of whiskey. He offered the glass to Nassar, which he accepted. Then Madison fixed one for himself. He sat back and said, "Your people have done very well in keeping quiet about the nuke."

Nassar nodded and replied, "Yes, they have done well. Al-Baghdadi has been pressuring the senior Muslim Brotherhood representatives, Al'alim and al-Ghazāli, to sell him the nuke. The caliph of the Islamic State, al-Baghdadi plans to expand the fighting into Saudi Arabia, Turkey, and farther west."

"Is he wanting to use it against one of them, Israel, or the US?"

Nassar sipped his drink, then said, "I do not know. Perhaps we offer him an invitation to join us in using it against the US."

Madison's eyes narrowed, and he said, "So, that's the purpose of this meeting. You're going to invite al-Baghdadi to join you in striking the US, and you want me to plan and lead it. Am I right?"

Nassar replied with a nod, "In essence, that is correct."

"You know Gareth tried to set me up. Right now, I'm focused on payback—Gareth and his go-fers for trying to set me up, and Kenworth for being a thorn in my side. I lost blood in Manhattan because of him and his people. It'll be a bitch for all of 'em."

"We will pay you the same as last time and assist you with your revenge," Nassar replied.

"I've already started my plan. Wes Brock was the first to go down."

When I read about Brock," Nassar said, "I thought that might be you."

Madison paused, then said, "If I agree, my price is double—half up front—and I call the shots. My timeline and my sequence of targets. I deal only with you, al-Ghazāli, and Al'alim. I don't want anything to do with al-Baghdadi."

"I will discuss it with al-Ghazāli," Nassar replied. "The bomb scientist, Fiqar, inspected the nuke again. He said the one in Manhattan should have functioned properly. He believes that Kenworth caused the malfunction."

Madison took a swig of his drink and said, "Hell, I could've told him that and saved him all the trouble." Madison picked up the bottle of Crown Royal and replenished Nassar's drink, then his own.

"No one is to say anything about me or the nuke," Madison said. "That goes for al-Baghdadi as well. Make sure al-Ghazāli and Al'alim understand. They must get al-Baghdadi's word. No leaks, no bragging, no nothing about the nuke."

"I will tell al-Ghazāli. Where will you set it off?"

Madison held up a finger and said, "I'll not discuss that now. As I said, it is my decision on the place and time. Otherwise, no deal."

Nassar nodded and sipped the whiskey. "Do you have another contact in the US government? We need to ensure the borders are kept open."

Madison grinned and chuckled. Then he said, "Not to worry. They're prostitutes—give them money, a few fringe benefits, and you get what you want. I have another senator, and he's just as sleazy as Chapman was."

"Can we trust him?"

Madison grinned again, and said, "Hell no. That's the first mistake people make—never trust a politician. But he's happy right now with the money, and I've got plenty of dirt on him. He'll do as he's told."

Madison was a professional mercenary in every way. His reputation was excellent; he was the man to call on for the most difficult assignments. Accurate and complete information had been a key component for his success. His informants were chosen with extreme care, and he kept detailed notes, recordings, and photographs—using them to his advantage to get results. Politicians were his first choice, as they were the easiest—they had the information and influence Madison needed.

"I am told that the CIA is looking for me and the nuke in the Middle East," Nassar said.

"Of course they are," Madison said. "You and me. Kenworth will be focused on getting the nuke back and Gareth on killing both of us. Do as I say and we'll succeed. Otherwise, we'll be dead."

Nassar maintained his focus on Madison for a moment, then sipped his drink.

"If al-Ghazāli, and Al'alim agree to my terms," Madison said. "I will have several things for you to do."

—◆◆◆—

Thursday, November 24, 2016
Headquarters, US Special Operations Command
MacDill Air Force Base, Florida

Most Americans were observing Thanksgiving—a special day for family and friends, but not for Max and his team. As with many other military, police, and emergency service personnel, this was a duty day. Very few knew of his mission, and to this dedicated and professional team, the fewer that knew, the better. Their holiday would be observed at some later date.

Special Agent Summers, having returned from her trip, briefed Max, Andy, and David. She was frustrated with her own agency, as it was more interested in protecting the administration than finding the terrorist responsible for the Manhattan incident.

"Mackenzie in New York and Hadley in DC will help us if they turn up anything," Gail said. "Mackenzie told me that Madison's accomplice in Manhattan hasn't changed his story and is out on bail. I asked him to arrange to have him brought back in so I could question him, but he couldn't make that happen. He's watching Gareth but can't stay on him full time."

"Madison's accomplice will probably skip out or turn up dead," Max replied. "That's Madison's way."

"That's what I thought too," she replied. "Hadley, in DC, thinks something is off in the investigation into Brock's death. It's a clown show. All the agencies—FBI, Homeland, Secret Service, and anyone else that wants to flex their muscle—are jockeying for the lead. Glowing reports before the new administration takes over and all that bullshit. They're trying to close it up fast as fentanyl overdose. Hadley isn't buying it. He said that they want it closed to keep from it getting out that Brock had an illegal housekeeper—embarrassment to the government. He told me off-the-record that the housekeeper was on vacation in Mexico, and he was told to wait until she returns to question her. She left the week before Brock died."

Gail paused, then held up the paper Hadley gave her with the housekeeper's address.

"You've got her address," Andy said with a grin.

"She's in Anáhuac, Nuevo León, a small city of about seventeen thousand," she said. "I'll go down there and interview her."

Max stepped to the map on the wall and searched for the city. Within a few moments, he stepped back to the others and said, "That city is in Los Zetas territory. I want David to check it out first. I don't like it. It could be a lead, though, or a trap. Just to remind you, Los Zetas is one of the most dangerous and ruthless cartels in Mexico. They're on to everything from drugs to kidnapping. That's just the type of people Madison would team up with."

Max looked to David and said, "Get the current situation there and see what the Zetas are doing in and around the city." Max looked to Andy and said, "See if you can locate the housekeeper and what you can find out about the family."

Max looked back to Gail and said, "No one goes there until we know the situation and where the woman is located. If we go there and start asking questions, we could have the Zetas all over us. Something just doesn't feel right with this."

"You're thinking Madison?" Andy asked.

"Right," Max replied. He paused to looked to each of them, then continued, "There's a rumor going around that Madison is dead. Don't believe it for a minute. It's possible Madison has the woman watched to see who shows up to talk to her."

"Do you think Madison has the nuke there?" David asked.

"No, but he could be there, or the Zetas know where he is," Max replied. "We can't just waltz in there and ask the Zetas about him. They've infiltrated the police and government. We'll need to be very careful. If Madison is working with them, they'll keep him informed of our every move or worse."

Max looked back to Andy and said, "Anything on the Muslim Brotherhood, or ISIL?"

"The usual battlefield intelligence and rhetoric from ISIL," Andy replied. "However, I did find one thing interesting. In al-Baghdadi's recent released audio message, he said, among other things, that he plans to begin fighting in Turkey, Saudi Arabia, and farther west. I think he's telling his followers to get ready, as he has something big in store. He could have teamed up with the Muslim Brotherhood and has access to the nuke. The reference to farther west could mean he has plans to fight in the US."

"You think it's more than the usual psyops?" Max asked.

"It's possible, but based on the current situation—the missing nuke in the Middle East, Madison, Nassar, and the other Muslims that have dropped out of sight for the last four months—we should pay attention to it," Andy replied. "They've had enough time to regroup and come up with another plan."

"OK, stay on it," Max said. "He could have just tipped his hand. I'll pass this on to Danya. I've got a VTC scheduled with her in about an hour."

———◆◆◆———

Max and Danya had been on the secure VTC for ten minutes as Danya gave her update. "We've been covering all of the known locations Madison has used before, but so far, nothing," she said. We've had twenty-four-hour surveillance on his place in Venezuela, but no one has been in or out of there since we've set up." She brushed her hair back from her face. "No one has admitted seeing Madison."

"Could he have slipped in there before your team got set up?" Max asked.

"Anything is possible, but it's highly unlikely in this case," she replied.

"Andy believes al-Baghdadi is getting ready for something," Max said. "He thinks it's possible that the Brotherhood and ISIL have teamed up. Al-Baghdadi might have the nuke, which could mean Madison is about to move or already has."

Danya made a note on her pad before she responded, "I was hopeful the FARC would offer up information on Madison, but they're saying they don't have anything on him. We do have teams checking out the known locations the FARC has occupied, but it's a lot of jungle to cover."

They continued their conversation for another twelve minutes. Then, using the last few moments of the scheduled time slot for personal talk, she closed with "Happy Thanksgiving. I love you."

———— ◆ ————

2:11 p.m.

Andy sat at the conference table with Max and said, "I just found out that Brock's housekeeper is dead."

"How convenient," Max replied, not surprised at hearing the news.

"The police found her body in Plaza Juárez, the city center," Andy said. "She was shot three days ago. They don't know if it was an accident or murder. I suspect it was the latter."

"I'm betting Madison had her killed," Max said. He took a sip from his soft drink and continued, "She had served her purpose, and no one showed up to interview her, so they got rid of her."

At that moment, David joined them at the table.

Max shot a glance at him and before he could speak said, "Ask Gail to join us."

David stood up, marched to Gail's desk, and said, "Gail, dahling, Max would like you to join us at the conference table."

She looked up from her notes and said, "I'll be right there, Sweet Pea."

David turned on his heels and returned to the conference table.

Gail arrived a moment behind David and sat beside him.

David, looking at Max, said, "We're not going to Mexico, are we?"

"No plans at the present time," Max replied. "Why?"

"Anáhuac, Nuevo León, is almost lawless. Los Zetas controls the entire area, and the situation there is not good at all. Bodies are found in the street all the time. Most of them are murdered and the others are killed in the crossfire. People are terrified and afraid to leave their homes."

"Thanks, David," Max said. "Andy found out that the housekeeper is dead."

Gail laid her glasses on the table, ran her hand through her hair, then said, "That doesn't surprise me, but I thought we might have a good lead. Shit! Back to square one."

"Oh my," David said. "Now what do we do?"

"Keep watching that area," Max replied. "That cartel is a key to Madison, and possibly the nuke. Danya said that no one has admitted seeing Madison in Panama, and neither he nor anyone else has been to his house in Venezuela. I still believe he's in Central America somewhere."

"I'll let Hadley know she's dead," Gail said. "I need to stay on his good side."

"Good idea," Max said. "Remind him we need anything he hears about the Muslim Brotherhood. You should get back with Mackenzie too. Now that the woman is dead, and with al-Baghdadi's comments, I'm more inclined to think Madison is on the move. He could show up anywhere."

"The CIA is still a dead end," Andy said. "So far, DIA and NSA are still trusted assets. I'll brief our contact at NSA on our current situation. I'll remind them that we think Madison is still in Central America."

"NSA has assured me they searched their transmission captures again back to 15 July," David said, "and they've given us everything. They haven't missed a thing."

"Gareth has been too quiet," Gail said. "That seems odd to me."

Max looked at Gail and said, "Why, what are you thinking?"

"Nothing in particular," Gail replied. "I was just thinking out loud."

Max paused and thought for a moment about her comment, then looked at Andy and said, "It's been a while since you've had contact with George in Turkey. Get back with him and exchange information. He may have more info on the Brotherhood."

# CHAPTER 4

Friday, November 25, 2016
InterContinental Costa Rica at Multiplaza Mall
San José, Costa Rica

THE PHONE ON the nightstand rang, rousting Madison from sleep. He looked at the clock, then picked up his cell phone and said, "Yeah?" Recognizing Nassar's voice, he said, "Hold on just a minute." He threw the covers back and sat up.

The nude woman next to him eased her eyes open and said, "What time is it?"

"A little after five," he said as he caressed her bare back, then draped the covers over her. "Go back to sleep. This is business, I gotta take the call."

She rolled over and tugged the covers up to her neck.

Madison stepped into the adjoining room, then looked back to ensure his companion was still in bed. Satisfied that she was not interested in his call, he took a sip of water from the bottle on the coffee table, sat in the wing backed chair, and said into the phone, "OK, go ahead."

"Your terms are agreeable," came the voice. "The money will be transferred today."

"I have several things for you to do. Meet me here Monday."

"I will be there." The connection ended.

Madison stood up, stepped back into the bedroom, and paused before he slid in next to the woman. He placed his arm across her back and lay motionless as he plotted his next move. With the Brotherhood assisting him, he had a broader range of options to execute his revenge plan, which was appealing. His mind raced with possibilities and options. Wide awake, he rolled over to face the clock and saw that forty-five minutes had passed since he gotten back into bed. He threw the covers back and sat on the edge of the bed. He had a lot to do before Nassar arrived. Grasping the water bottle from the nightstand, he downed the remainder, then headed for the shower.

———• ◆ •———

Monday, November 28, 2016
InterContinental Costa Rica at Multiplaza Mall
San José, Costa Rica

Nassar, meeting again in Madison's suite, sat across from him on the sofa. Madison poured hot water into the cup over a Ceylon tea bag with mint and sage for Nassar, then poured one for himself. He set the pot down and said, "It's not Middle Eastern, but it's close."

"It will be fine." Nassar said, lifting the cup to his lips.

Madison did the same, then withdrew a slip of paper from his shirt pocket, handed it to Nassar, and said, "Take care of him. He's the one that helped me in Manhattan but got caught. That's the contact info to find him. He's out on bail and I don't want him to go to court." Madison held his eyes fixed on Nassar as he sipped his tea.

"I will take care of it," Nassar said. "Al-Ghazāli wants this completed before the new administration takes over. He believes we will miss the opportunity after they get in office."

"I told you that it must be my timeline. Now he wants to put a deadline on it? I don't like it."

"I am to provide you whatever you need," Nassar replied as he sipped his tea.

"My expenses will go up with this short of a timeline."

"That is acceptable."

Madison stood and paced around the room. A few moments later, he returned to the chair and sat. "OK, I can do it. Here's what I want you to do. Start a rumor in DC that Jenny is blaming Stew for her losing the election and she is seeking someone to assassinate him. With her husband out of the way, she will play the grieving widow and carry on as her loving husband would want. Start the rumor immediately, then monitor the progress. I want Stew to hear the rumor within the week. The next week, start another rumor that Stew knows of Jenny's plan and he has hired an assassin. I want her to hear that Stew plans to assassinate her."

"Just a rumor?" Nassar asked. "What will that do?"

"It'll eat 'em both alive and keep 'em off guard."

"You want them to hire someone to kill the other one?"

"Not necessarily, but if they do, all the better. I want 'em to expend energy focusing on each other and not me. They're so evil, they will."

Nassar lifted his eyebrows and sipped his tea.

Madison paused for a moment, then fixed his eyes on Nassar and said, "Are the two jets we took from Incirlik still in the warehouses?"

"Yes," Nassar replied, and his eyes narrowed.

"I need you to get those two planes checked out and serviced. Repaint the tail flash with WW."

"Tail flash? I do not understand."

"On the tail of the two jets you have, SP is painted on the tail. Repaint them with WW so they will look like the jets of the 13th Fighter Squadron flying out of Jordan."

"What do you want to do with them? Al'alim is going to sell them to the Iranians or Chinese."

"I know he's going to sell 'em, but I plan to use them first."

"No, Bart. Al'alim will not allow it."

"You said you are able to provide whatever I need." Madison said with a stern tone. "I need to use those planes."

"Well…I do not know. I must talk to Al'alim."

"Ok, you talk to him. I'll use 'em, then fly 'em to Iran. It'll happen in three weeks if you get me what I want."

"Three weeks?" Nassar replied. "That is not much time."

"You just got through telling me al-Ghazāli wants this finished by the time the new administration takes over. I suggest you move your ass and not let the grass grow under your feet." Madison paused, then said, "I want you to hire two American F-16 pilots for this mission. You'll be able to find a lot of them in the US, working as contractors flying F-16s."

Nassar smiled and chuckled. "You call them contractors?"

"Yeah, that's a more palatable term for the politicians than mercenary."

"We have the pilots now, the ones that flew them out of Turkey."

"No, they won't do, they're Turkish. They must be Americans."

"But American pilots will be expensive."

"If the pilots aren't Americans, they'll be discovered as hostile aircraft as soon as they open their mouths, and you will lose two F-16s. They'll be challenged by tactical air control as soon as they're identified on radar. They have to sound like Americans. Otherwise, they'll be shot down. When you hire the pilots, get 'em in country, and I'll talk with 'em."

"How much do I tell the pilots to hire them?" Nassar asked with a serious tone.

"No more than necessary. If they persist, tell 'em it's classified. That'll stop a lot of questions. They'll think they are being hired by the CIA."

"What if they ask for something official, or proof?" Nassar asked.

"They won't. But if they do, tell 'em to call the director of operations at Langley, but unfortunately, the CIA won't confirm or deny anything."

A slight smile appeared on Nassar's face.

"Just tell 'em they're being hired for one mission—to shoot down an aircraft. They'll land their jets in Iran to complete the mission. Ensure you do get 'em safe passage out of Iran and back to the US. They'll want that assurance."

Nassar nodded and said, "I understand."

"The pilots'll need information from the Air Tasking Order and the Airspace Control Order. Have someone ready to get the information from the Combined Air Operations Center, Al Udeid Air Base, Qatar. Your person must be quick and transmit it to the pilots right away. The orders will be posted and available twenty-four to forty-eight hours before the mission. I'll give you that date soon. I am expecting it from the senator."

"I will tell Al'alim."

"Get the crews on board and instruct them not to speak a word about what they are doing. I'll give you more instructions later."

"What are you planning?" Nassar asked, then sipped his tea again.

"I told you the pilots are to shoot down an aircraft, and that's all I'm saying for now. I have several things to work out first. In the meantime, identify people that can be trusted to deliver the nuke to Los Zetas. We'll use the drug routes again, and I have already coordinated with Los Zetas to take it into the US."

"What else do you need?"

"The senator told me Kenworth is in Tampa. He didn't know whether Kenworth's girlfriend was with him or not. Have someone find out if she is there or somewhere else. I'll let you know what else I need."

———— ⋅ ◆ ⋅ ————

Wednesday, November 30, 2016
Headquarters, US Special Operations Command
MacDill Air Force Base, Florida

Lieutenant Colonel Johnston and George had been on a secure phone connection for several moments with George providing the latest update. "A man matching the description of Nassar boarded a flight out of Istanbul to Bogotá on Saturday," he said. "He was traveling under an assumed name, and we lost him. I don't know his final destination. It could be Bogotá or somewhere else."

"Was he traveling alone?" Johnston asked.

"No one appeared to be with him. It's my estimation that the Brotherhood is starting to move."

"It does sound like something is going on," Johnston said. "He might be meeting with Madison. We've thought all along Madison was in Central America somewhere. Bogotá is not that far away from Madison's old stomping grounds when he was with the FARC, or his place in Venezuela."

"I won't be of any help in that area," George said. "The CIA still has things blocked off."

"Danya is in Panama and can pick it up. This is more than we have had in several months. Anything else on ISIL or the Brotherhood?"

"Nothing really outside of the battlefield intel," George replied. "There was a little spike in the internet traffic just before and over the weekend, but nothing specific. In light of the spike in traffic and al-Baghdadi's comment on the audio he released the other day about expanding his fight, I believe ISIL and the Brotherhood are getting ready to make a move. It's possible they are planning something with the nuke. Oh, there is a rumor floating around that Madison is dead."

"Don't believe it," Johnston said. "We think it's just to throw us off."

Johnston told George about Brock's housekeeper, and that she was dead. After several more minutes, he ended the call, reviewed his notes, then sat at Max's desk. "George said a man matching Nassar's description boarded a plane to Bogotá, but he didn't know his final destination," Johnston said. "He was using a phony name. I thought you might want to contact Danya."

"I'll call her. She'll want to charge out looking for him. I know I'll be wasting my breath, but I'm going to encourage her to send someone else out on this. Alert David and have him start looking in Venezuela, Colombia, and Panama. I'll prepare a message to our Special Forces teams in that area to be on the lookout for Nassar or Madison."

As Max suspected, Danya was ready to lead the charge looking for Nassar when he told her. With his urging, she agreed to coordinate the efforts of the Mossad agents in the area to locate Nassar, although the triangle of where Max suspected Madison was located was still a huge area. "No one has been to his house in Venezuela," Danya said. "We haven't turned up anything in the places he has been, but we are still searching. We are still watching the airport."

"Damn," Max said, more to himself than her. "I thought that Nassar going into the area might cause some activity. Keep me posted."

——— ◦ ◦ ◦ ———

Wednesday, November 30, 2016
Gareth Residence
New York, New York

Stew Gareth mouthed a cigar as he picked up the phone and punched in the number to Acting CIA Director Jonathan Wellington's office. As soon as Jonathan answered, Stew said, "What's the status of Nassar and Madison?"

"We still don't have a good location on either one," Jonathan replied, anticipating Stew's reaction.

"I told you two weeks ago to put a priority on finding them. What the hell is the problem?" He pulled hard on the cigar, blew the smoke upward, then took it from his mouth and held it between his first two fingers. A blue haze formed above his head.

Jonathan paused, then said, "I have people looking for them. We had a lead on Nassar but lost him."

"You lost him? Shit." Stew slammed his fist on the desk, and a large ash dropped from the cigar.

"We're covering Central America and Turkey, which is still under martial law," Jonathan said. "It takes a lot of resources and time."

"Offer up more money. I don't want to look up and see another bomb blast or bullet coming at me."

"I'll get back with you," Jonathan said, and then the phone went dead.

At that moment, Jenny appeared in the doorway to Stew's office—wearing a beige robe over her pajamas. The belt struggled to keep the robe closed. "What day is it? Do I have anything today?" she asked.

"Wednesday and no," he replied.

"Oh." Jenny made her way to the cabinet, set a tumbler on the counter with a clack, then half-filled it with Scotch. After taking a gulp, she made her way to the chair in front of Stew's desk and plopped in it.

"You need to back off that stuff," Stew said. "You haven't eaten a decent meal or bathed in over a week. I'll…"

"I need a drink. Just leave me be."

"You need to clean your ass up so we can get back out into the public," he said as he puffed the cigar.

"Why? So, I can be humiliated again?" She upended her glass and laid her head back on the chair.

Stew started to speak, then saw the glass fall from her hand. His words would be wasted.

# CHAPTER 5

Friday, December 2, 2016
La Sabana Metropolitan Park
San José, Costa Rica

S ENATOR JOSH ALEXANDER swaggered to a metal bench at the edge of the lake in the 178-acre park. He sat where he was instructed, and although a few people occupied the area, none were close enough that he could recognize. He scanned the area and waited.

The sky was populated with cumulus clouds, and the temperature was seventy-seven degrees in the Central Valley—a beautiful day in this tropical paradise. From a distant bench, with a newspaper shielding his face, Bart Madison identified the nervous senator as he entered the park and found the meeting spot. The young man—in his late thirties—wore Ray-Ban sunglasses, a trim-fit shirt, and slim-fit slacks. He fidgeted and looked around as he sat waiting for Madison. He stood out in comparison to the others.

Madison—wearing shorts, T-shirt, soft-brim hat, and sunglasses—exercised caution and studied the area, looking for anything that was out of place or signaled a threat. He wasn't about to drop his guard, as the senator could have led a bounty hunter or the authorities to him. Madison's eyes landed back on the senator. Alexander was becoming restless and fidgeted. He took a handkerchief from his pocket and dusted his already shiny shoes. He replaced it and smoothed his hair with a sweaty palm. Madison allowed several more minutes to pass and scanned the area again before he stood and walked to the senator. He sat next to him and said, "Beautiful, isn't it? The locals call the park, 'the lungs of San José.' It's the largest urban park in the country. This site was previously the location of the first international airport, and in 1977 La Sabana Metropolitan Park was dedicated."

"Spare me the history lesson. Where have you been? I was about to give up on you. We were to meet a half hour ago."

"Relax. I just made sure you were alone."

"I am," Alexander replied, his tone signaling his displeasure in waiting.

With the man's curt reply, Madison shot him a look that could have drawn blood. "I don't rush things. Do you have the itineraries I told you to bring?" He withdrew a bulging envelope from his pocket and slid it to the center of the bench, between them.

Alexander's hand went to the envelope. "What do you want them for?"

Madison's hand slammed on top of the senator's. "Don't worry about what I ask for. You just do as you're told."

Alexander got the message. He withdrew a folded sheet of paper from his shirt pocket and handed it to him.

Madison held his gaze on the man for a moment, then lifted his hand and took the paper. He read the information, then looked at his watch. "Wellington moved up his trip to 14 through 16 December, and Fitzgerald is still scheduled for Nantucket 2 through 11 December," he said. "If there is a change to any of this, you are to contact me immediately. Do you understand?"

"I do," Alexander replied.

"What is the status of the southern US border?"

"No change. Still open, and no plans to close it."

"I want you to provide me with information on what the Intelligence community is doing, specifically in the Middle East and Central America. I want to know about any significant activities. That's a complete summary each week. Do you understand?"

"I don't know. That's risky."

Madison locked his eyes on Alexander's and said, "You're on the Senate Select Committee on Intelligence and the Senate Committee on Armed Services. I just got through telling you that you're to do as you're told. You do remember me telling you that, don't you?"

Alexander dropped his head. "I understand."

"Good. The team that Max Kenworth is heading up at SOCOM that I told you about is looking for a missing nuke from Incirlik Air Base in Turkey. I want to know what he's doing. Where he goes and what he is planning."

"I'm aware of the stolen nukes from Turkey. I thought they were all recovered."

"No, one is still missing."

"The information you requested is going to be harder to get and more sensitive."

"Get the information and don't get caught."

Trying to change the subject, the senator said, "You asked about Kenworth's girlfriend. She's not with him at SOCOM. She went back to Panama. And she's not his girlfriend; they got married back in August."

Madison stood and looked down at the man as a slight smile started to appear on his face. He paused, then said, "Let's walk over to the Costa Rican Art Museum." He pointed toward the building. "It's the old airport terminal."

Alexander stood and stepped out with Madison.

"Dinner reservations are for six o'clock at the Pimento restaurant in the hotel. It's Italian," Madison said.

"Do I need to dress?"

"No, Senator. Casual is fine."

Madison kept Alexander engaged in conversation, mostly about what was happening in DC and the people's attitude. Madison listened to each thing the senator said and how he said it. To Alexander it was idle conversation, but to Madison it was intelligence gathering. As he anticipated, everyone was geared up for the holidays and little was getting accomplished. No new initiatives were being instituted. It was a typical holiday season.

———— ✦✦✦ ————

Madison sat in the spacious lobby with a glass of bourbon as he waited for Senator Alexander. People from around the world came to Costa Rica for many reasons—vacations topped the list. At this time of day, the lobby was busy with guests checking in, returning from tours and the beach, and countless other activities. As was his custom, Madison kept alert for anyone entering the hotel who might pose a threat.

Alexander exited the elevator at 6:00 p.m. He paused in front of the large mirror and gave himself the once-over, then a cursory inspection of his teeth—a ritual he observed at every opportunity. Satisfied his appearance was up to standard, he swaggered to where Madison sat. Alexander nodded and smiled at each person he passed, ready to greet anyone who might recognize him. No one did.

Madison watched the self-absorbed man and was somewhat amused. He stood, glass of bourbon in hand, as the senator neared and said, "This way." He ushered Alexander to the restaurant.

As they entered the Pimento restaurant, the maître d' greeted Madison and said, "This way, gentlemen." He escorted them to a lone table by the large window where an attractive brunette sat. Her tight, low-cut dress left nothing to the imagination. A delicate gold chain around her neck supported a small pendant suspended in her cleavage. Madison set his glass on the table, then sat next to the woman. He looked to her and said, "Nina, this is Josh Alexander."

She extended her soft, manicured hand to Alexander and said, "Senator, a pleasure to meet you."

Alexander—surprised—took her hand and replied, "The pleasure is mine."

A waiter approached and set an ice bucket with a bottle of Pinot Blanc beside the table. He filled Nina's glass, then the senator's.

Madison took a sip of his drink and said, "I have business to attend to and won't be able to stay. Enjoy your evening. I took the liberty of ordering for you." He drank the rest of the bourbon, leaned over, and kissed Nina's cheek. Then he stood and walked out of the restaurant.

⸱ ⸱ ⸱

Friday, December 2, 2016
Headquarters, US Special Operations Command
MacDill Air Force Base, Florida

At the conference table for a review of the week sat Max, Andy, Gail, and David. Danya was on a secure VTC from Panama. The paucity of information on Madison and the nuke was taking its toll on the team.

Tempers were becoming short, and people were on edge. Max and his people knew something was happening, but they didn't know what or where.

Max led off the meeting and, with his first words, revealed his frustration at their stalled progress. "OK, people, we've gone over everything countless times. We know it's uncharacteristic for ISIL or the Brotherhood to remain quiet about the nuke for so long." He gave a quick overview of the situation to date. "The Special Forces teams in Venezuela, Colombia, Panama, and Syria haven't reported any information that pertains to us—nothing on Madison or the nuke. Each of you have been busy on the phones this morning; I hope you've turned up something. Gail, whatta ya got?"

"Captain Mackenzie called me this morning. Madison's accomplice is dead. They found his body last night. There goes that possible lead."

Max nodded, wrinkled up the corner of his mouth, and said, "We thought that might happen. Has Captain Hadley picked up on anything?"

"No," Gail replied. "However, the lab believes the fentanyl that killed Wes Brock came out of Mexico. As we suspected, Hadley believes the housekeeper put the fentanyl in Brock's prescription bottle. He just can't prove it. The feds want to close the case, but he's stalling them. On another note," she continued, "my contact on the border told me one of the top lieutenants of Los Zetas has disappeared, and they've been seeing a lot of Russian arms turning up. It appears they are being supplied weapons ranging from RPGs, machine guns, pistols, and ammunition."

"Was the lieutenant killed, arrested, or what?" Max asked.

"It's doubtful he was arrested. Nothing indicates he was killed. He's just disappeared."

"This could be a sign that Madison is moving," Max replied. "He used the Zetas before and would logically use them again. The lieutenant and Madison could be meeting someplace." Max looked at the VTC screen and said, "Danya, alert your contacts in the area. The two could be meeting in your area."

Danya nodded. "Will do."

Max looked back to Gail and said, "I don't like it that they are getting Russian arms. Stay on this."

"There has been an uptick in internet traffic in the Middle East," Andy said. "George told me the CIA has a hit team after Nassar and Madison. He suspects the team is already in Turkey."

"That means we must find them first," Max replied. "The increase in internet traffic may mean the Brotherhood and ISIL are moving or have already moved the nuke." Max looked to David and said, "Keep a close eye on this."

David nodded.

"We haven't turned up anything on Nassar," Danya said. "Although I don't think he stayed in Bogotá, we're still searching the city. No one has been to Madison's house in Venezuela either. If he is in Venezuela, Colombia, or Panama, he's keeping a low profile, but I don't think he's in any of those countries."

Max covered all their leads and recapped what they had to date. Very little new information had been uncovered. Max, still frustrated at the lack of progress, ended their meeting. Danya and Max used the last few minutes of the VTC for personal communication. The others returned to their desks.

⎯⎯⎯ ◆◆◆ ⎯⎯⎯

Friday, December 2, 2016
Mossad Safe House
Balboa, Panama

Danya, at the conclusion of the VTC, went to work contacting her sources who were tied to drugs and human trafficking in the region. When she inquired about a meeting that involved several cartels, most were reluctant to talk. With some persuasion, she was able to get them to agree to notify her if they heard of such a meeting. Just as she was shutting down for the evening, she received a call. Recognizing the number, she was surprised to hear from one of her contacts so soon. Her excitement rose.

This particular person seemed to have information on what she inquired about. She had used him numerous times before. Although his information had never been wrong, Danya didn't trust him.

"That's right," came his voice through the phone. "There is a big meeting in El Salvador. I think that might be what you are looking for. Those are bad people there, and you do not want to go."

"What kind of bad people?" she asked.

"All kinds. The cartels from all over. They go there for special kinds of people."

"What do you mean?"

"The cartels that traffic in humans meet there for special requests. If a rich person or politician wants a certain type of woman, male, or even a child, the cartel goes there for them. It is, like you say, a wholesale house. They also collaborate on large drug operations. A lot of money changes hands there."

"How long are they there?"

"Who, the cartels?"

"Yes, how long are the meetings?"

"About a week or so. They have a big party and make it a holiday."

"How nice. Where in El Salvador is it? Will you take me there?"

"No, it is too dangerous. Do not go there."

Danya talked with the man for several more minutes extracting information. He was adamant that it was too dangerous to go there, and he refused. In a last attempt, she pushed harder, and he agreed to provide her directions. They arranged to meet an hour later.

———— ◆ ◆ ◆ ————

Saturday, December 3, 2016
Walled Estate
El Cuco Beach, El Salvador

Danya took an early morning flight to San Salvador, El Salvador, then drove the eighty-six miles to El Cuco Beach. She had planned to make it a quick trip—identify her target and return to Panama.

El Cuco Beach, on the Pacific coast, is a long and beautiful beach of smooth dark sands and calm waves. It is difficult to get to as the small village, by the same name, is underdeveloped and visited mainly by locals.

El Salvador, "The Land of Volcanoes," is about the size of New Jersey and has a tropical climate. The country suffers from frequent—sometimes destructive—earthquakes and volcanic activity, and it has the distinction of being the most violent nation in the Western Hemisphere. The government has been plagued by corruption. Gangs and cartels have spread into the country, resulting in high murder, extortion, and human and drug trafficking rates. It is also a transit country for illicit drugs destined for the United States.

Danya's destination was the large, walled estate that looked onto the beach from the well-manicured grounds. The sprawling house had nine bedrooms and nine bathrooms. The open floor plan had high ceilings and ceramic floors, and there was a swimming pool between the house and beach. Aside from being a beautiful estate, it was a walled compound.

By early afternoon, Danya took up a position on the beach where she could observe a large portion of the estate's back grounds and pool. People of all ages, shapes, and sizes populated the beach, doing the myriad of things you would expect—swimming, floating, boating, and playing in the water. Umbrellas dotted the shoreline. Danya had no trouble blending in. Lying beneath an umbrella, she took note of the layout of the house, posted security, catering staff, and the number of what she believed to be guests. Her objective was to identify one man— Bart Madison.

As the sun warmed her body, Danya was reminded of her wedding and honeymoon on Saint Lucia in August. She and Max had spent ten wonderful days on the island, and they vowed to return. After allowing herself a few minutes of mental escape, she snapped back to the job at hand. She had been stationary for almost two hours, and it was time to find another observation position.

She strolled along the beach until she was out of eyesight of the estate, then cut into the foliage and circled back toward the property. She weaved in and out of the flora as fast as she dared, making as little noise as possible as the colorful plants brushed her arms and legs. The sweet smell of mangoes and tropical flowers was thick in the humid air. Perspiration streaked her face. She found a place where the foliage thinned out, revealing the side of the estate.

Examining that portion of the grounds and pool, she saw several men observing a group of young women being paraded around the pool as if they were cattle at auction. The men watched, drinks in hand, as several nude women played volleyball in the pool. Three others lounged in the sun beside the pool. Danya took her time to examine each man, but none of them was her target. More men entered her field of view as the others left. Caterers circulated, offering drinks and hors d'oeuvres. She realized the sun was starting to dip and decided to move to her next observation point. She backed out of her position and began the slow, methodical trek to what would take her to the front of the property. *There's got to be a way to get inside,* she thought. *Maybe after the sun goes down.*

She reached the front corner of the property and saw a gravel road ending at the closed driveway gates at about the midway point of the wall. A detached garage and trees blocked her view of the rear. She did have good visibility of the front entrance, but all of the activity was in the back. In order to move farther around the front, she had to cross the gravel road, which would expose her in the time it took to dart across. If one of the security personnel should see her, that would signal an alert and put her in a situation she didn't want. *Just wait until after sundown,* she thought.

The sun set and the exterior lights of the estate illuminated the property. Danya picked a place to cross the road—a slight bend, twenty-five meters beyond her position. She watched and listened for anything that signaled she had been seen. After several minutes, she moved on to the far corner of the perimeter, then stopped at the corner of the house to observe the rear of the property from that side. There she could see several men and women standing and sitting about. The lights provided excellent visibility. Several tiki torches burned around the grounds and at the pool. A firepit burned beneath a pavilion and appeared to be ready for cooking the evening meal. Music filled the night air.

She scrutinized the area and studied the security guards. *They are a bit lax and too focused on the women,* she thought. *Good.* At the corner of the house, a shadow was cast to the wall, creating a dark spot. Taking advantage of the shadow, she eased herself upon the wall, then down, and moved to the side of the house. Crouching, she moved behind a hedge that ran the length of the swimming pool to a position where she had a good view of the pavilion and most of the rear property. She watched as more people filled the grounds and caterers circulated serving drinks. From her vantage point, she was mere feet from some of the most notorious and ruthless cartel representatives in the world. *Wait, watch, then get the hell out of here,* she thought.

# CHAPTER 6

Saturday, December 3, 2016
Walled Estate
El Cuco Beach, El Salvador

HER CLOTHES WERE saturated—as much from the tension as the humidity—while she lay motionless in the shadow behind the hedge. A slight move could attract someone's attention and cause them to investigate, resulting in her discovery. Danya used disciplined restraint in ignoring the beads of perspiration that trickled down her skin and the occasional insects that crawled over her.

The aroma of meat and fish on the firepit filled the air. Danya watched as the guests strolled up to the grill, where the chef served them plates they preferred. Some found seats at a table, while others sat in chairs by the pool. Her eyes locked onto one man ambling toward the hedge—a plate in one hand and a drink in the other. *This is not good,* she thought as she watched him sit on the step separating the hedge. The man was eight feet from her. She couldn't move without being discovered. She watched—almost envious of his plate—as he stuffed his mouth.

A second man approached carrying his plate and drink. He sat on the step next to the other man. *Madison,* she thought as her eyes stayed fixed on the bearded man. Her adrenaline spiked. It was all she could do not to shoot the son of a bitch who put her through hell and almost killed her and Max. Shooting him would exact revenge for what he had done and rid the world of a deadly mercenary. *It would be an easy kill,* she thought. *But it would be suicide. I'm outgunned, and this hedge provides no protection. He's the key to recovering the missing nuke. I have no choice but to allow him to die another day.*

She remained motionless and listened to the two men engaged in idle conversation. For over ten minutes they talked about the women, the party, scuba diving, and fishing. From their conversation, Danya identified the man next to Madison as the Zetas lieutenant Gail mentioned in their meeting.

The lieutenant looked to Madison and said, "We have received the first payment and scouted the route."

"Good," Madison said with a nod. "Make sure your mules understand what to do and are reliable."

"Not to worry."

"I'll know in the next few days when the package'll be delivered to you," Madison said. "I have a couple of things to take care of before I can be at your location. It'll probably be the week of Christmas."

At that moment a man with a shapely woman on his arm approached the two. Danya concentrated but couldn't make out what he said—his back was to her. *He must be important,* she thought. *What is he saying?* Madison and the man beside him stood and walked away with him. Watching them as they strolled away, she saw the man say something to the woman and pat her on the butt. She stepped away from the three of them. *If I could just hear the conversation.*

Deciding not to push her luck, Danya eased to a crouch, turned around, and began her slow methodical withdrawal. She identified two security men ten feet from the end of the hedge, then froze again. After a moment the two stepped toward the firepit. *Now is my chance,* she thought as she exhaled. Danya retraced her steps to the corner of the house and into the shadow. Without stopping, she hopped up, grasped the wall, then pulled herself up and threw her leg over. Just as she was atop the fortification, a man shouted. Just as she dropped on the other side, a shot rang out. Danya sprang to her feet and ran as fast as she could. It was twenty-five meters across open terrain to get into the dense foliage. *They are about that far behind me,* she thought, *and they have to negotiate the wall.*

Danya pushed and pumped her arms. It was a sprint for her life. *I'm dead meat if they catch me,* she thought. Straining with all her might, pushing her body forward, she could hear two sets of feet pounding on the gravel behind her. The sound of a pistol thundered, then another shot.

The bullets ripped through the leaves next to her, signaling the men's deadly intent. Danya had entered the dense jungle growth, and her chances of escape increased.

She zigzagged, moving as fast as she could. She no longer heard the men, but she knew they were still following her. She stopped and took a knee. Scanning and listening, the only sound she heard was her own breathing. Nothing in the foliage moved. Danya had managed to lose them. Taking no chances and keeping vigilant, she proceeded, making a wide circle to where she left her car. *I've got to get out of the area before they stop searching for me in the bush and take to the roads,* she thought.

Perspiration streaking her face, Danya reached the car, flung the door open, and got in. She started the engine, shifted into drive, and—without headlights—followed the road out of the beach area into the town of El Cuco. Once in town, Danya switched on her headlights and made her way back to San Salvador.

— ◆ ◆ ◆ —

Saturday, December 3, 2016
Quality Hotel Real Aeropuerto
San Salvador, El Salvador

It was almost midnight when Danya arrived at her room in the hotel near the airport. She wanted to shower, but her priority was to brief Max on what she had discovered. She sat at the desk and opened a cold bottle of water. She drank half of it, then called Max on her cell. "I located Madison; he's coordinating with Los Zetas, just as Gail thought."

"Where've you been?" came Max's groggy voice. "I've tried to call you all day. What did you say? You located Madison?"

"Yes, I located Madison and he's coordinating with the Zetas."

"Where is he?"

"He's at an estate at El Cuco Beach in El Salvador. It's a big meeting for the cartels that traffic in humans for special requests and big drug operations. They make it a week-long party."

"Is this actionable? Has it been verified?"

"Yes, they have been there for a few days, so we will need to move fast if we are to get Madison."

"Where are you now?" he asked.

"At a hotel in San Salvador by the airport."

"You went to El Salvador and verified Madison was there?" Max's tone changed.

"Yes, I had to act fast."

In a harsh tone, Max replied, "You went to El Salvador and didn't tell anyone? That's not very smart, and we agreed you wouldn't take these kinds of chances."

"Max, it was short notice, and no one was available. My contact told me the meeting was in progress. I had to get there fast to see if Madison was there."

"You know better than to go alone. If you had gotten into trouble, no one knew where to find you. If they had captured you, they would've killed you, or worse. El Salvador is rough territory. We agreed."

"It's my damn job to get information. I did. Do you want me to give you the information so you can send in a team, or not?"

"It may be your job to gather information but not to take unnecessary risks or do dumb things. Dammit sweetheart, I don't want to be a widower so soon after being a groom."

"OK, Max. But it was a piece of cake. I just took a peek, saw Madison talking to a guy I believe is the Zetas guy Gail mentioned, then left. No problems."

She spent the next half hour briefing Max about the estate and the people there. She gave him the coordinates so he could locate the estate on a geospatial image. As soon as he felt like he had sufficient information to brief his boss, Max planned to recommend sending a Delta team to El Salvador to capture Bart Madison.

Concluding his call with Danya, Max said, "Promise me you're taking the first flight back to Panama in the morning."

"I promise," she replied, her voice soft and sincere. "I love you."

"I'll call you about noon tomorrow. I love you too."

Max called Major General "Chugs" Matherson, Director of Operations, or J3, at SOCOM, and he picked up on the third ring.

"Max, you're working late," he said.

"We've located Madison," Max replied. "I want to send a Delta team to capture him alive." Max spent the next several moments briefing the J3 on the situation.

Chugs agreed that they should apprehend Madison. He thought they might get him to tell them where the nuke was located. If he was in custody—or killed—it might be a little more difficult to execute his plan. "I'll alert the Delta commander and tell him to prepare to deploy to El Cuco, El Salvador, and capture Bart Madison."

———— • ♦ • ————

Monday, December 5, 2016
Headquarters, US Special Operations Command
MacDill Air Force Base, Florida

Max, Andy, Gail, and David sat in the background of the Sensitive Compartmented Information Facility watching the monitors and listening to the operation as it unfolded on the ground at the estate on El Cuco Beach. The Delta team had surrounded the estate and established a blocking position on the gravel road leading to the front of the estate in case anyone tried to flee.

Tension was high as the operators began their operation, and Max's team listened as the reports flowed in. The soldiers took a slow and methodical approach, searching for any booby traps or concealed cameras. However, they were progressing faster than they had anticipated. The team breached the gates at the front and the wall around the perimeter from the rear. There were no vehicles in the front parking area, and a single pickup was parked in the detached garage. No tiki torches or firepit burned in the back. The grounds were immaculate, without a single shred of litter.

The operators continued and entered the house. Each room was searched without finding anything. The nine bedrooms were searched, and each of the beds was made with fresh linen. The nine bathrooms were clean, without a drop of water in the lavatories or showers. There wasn't even a single tissue in any of the trash bins.

"This place is clean," came the commander's voice over the radio. There aren't even any ashes in the firepit. Either we are at the wrong estate, or they knew we were coming."

The operations officer turned to look at Max and saw him nod his head in agreement.

"They knew we were coming," Max said. "Withdraw the team."

The operations officer nodded and gave the command into his radio.

———— ◆ ◆ ◆ ————

Monday, December 5, 2016
Fitzgerald's Vacation House
Nantucket Island, Massachusetts

Nantucket Island is approximately thirty miles south of Cape Cod. It has a land area of forty-five square miles and a year-round population of just under 12,000. In the summer, the population swells to over 50,000.

The Christmas season was underway. The traditional tree lighting on Main Street was held the week before. The annual Christmas Stroll Weekend was the past Friday through Sunday. During the Stroll, all the shops were open late, and the shopkeepers provided wine, hot chocolate, mulled cider, fruitcake, and cookies to their customers. The town was turned into a Christmas wonderland, with a Santa's Village marketplace, live entertainment, craft shows, Christmas carolers, a visit by Santa Claus, and many more festivities. The holiday spirit was in full force on the island.

Deputy Secretary of State Aaron Fitzgerald owned one of the pre-Civil War houses overlooking the water. As in previous years, he, his wife, and their two teenage boys started their holiday season with a week on the island. They took part in the festivities, and the secretary was often one of the judges for various contests—a routine occurrence for the island's senior federal executive. Although the main event was over, more entertainment was scheduled for the rest of the week. Weather permitting, he and his sons planned to take their sailboat out for a few hours each morning. Monday morning was a good day to be out on the boat.

The seas were good when they headed out, but it was a cool forty-three degrees and cloudy. There were several other sailboats out trying to get in a few hours of sailing. The only other boats they saw were a Rampage 41 Express, a Robalo Center Console R222, and a Sailfish 320 Center Console. The occupants of all three appeared to be fishing. After a weather alert predicting fog by two o'clock, Fitzgerald decided to head back to the slip.

Christmas music from around the island greeted them as they arrived. Just as they got the boat secured, dense fog rolled in—a common occurrence for the area.

Later that evening the Fitzgeralds, along with their security, attended a performance of *A Christmas Story: The Musical*, put on by the Theater Workshop of Nantucket. It seemed like the entire island turned out for the event. The family was well-known there, befriending many of the inhabitants over the years. Greetings were exchanged with a number of those friends.

The week was filled with the same types of activities—festive fun, relaxation, and being with family. Eggnog, pastries, cookies, and holiday candies were in abundance and shared with visitors who dropped by. Tuesday and Wednesday were not good days for sailing, but the disappointment subsided when several other teenagers from the island took the boys into town for the day. The adults stayed at home by the fire, reading and listening to Christmas music. On Thursday, Aaron and his sons, accompanied by two attractive girls from the island, went sailing again. Several other sailboats were also taking advantage of the weather along with several powerboats containing fishermen.

Friday was planned as another sailing day, but the weather did not cooperate. The girls who had accompanied the boys sailing took them into town for the day, leaving the adults to the cozy fire and music. Although the day was sunny, the thirty-eight degrees outside kept the holiday spirit alive.

Opting not to go out that evening, Aaron and his wife stayed inside by the fire and watched Christmas movies after dinner. The security detail made their evening checks. Satisfied everything was as it was supposed to be, they went out to the front yard and played football with the boys. It was a cozy evening and a time to relax. She sipped a hot chocolate with marshmallows; he sipped a cognac.

The fire began to dwindle. Aaron rose from his chair, put another log on the fire, and poured another drink. He glanced at the clock as he stepped back to his chair. He sipped his drink then set it on the end table. "I'll be back in a few minutes," he said. "I want to check the boat."

"OK," his wife replied, not paying that much attention to him.

Aaron stepped to the front window and watched one of his sons throw a pass to the other. Opting not to interrupt them, he donned his muffler and coat, went out the back of the house, and headed down the walkway to the dock.

———◆◆◆———

Fog, thicker in places, covered the water and boat slips. A Robalo R222 with a Yamaha 250 outboard motor—without lights—eased out of a slip and made its way along the coast, closer to Fitzgerald's property. Christmas music filtering through the night air covered the low rumble of the engine. The three men in the boat were dressed in black. They had studied the area and their target's location for several days, waiting—like a predator—for the right time to strike.

Two men were at the bow of the boat—one a spotter with a thermal scope, the other a sniper armed with a suppressed Wilson Combat SS-15 Super Sniper rifle in .308 Winchester, with a Pulsar thermal riflescope. Sandbags steadied the rifle. A dark wool blanket was spread over the prone sniper—as much for warmth as for concealment.

Through their thermal scopes the men observed their target's property, taking their time and calculating every move. Like a lion stalking its prey, they were skilled and disciplined in their trade. They had anticipated that at some point, Fitzgerald would get complacent and drop his guard—people usually did. It only takes that one instance for the predator to strike.

The boat sliding along in the fog was 150 meters from the property when the spotter identified Fitzgerald walking down the path to his dock. The sniper confirmed he identified the target. Fixing the crosshairs of the thermal scope on his target, he practiced his trigger pulls, timing them with the slight movement of the boat. Satisfied, he squeezed off a round, then another. Both he and his spotter saw Fitzgerald's body fall to the ground. The spotter motioned to the coxswain, who turned the boat and headed out of the area.

———◆◆◆———

Fitzgerald's wife realized it had been almost an hour since her husband said he was going to check on the boat. Thinking she might not have heard him return, she walked through the house without finding him. She looked outside and didn't see him. She stepped out front and told one of the security men her husband had not returned from checking the boat. He in turn instructed her and the boys to go inside while they searched the property. Within a few minutes, they found the lifeless body of Deputy Secretary of State Aaron Fitzgerald on the path to the boat slip. He had two large-caliber wounds, one to the head and one to the chest.

# CHAPTER 7

Saturday, December 10, 2016
Gareth Residence
New York, New York

Acting CIA Director Jonathan Wellington called Stew to notify him that Deputy Secretary of State Aaron Fitzgerald had been killed the night before. Wellington knew that Gareth was on the verge of paranoia at the death of Deputy Secretary of Defense Wes Brock, and with the news of Fitzgerald, he anticipated Gareth would be worried.

"What happened?" Stew said as he snuffed out his cigar.

"What we know now is that Fitzgerald, with his family, was at their place on Nantucket Island for the week," Wellington said. "Early last evening he went out the back of his house to check on his boat, and he was shot twice—once in the head and once in the chest, with 30 caliber bullets."

Stew fingered his cigar, then asked, "Who did it?"

"Unknown at this point. They're still working the scene. So far, no one has been located that saw or heard anything. No additional evidence has been found. Whoever did it knew what they were doing. It was professional."

"Madison," Stew said in a stern voice, then placed the cigar in his mouth. "I told you to kick your people's asses and get that *sonsabitch*. He's coming after us one at a time, and you do understand, don't you, that he's coming for you too? First Jenny blames me for her losing the election, and now I have a terrorist after me. I want you to get me a couple of trusted security men."

Wellington took a deep breath before replying. "Calm down. We don't know it's Madison."

"You're right, you don't know. Your agency doesn't know. What the hell is the matter with your people? Madison is probably set up in some fancy hotel here in the city, watching me."

"We don't have evidence he's in the States, but we'll find him."

"When? Will I spot him at your funeral? Or worse—you spot him at mine?"

"I'll get you a couple of good security men. Please, calm down."

"How the hell can I calm down when there is a terrorist running around out there with me in his sights? Find the bastard!" Stew slammed the phone into the cradle then lit the cigar. He stood and walked to the liquor cabinet. He grabbed a glass and the bottle of Scotch, then sloshed the glass half full. He stepped to the door of the study, closed it, and locked it. Puffing his cigar, he went to an easy chair and dropped into it.

———•••———

Saturday, December 10, 2016
Headquarters, US Special Operations Command
MacDill Air Force Base, Florida

The news of Deputy Secretary of State Aaron Fitzgerald's death reached Max and his team that morning. Learning of the assassination was a blow—not because Fitzgerald was well-liked and admired, but because an assassin was able to penetrate the senior leadership of the government. Precautions were always taken, as they are a symbol of the United States—attacking that symbol was something terrorists and enemies of the United States were always trying to do. When they succeed, it is a heavy blow with a psychological impact. It seems to have a bigger impact on those sworn to protect the country.

Seated at the conference table with Max was the team, and Danya was on a secured VTC. Max had read the official statement to the others notifying them of the death. Looking at Gail, he said, "Check with Captain Mackenzie and see if they've heard any rumors on the assassination. Then find out who is heading up the investigation on the island and see what evidence they have. Go to Nantucket if you need to."

Gail sipped her coffee, then replied, "I'm on it."

"Andy, see what you can find out through your channels."

"Yes sir."

Max looked to David and said, "See if there is any traffic about this. Get with your contacts. Also, check with NSA and see if they captured any communications related to the assassination. Andy and I will help you come up with a keyword search for NSA."

Max looked to the VTC monitor and said, "Danya, circle back with your sources and see what you can come up with. Maybe you'll have the same luck you did with the meeting in El Salvador."

Gail laid her glasses on the table, then said, "Max, are you thinking Madison did this?"

Max took a sip of his coffee, then said, "I don't have any evidence. I just have a feeling he did. It is just too coincidental for me. If he did, we need to know about it and get on his trail before it goes cold."

"I'm rubbing off on you," Gail replied. "I was thinking the same thing."

"It may turn out that he didn't do it," Max said. "So, everyone, don't let this derail you from your primary mission. Danya found out that Madison and the Zetas lieutenant were together. My guess is that he plans to move the nuke with their help again. Gail, see if the lieutenant is back in the border area. We need to watch him."

"Do you think Madison would be moving it and take out Fitzgerald at the same time?" Andy asked. "It seems to me that he would stay in close proximity if the nuke was being moved."

"It could still be in the hands of the Muslim Brotherhood and hasn't made it to this side of the Atlantic yet." Max replied. "But don't take anything for granted."

———— ♦ ♦ ♦ ————

Monday, December 12, 2016
Damaged House
Raqqa, Syria

Madison, al-Ghazāli, Al'alim, and Nassar met at an undisclosed location in the city of Raqqa, located on the northeast bank of the Euphrates River, 160 kilometers east of Aleppo. Raqqa had been under ISIL control since January 2014.

The four men sat cross-legged on a worn rug in the center of the house, which had once been owned by Christians. It had suffered from the effects of the war—thick dust covered everything, and debris littered the floor. Al-Ghazāli, honoring his agreement with Madison, kept al-Baghdadi from the meeting, but he had him select the fighters to guard the property and several neighboring blocks. Al-Ghazāli motioned with his hand, and a young Arabic boy served the men tea.

Nassar lifted his cup to his lips, then said, "I have secured two American pilots and will take them to the location of the jets in two days. They want to inspect the F-16s."

"Good," Madison replied, then sipped his drink. "I figured they would want to do that. Did you tell 'em exactly what they were supposed to do?"

"Yes."

"Do you have someone ready to get the Air Tasking Order and the Airspace Control Order? Remember, if the pilots don't have those documents, they don't fly."

Nassar sipped his tea, then replied, "I remember. They will receive them."

"What about the tail flashes? Did you get them repainted?"

"Our people did a most excellent job. They look just like the other American planes in Jordan. They are serviced and ready to fly."

Madison shot a glance to Al'alim, then focused on al-Ghazāli and said, "Have your fighters clear and seal off the entire section where the F-16s will take off. Start Wednesday evening. I don't want any traffic or movement beforehand. The jets need a minimum of six thousand feet to take off. Eight thousand is better. The Americans have their satellites and Predators scanning the area, so tell your people not to disturb a thing before Wednesday evening. If the American reconnaissance notices any changes, then it'll be too late for 'em to react."

Al-Ghazāli nodded, sipped his tea, then returned the cup to the saucer on the floor in front of him. He held up his hand, indicating for Madison to stop. He remained silent for a moment, then said, "Your plan, it is very…aggressive. We have two planes that will bring us a lot of money. The pilots must fly them across Syria and into Iraq, where they will then shoot down a plane. Then the pilots will fly into Iran. Our brothers have concerns that the pilots will not succeed."

Madison hesitated before he replied. "You must trust me. *Bold* is a better word. Everyone must do exactly as I have prescribed in my plan, and no one can mention a single word about it. I'll meet the pilots before they take off and have them brief me to ensure they know every detail of what's expected. We will exploit a vulnerability of the American Air Force. They have air superiority in Iraq, and our pilots will go in, looking and sounding like the other American pilots. By the time the Americans realize there's a problem, our pilots will be crossing the border into Iran. The Americas will not be allowed hot pursuit into Iranian airspace."

"I will tell our brothers. They are concerned that we will lose the two jets," al-Ghazāli replied, holding his gaze on Madison.

"Yes, that is possible. But I have done everything and planned this operation to the smallest detail to minimize that risk. The Americans are looking for those F-16s, and it's just a matter of time before they find 'em. With every passing hour that you have 'em, the probability of their discovery increases. Aside from the CIA and military looking for 'em, you can bet your ass that half the people in the region want to collect the reward the US has posted for information on those jets. When the US finds out where they are, you won't have 'em for long; a Predator strike will destroy 'em."

Al'alim's eyes widened and he replied, "The US will blow up their own planes?"

"Make no mistake," Madison replied. "They're pissed off about the Brotherhood stealing their F-16s. I'm sure they believe you're going to sell them to either the Chinese, Russians, or Iranians. They won't let that happen."

A flurry of Arabic erupted between the Arabs for a few moments.

Madison continued when they fell silent. "Get the nuke out of the country by Thursday. My Los Zetas contact is ready to take the nuke into the US and is waiting on us. When the plane is shot down, it'll be like we stirred up a hornet's nest. We won't have a chance anytime soon to get it out of the country."

"It will be done," al-Ghazāli replied, then reached for his teacup.

"Not a word can be said about any of this—the F-16s, the nuke, or anything about the plan. Not even to al-Baghdadi. When I was in El Salvador coordinating with Los Zetas, we had a visitor. I'm not sure who it was, but I suspect it was one of Kenworth's people. I don't know how long the person was inside the compound. The person was seen leaving and got away. I believe Kenworth is getting close to us. We must move now, and with great secrecy."

Could that person have been the American CIA?" Al'alim asked.

"It's possible, but I'm betting it was Kenworth," Madison replied.

"Perhaps I should meet with your new senator…Alexander, Josh Alexander," Nassar said. "I haven't met him yet, and this might be a good time."

Madison shot a glance to al-Ghazāli, then back to Nassar, and said, "Go ahead. I've got too many things to do this week to set it up. See what you can get out of him. But don't meet with him in DC. He's an arrogant little shit."

A smile spread across Nassar's face, and he said, "I can handle him."

"We have only one chance to pull this off. Everyone must do exactly as I have stated. Each action must be accomplished as I have indicated in the time sequence of events."

———— ◆ ◆ ◆ ————

Monday, December 12, 2016
Gareth Residence
New York, New York

Jenny dragged herself out of bed and made her way into the shower. She was unsure when she had showered last, but she put that concern out of her mind as she adjusted the water. She allowed the hot water to flow in rivulets over her large frame, hoping to clear her head. She didn't recall having any appointments. *Hell, I don't even know what today is,* she thought. She had not been out of the house for over a week. Her head began to clear—somewhat—after the long interlude of the hot shower. As she toweled dry, the foul taste in her mouth captured her consciousness—washing it out was the next priority. She picked up her dingy night gown and robe, *That stinks,* she thought, holding the garments away from her body. *When was the last time this was washed?*

54

Food was not appealing to her, even though she didn't remember her last meal. *Coffee,* she thought. *I need some coffee.* She dropped the clothes by the door, withdrew a teal-colored muumuu, then sat on the edge of the bed. She slipped on the shower-curtain lookalike. As it slid across her face, she sniffed to ensure it was clean. Satisfied, she stood—steadying herself with the bedpost—and adjusted the garment. Her eyes landed on two empty Scotch bottles and three glasses sitting on the dresser. *When was the last time the maid cleaned up this place?* she thought. *The damn staff isn't doing what they're supposed to. Worthless illegals. Time for coffee.* Jenny kicked the smelly garbs out of her way and went downstairs to the kitchen.

She made a brief search for Stew and saw that his office door was closed. Avoiding him was her objective; making the coffee was her focus. As it brewed and filled the air with its aroma, she searched for her phone. When she returned to the kitchen, the coffee was ready, and she laid the phone on the breakfast table. She withdrew a mug from the cabinet, set it by the pot, and paused as she noticed the spilled coffee grounds on the cabinet. Jenny managed to fill the mug with coffee, cream, and sugar without spilling too much. At that point, the mess didn't bother her, as she desired the brew. With the mug in her right hand, she steadied herself on the breakfast table as she stepped around and took a seat on the opposite side, where she could see the door. Jenny emptied that cup, then most of another. Although her thoughts seem to be a little clearer, she paused to briefly think about the call she was about to make. Pushing the buttons, she heard the phone ring as she placed it to her ear. When Jonathan Wellington came on the line, she said, "Jonathan, I don't know who else to call, but I knew you could help. I need a bodyguard. Someone is going to try to kill me."

Wellington paused before answering. "Jenny, we had this conversation last week."

"We did?"

Wellington knew she was drunk at the time and tried to tell her Stew wasn't going to kill her. He, like most of the others inside the 495 Beltway, knew she had crawled into a bottle after losing the election. Reasoning with a drunk is impossible. *She sounds a little more coherent today,* he thought. "I've had a couple of people checking around, and they haven't come up with anything."

Jenny slurped her coffee, then replied, "Dammit, Jonathan, what the hell am I going to do?"

He heard her sniff and clear her throat. "That's just a vicious rumor someone started," he said. "I've talked to Stew, and he denies it. He heard you were blaming him for losing the election and wanted him killed. Are you blaming him?"

"No," she replied in a harsh voice.

"I'll get someone to stay with you for a while. Stay away from the booze and get cleaned up."

"Don't take all fucking day," she shot back.

"Stew said you were going to start working on the new campaign after the first of the year. You're going to have to start getting out and making appearances. You can't do that if you're drunk."

"Oh, fuck off."

"Forget about this election and focus on the next one. People have short memories and will forget all about this one. Show 'em that you are a fighter and not a washed-up drunk."

"Shit. What about Madison and Nassar?"

"We're looking for 'em. I don't think either one poses that big of a threat. I've got people in the Middle East dedicated to looking for 'em. We'll get 'em. Don't worry."

Jenny downed the remainder of her coffee—along with the grounds in the bottom of the cup. "Shit!" she said as coffee dripped on her chin and onto her muumuu. She slammed the phone down and stroked the side of her face, feeling her hair. *I need to get a hair appointment. I'll go by Neiman's and pick up a new lipstick.* She stood, ambled to the counter, and fixed another cup of coffee.

She was over the hill, and Wellington knew it. If she cleaned up her act, she might have a shot; otherwise she wouldn't. It would be a long four years until the next election, and he knew it would be an uphill climb for her. Keeping his foot in her camp would keep his options open, just in case.

# CHAPTER 8

Thursday, December 15, 2016
Abandoned Truck Service Yard
Palmyra, Syria

IN THE EARLY morning hours of 17 May, after the B61 bombs were unloaded from the F-16s, the Turkish pilots flew the aircraft out of Turkey—below radar coverage at 100 feet. They continued at that altitude for twenty minutes and landed on a straight section of the highway south of Palmyra on Route 90. The Muslim Brotherhood controlled the nearby gas station and vehicle service yard where the jets had landed. Scattered around the walled yard were old truck parts, trailers, and several tractors in various stages of disrepair. There were two garages in the yard that were used for servicing large trucks. One had been converted into a temporary hangar. The F-16 was small—only 33 feet wide and 50 feet long—making it easy to hide in the footprint of the building.

Nassar had brought the two pilots to the yard at 0545 hours in order for them to review the last few details of the mission and be prepared to brief the others at 0630 hours. The mission briefing was conducted in the second garage, with the F-16s in the background. The sleek aircraft were a stark contrast to the surroundings. A timeworn, oil-stained workbench with a tall back—where tools once hung—was turned around, and a large map depicting Syria, Jordan, Iraq, and Iran was tacked to it. Three old and rusted metal frame chairs and two wooden crates were arranged together as seats for Madison, Al'alim, al-Ghazāli, and Nassar. The other seat was for the second pilot.

A copy of the Air Tasking Order and the Airspace Control Order, along with Madison's plan, had been provided to the pilots the day before. They studied the materials and formulated their tactical plan.

Also, they developed a script to further their ruse when they contacted the tactical command-and-control.

This meeting was the transition into the tactical portion of Madison's plan. For his plan to be effective, it all came down to the precision and details of the mission laid out and the execution of the two pilots, who were the primary focus of this briefing. Bart had met with the two pilots prior to the briefing to calm their concerns with their payment and to verify that their safe passage provisions had been solidified.

"As Nassar told you, payments'll be made to four accounts under two different aliases in banks in Singapore and South Korea," Bart said. "One-quarter of your fee was deposited this morning for both of you, for being here for the brief. A second transfer'll occur upon target destruction, and the remaining half'll be transferred upon crossing the Iranian border." He handed both pilots a slip of paper with the names, account numbers, and banks. He held an authoritarian gaze on them for a brief moment as a caution to not renege on the contract. The pilots got the message.

"Al'alim has assured your safe passage from Iran," Madison said. "When you land across the border, follow the instructions that were in the material Nassar gave you."

Pilots have a certain format they communicate in to reduce confusion and unnecessary words. Madison had told Al'alim, al-Ghazāli, and Nassar to anticipate the briefing might seem to be in code and unclear. The briefing was another rehearsal for the wingman to know what to do.

John "Cuffs" Handy was the flight lead and mission commander, as well as the lead planner. The lean, dark-haired man stood in front of the F-16s with the map of the area to his left—notes, times, and props decorated the edge. He held a long, narrow stick in his right hand to use as a pointer.

Cuffs—an American expat, living in Amman, Jordan—was a former United States Air Force Academy graduate, fighter pilot, and F-16 instructor pilot. In early 2015, he had deployed to Jordan in support of Operation *Inherent Resolve* and was tasked to the Jordanian Air Force. Soon thereafter a Jordanian pilot was shot down over Raqqa, Syria, and his murder—by being burned alive—was shown in a live video stream. This event, and the lack of a coherent, aggressive war strategy by the administration at the time, soured Cuffs's perspective. He was beyond his years in the Air Force—passed over for promotion and going nowhere. His wife divorced him years ago and was granted permanent custody of his two sons; he didn't have visitation rights. All he had was his ability to command a fighter jet in ways most men only dreamed.

Cuffs left the Air Force at the end of his tour and stayed in Amman. He had made enough connections within the State Department and Jordanian Defense Ministry to write his contract for F-16 flight instruction. When contacted by Nassar, he agreed—subject to his trusted and former wingman, Jason "Swat" Howard, agreeing to join him. No fighter pilot walks into a fight without someone he trusts to check his six. For Cuffs, it was Swat.

Swat was a short, wiry cowboy from Wyoming—just the opposite of Cuffs. He had a flair for anything dangerous or that might lead to a fight. There wasn't a country song he didn't know and there was nothing he wouldn't try to ride—women, jets, livestock, the bottle…nothing. His trademark strawberry-blond mustache, with hints of red and gray and twisted at the ends, sat above a hefty pinch of Copenhagen in his left cheek.

Swat and Cuffs met at Osan Air Base in South Korea as young fighter pilots. Their friendship solidified and their trust of each other grew deep. If they weren't flying, they were chasing the local talent, keeping up foreign relations. Their squadron motto, *Harrumph,* became more than just a word; it was their unifying bond—thicker than blood.

Swat left the Air Force before Cuffs and established a lucrative business in South Korea coordinating defense contracts and occasional flight instruction from Kunsan Air Base. Cuffs had made the initial contact with him after Nassar's offer. Swat hadn't been in a cockpit for quite a while, and with Cuffs' call, he jumped at the chance to fly again with him. They both knew the terrain and the normal flight corridors for US missions from Muwaffaq Salti Air Base (MSAB) inside Jordan.

Cuffs started the briefing on time. "Our mission is to infiltrate and assume the identity of a US mission of the 13th Fighter Squadron, "Panthers," launched from MSAB, long enough to penetrate the Iraqi airspace and conduct a precision strike on a distinguished visitor (DV) C-17."

Madison listened to each word to ensure it was in accordance with his intent. Timing was critical and had to be in accordance with his time sequence. Senator Alexander had kept Madison up-to-date on Acting CIA Director Jonathan Wellington's itinerary. He was scheduled for a meeting with local warlords in Kirkuk at 1000 hours. The C-17 carrying the director was scheduled for takeoff at 0900 hours from Baghdad International Airport to be at the meeting as scheduled. This was the pilot's time on target.

So as not to prolong the meeting and keep to the strict time schedule, Madison anticipated the words and phrases that would need to be translated for the Arabic men.

"This mission will be EMCON zero," Cuffs said. "No radio transmissions of any kind. All emitters are to remain off, COMM Out signals only." His eyes landed on his wingman.

Swat nodded.

It was imperative that US Intelligence platforms would not detect, either electronically or via radar, their departure. These emission control measures and radio silence techniques avoided that detection. "Takeoff will be fifteen seconds max afterburner interval. Do not climb higher than 100 feet above ground level. Rejoin to line abreast, left side. Ingress speed will be 540 knots."

Madison turned his head and in a low voice said to the Arabic men, "They'll take off and use a fifteen-second burst of their afterburners. Once airborne, both jets will form up in their formation and fly no higher than 100 feet at 540 knots."

"Takeoff time is 0800 hours," Cuffs said. "We will navigate below radar coverage to the border of Jordan and Iraq within the US transition corridor." With his pointer, he traced their route on the map from Palmyra to the corridor. He continued, "According to the ATO, the actual jets are fragged for a mission departure time of 0840 hours as *Weasel 31*, placing them in the corridor around 0850 hours."

Madison leaned toward the others and said, "Weasel 31 is the call sign of the command jet, and Weasel 32 is his wingman. ATO is the Air Tasking Order."

Al'alim nodded that he understood, then turned his head to see al-Ghazāli and Nassar nod.

"We will assume this mission and feign aircraft malfunctions for the mismatches between Identify Friend or Foe (IFF) encryptions and requirements on the ATO. We will be exploiting complacency in the Air Force. For twenty years we have had air superiority in the region and without a credible adversary. This has caused rot within the Air Force."

Cuffs paused for emphasis. Both Al'alim and al-Ghazāli smiled at his words. No translation from Bart was necessary.

"At point alpha"—Cuffs touched the map with his pointer just inside the Jordanian border along the Baghdad International Highway, ten miles from the Iraq border—"this is a radar coverage weak spot and the check-in point for missions flowing into Iraqi airspace from MSAB with the tactical command-and-control, known as *Kingpin*. We will *Gate*, reform into *ResCell*, and climb to twenty thousand feet."

Bart turned his head and said, "When they get to the highway, both jets will go vertical with afterburners and will reform in their formation in the single resolution return of the radar and climb to twenty thousand feet."

The Arabic men nodded.

Focusing on Swat, Cuffs said, "Passing thirteen thousand feet, cycle your IFF on and off for two seconds, but no Mode C. Remain off until level at twenty thousand feet. I'll make our first transmission at seventeen thousand feet…Kingpin, Weasel 31, Bullseye 310/69, twenty thousand, as fragged, fifteen early, Parrot Sweet, India Sour."

Al'alim turned his head, leaned into Bart, and said, "I don't understand."

"As the jets climb past thirteen thousand feet, they'll switch off and on their IFF for two seconds," Madison replied. "This starts the ruse. Leaving Mode C off will prevent any altitude verification with air traffic control. Their actions in the cockpit'll cause the electronic signal received by Kingpin to look like they are having equipment malfunctions. He's telling them they're sixty-nine miles from the point known as *Bullseye*, which today—in accordance with ATO—is Al Assad, Iraq. He's on a bearing of 310 degrees, and they're fifteen minutes early. It's a way for the radar controller to find their aircraft. *Parrot* Sweet means they have good unclassified communications. *India* is the code word for their encryption of the electronic identification. In this case, their classified transmissions—IFF—are not working."

Al'alim nodded and rubbed his chin. His attention returned to Cuffs. Swat stroked his mustache. "Roger."

Bart sat back to analyze Cuffs's briefing and compare it to his plan. So far, he was spot-on. His plan wasn't foolproof, but he believed this was the best way to spoof US fighters and gain access to contested airspace long enough to generate the kill shot. Counting on complacency and poor maintenance capabilities to be the fall guy was entirely believable after the previous administration's gutting of defense budgets. He had confidence in the pilots' skill to execute the plan to success.

Bart's attention snapped back to Cuffs when he said, "Contingencies." He paused, then continued: "This mission cannot delay more than ten minutes. We will launch a single ship, if necessary, to meet the timeline. In the event of aircraft malfunction or battle damage preventing successful low-altitude egress east into Iran, assume EMCON zero again, snap 130 degrees heading toward Karbala, punch out southwest of the city."

"Snap?" al-Ghazāli questioned.

"Turn to a heading of one hundred thirty degrees, then bail out southwest of Karbala," Madison replied.

"You'll have to escape and evade north," Cuffs said. "Proceed to the small mosque listed on this card. Ask for 'Shefadt'—he'll take you to the imam and coordinate your crossing of the Iranian border." Cuffs hadn't developed the backup egress plan and didn't have a relationship with any of the players on the ground. He didn't trust the unknown, but there was no other option. The thought of Swat relying on this for survival concerned him.

Cuffs looked to Bart, seeking input if he had misspoken or omitted any part of the plan. Before Bart replied, he glanced back to Swat and said, "Swat, if you can't make Karbala, flow west, leave as little intact wreckage as possible, and save me a seat at JJ's with the best woman you can find."

Swat smiled, but the grim undertones were not easily covered by the casual joke of a fighter pilot's version of heaven.

Bart nodded his approval but didn't say a word. Arabic erupted among the three men next to Madison—their mannerisms animated. The brief flurry ended as fast as it began.

"Any questions?" Cuffs asked.

Bart looked to the Arabs, then back to Cuffs, and said, "No, it's complete."

"We step in fifteen, start in forty," Cuffs said, and he flipped his pointer onto the workbench.

Both pilots stepped to the back of the room to put on their flight gear. Swat, with his Copenhagen smile, slapped Cuffs on the back. "*Harrumph!*" That was about the extent of their small talk.

Cuffs turned his head and with a broad smile replied, "*Harrumph!*"

Al'alim motioned with his hand, signaling for his men to prepare for the launch. Several men darted to their vehicles and raced in both directions on Route 90. They inspected it for debris that might have found its way onto the pavement from the night before. At the 8,000-feet marker, the vehicles stopped and set up their roadblocks.

Inside the garage—which had been modified several days earlier to allow for an engine start—a few young men searched for anything that could be blown about. Satisfied when the task was complete, they slid open the front and rear doors.

Both pilots conducted the preflight of their F-16s. Bart—walking alongside Cuffs as he conducted his inspection—admired the deadly machine that sat at peace. Words were not exchanged. Cuffs was here to do a job, nothing more.

Both aircraft were armed with two AIM-120B radar-guided air-to-air missiles and two AIM-9M heat-seeking missiles. The heat-seeking missiles could be decoyed or defeated by flares. For that reason, the AIM-120s would be the lethal culmination of the mission.

Swat completed his preflight at the same time as Cuffs. He didn't say a word to the ground crew—he could not care less. This was the last time he'd see this godforsaken desert. Swat reached into the upper pocket of his flight suit, pulled out a soft pack of Camel Crush Menthol cigarettes, and checked the contents. *Thirteen left*, he thought. *That's good luck.* He slipped one between his lips, lit it, and pulled a slow drag. He was a bit of a fighter pilot historian of sorts. World War II aces used to smoke

Lucky cigarettes, and Swat used that phrase, "to smoke a Lucky," when teaching. Today it was Camel Crush. For some reason, the Arabs loved them, and Swat always carried a pack to barter his way out of trouble, if he ran into any. He didn't trust Bart, their Arabic employers, or their contingency plan in Karbala, if something were to happen. But he trusted Cuffs and figured the Camels gave him an advantage.

Cuffs started to ascend the ladder to the cockpit, then he stopped and turned to face Madison.

"The money and our exfil had better be there," Cuffs said. It was a warning from one mercenary to another.

Bart understood the meaning of his statement. "It will be. Just don't miss."

"I won't." Cuffs said, his tone serious and full of confidence. He turned and continued to the top of the ladder. With care, he settled into the cockpit, as if descending into a warm bath.

The F-16 cockpit fit like a glove, wrapping around Cuffs and grafting together as no man or machine could be closer. As the clock hit 0740, he hit the *Start 2* toggle. He heard Swat's jet roar to life as well—on time, nothing less. As the engine whines to life and the canopy descends around Cuffs, the worries of the world disappear. He'd done this a thousand times, and this was just another mission.

Within five minutes he was ready to go. With a gentle touch, he advanced the throttle and emerged from the garage, filling the cockpit with sunlight. To reach the runway, Cuffs and Swat had to taxi out and around the other long garage blocking their view from the highway. Swat inched forward as well. They had already started their EMCON zero procedures—hand signs only. With a thumbs-up from Swat, Cuffs idled toward Route 90. He glanced to Bart, standing next to the Arabs. Al'alim and al-Ghazāli appeared to be spellbound by the spectacle of the two aircraft making their way out of the building. Nassar rotated his head as he scanned the area. Bart, in a commanding stance, gave a final thumbs-up, and Cuffs replied with a sharp salute. He turned his eyes forward, finished his pre-takeoff checks, strapped on his mask, and slid the bayonets until they clicked twice.

Approaching the entrance to the road, Cuffs saw a dirty-faced boy of no more than fifteen holding a hand radio. He gestured OK and gave

Cuffs a thumbs-up. Cuffs had never seen the boy before. *The commander of urchins,* he thought. He set the parking brake, and a flurry of other boys ran to the missiles on the wings. *The commander's troops.* They pulled the last remaining arming pins, then scattered.

The hair on the back of his neck began to rise as Cuffs looked back at Swat's jet. As they took their positions on the road, Swat pulled up on the left side, just aft and alongside Cuffs. The noise of an idling F-16 is distinct and garners the attention of anyone nearby. He checked his watch and read 075936, then looked at Swat, who returned an exaggerated nod, followed by a thumbs-up. Cuffs gave the final signals—*run 'em up,* thumbs-up, a two-handed, index finger and pinky finger extended gesture—a silent *Harrumph!*

The F-16 roared to life as 60,000 pounds per hour of fuel-flow poured into the ignition section of the afterburner, generating 32,500 pounds of gut-churning thrust, forcing Cuffs back into the seat. Within seconds, the jet was off the ground, accelerating through 200 knots, gear retracting, and not cresting fifty feet off the deck. Swat was right behind him. More than anything else in his life, that exact moment of takeoff roll and instantaneous acceleration was one ride he could never get enough of. Not even the best sex could match the thrill, or power, of a General Electric GE-129 roaring past 400 knots.

The two F-16s flowed southwest, eluding radar detection, before turning directly toward point alpha. Swat rejoined as briefed and flew a perfect wingman position. This initial portion of the mission was more task-intensive than most. At 100 feet and over 500 knots, it only takes one second of inattention to kiss the earth, ending a life and destroying a good jet. On top of that, Cuffs had a specific route to follow, utilizing the terrain to avoid detection. Swat had the harder job. Not only did he need to be attentive enough to not kill himself, but he also needed to be in position at the time of the pull-up to hide within the resolution cell of the radar return of one aircraft. Not an easy task, but one that lit his adrenaline and had him on the optimum performance curve between stress and desired output.

The preflight intelligence Nassar had obtained provided Cuffs the frequencies that Weasel 31 would be using for the day. Cuffs listened for clues as to their status. Hearing that the actual Weasels were slightly delayed meant the window for this ruse was available. At five miles from point alpha, Cuffs slowly lit the afterburner, accelerating to 600 knots, and with the flick of his wrist on the side stick, two hardly noticeable F-16s ascended vertically into the vast blue sky. Both fighter pilots switched frequencies, as briefed, to their tactical check-in and inter-flight channels. Swat began cycling the IFF.

Cuffs made a broken check-in. "King…in…31, thousand, fragged…"

# CHAPTER 9

Thursday, December 15, 2016
Air Corridor
Inside Iraq

"WEASEL 31, KINGPIN, is that you trying to check in? Negative radar contact, broken unreadable."

Cresting 20,000 feet, the two fighters established formation and began turning on various systems that would validate their identity. Next, they began setting up the weapons systems for use.

"Kingpin, Weasel 31, Bullseye 310/69, twenty thousand, as fragged, early, Parrot Sweet, India Sour," Cuffs replied, his voice calm, as if this was his hundredth mission as a Panther.

"Weasel 31, Kingpin, good bullseye, standby for further identification," the tactical controller responded.

This was the start of the ruse and the first test Cuffs had to pass, or their cover would be blown. He followed his script: "Kingpin, Weasel 31, unable, our maintenance guys got the wrong crypto last night, and we launched knowing it's gonna be an issue. We're having a rash of maintenance problems with this deployment. You are showing me Parrot sweet though, right?"

"Weasel 31, affirmative, Parrot sweet. Sorry to hear about the maintenance issues." The controller's initial, cautious tone eased. This was the chance.

"Kingpin, do y'all still get three drinks a day down there? Can you still *shoot the moon* and knock down three before midnight and the next three right after 0001?"

Kingpin's tone relaxed further. "Weasel, yeah we sure do."

"Dang, if they'd let our maintenance guys tie one on every now and again, I'd bet we'd get better jets…just saying. Weasel 31, request direct on course."

"Weasel 31, Kingpin, proceed as requested, and you're probably right about maintenance. Happy hunting, boys."

Cuff's ploy worked with air traffic control—the trap was set. He breathed a sigh of relief that he had passed the test and didn't have to worry about other Panther aircraft—for the time being. Any suspicions had been dissolved. The airman on the radio had no reason to suspect the pilot he was talking to was not who he was supposed to be. One hundred fifty nautical miles lay between the two mercenaries and Baghdad International Airport.

At one hundred nautical miles from the airport, Swat tuned his IFF interrogator to the transponder code of the C-17 designated for Acting Director Wellington's DV transport, call sign Reach 72. He slewed his radar cursors out to an eighty nautical mile scope and centered them on the bullseye location of the airport. He checked his watch and read 0845. Reach 72 was scheduled for an 0900 departure. That meant that the C-17 would turn on its transponder and request taxi at 0850. Swat would be able to *paint* their return, verify their location, and correlate it to their radar track when they lifted off.

Cuffs tuned to several different frequencies to verify that they had not been detected. Listening to the traffic, he verified Reach 72 was *green* and on time. He set his autopilot and soaked in the quiet tranquility. In a few minutes he would unleash a level of violence that had never been seen before the creation of this aircraft. At his fingertips, Cuffs had the power to create utter mayhem and destruction, but for now he relaxed, gazing out the bubble canopy. It was as if God had reached out and prepared the path before him. In fifteen minutes, the solitude and perfection of man and machine would transform, in near Jekyll and Hyde fashion. Cuffs and his Viper—the most technologically advanced fighter in the world—would rain fire and destruction in a surprise attack, camouflaged by the fog and friction of war and the remains of the fallen government of Iraq.

At 0850, Swat saw the transponder code illuminate and heard on the Baghdad ground frequency, "Reach 72 Information Whiskey, request beacon and engine start."

"Weasel, green 'em up," Cuffs said as he shot a glance to Swat.

Both pilots reached forward in their cockpits and toggled the Master Arm switch from Off to ARM. As planned, Swat was the main shooter. He needed to allocate his radar, shoot, and monitor his missile for effectiveness. Radio communications—check-ins and coordination with Reach 72—were conducted by Cuffs.

As the missiles came to life, electricity shot through the wiring in both aircraft as the master computers initialized all of the missiles, completed their built-in tests, and replied with their status on the weapons page.

Cuffs set his radar elevation to the surface—twenty miles in front of him—and scanned for any targets. There were multiple other missions ongoing—most were Army helicopter operations that took place below 3,000 feet. One particular mission—which worried him—was that of Weasel 21. It was a pre-dawn mission supporting a special operations task force *snatch-and-grab* mission to the south in the Basrah Province, near the city of Basrah. If not successful by daybreak, the mission was to be scrubbed. That would put WEASEL 21's return to base at approximately 0930 over Baghdad, after a post-mission air refueling. However, if the mission went *Jackpot*, Weasel 21 would remain on station until all of the intelligence was gathered. The presence of Weasel 21 was a potential flash point for Cuffs and his wingman.

Cuffs was concerned with the status of the actual Weasel 31—whether it got airborne or not. He would only know about Weasel 31 through radio chatter, but he could radar search for Weasel 21. As planned, Swat would scan for their transponder codes.

Cuffs heard the controller telling them to switch frequencies. "Weasel 31, Kingpin, push tactical Cobalt 4, Reach 72 green, Mission GO."

"Kingpin, Weasel 31, Roger, push Cobalt 4."

Hearing the controller, Swat ran his finger down his mission card, found the correct frequency and tuned to the proper channel.

Baghdad International was easily visible from twenty miles away. Traveling at 400 knots, or eight miles a minute, Cuffs and Swat were right on time when Reach 72 took the takeoff position.

Cuffs made radio contact with the C-17, as expected. "Reach 72, Weasel 31, on Cobalt 4, as fragged, visual, established at Angles 13."

"Weasel 31, Reach 72," the copilot's voice cracked as he began to speak. It was his first downrange mission since becoming qualified. "Copy all, rolling, cleared on course direct, flight level 250."

*Perfect,* Cuffs thought, and a slight smile emerged on his face. The copilot's inexperience and distraction with takeoff roll caused him to overlook a verbal authentication with the fighters. Cuffs had planned for the challenge and had a reply prepared, but the copilot missing the authentication request spared him the trouble of complying with the procedure.

Swat locked his radar just as the C-17 lunged its T-tail into the air. The huge aircraft gained altitude and retracted its landing gear. He fired the missile—the countdown began. It transitioned to active, and Swat canceled the radar lock.

Swat—who didn't talk on the primary frequency—said, "One!" It was the signal to Cuffs that ten seconds remained.

Hearing his transmission, Cuffs said in a commanding voice, "Reach 72, break left, Flare, SAM, left seven o'clock!"

The C-17 contorted like a pole dancer and belched out over one hundred flares in a dramatic display of fire. This combination of defensive maneuvers—including the entire belly load of flares—would defeat any heat threat, but this silent killer was an AIM-120 missile. It was immune to flares and tracked—as expected—on the target.

Cuffs continued with his prepared script and said with excitement, "Kingpin, Weasel 31, SAM launch—" He continued his transmission, "Weasel 2, break right, Flare, SAM, right three o'clock!" The additional call to Swat—for Kingpin's benefit—alerting him of an additional launch call would send Kingpin into even more confusion. His tone and precise communications disoriented the command-and-control structure, other fighter jets, and Reach 72, until impact.

A new voice—high pitched and excited—came over the radio. "Weasel, Kingpin…did you say SAM?"

Cuffs—ignoring Kingpin's transmission—continued the charade as planned. "Two, Flare, break right…"

The warhead of the AIM-120 reacted to its proximity sensor, sending 10,000 titanium shards through the skin of the C-17—at an oblique angle beginning with the cockpit through the wing box. The upward trajectory of the flight path slowed and apexed, then began to drift toward the earth. The wing box penetration ignited the cargo jet's main fuel cell and severed the right wing. As it folded, and the fuselage began to roll, the 300,000-pound C-17 careened to the sandy desert south of the runway. The secondary explosion upon impact and dark black, jet-fueled smoke left no doubt that all fifteen souls on board—including Acting CIA Director Wellington and the copilot on his first mission—were Killed in Action.

Cuffs replied, "Kingpin, Weasel 31, mark Bullseye 091/87, Reach 72…additional possible MANPADS five miles north of Baghdad, up to Angles 18."

Over the radio came the routine check-in, "Kingpin, Weasel 31, mission number 3613, Bullseye 310/69, Angles 20, as fragged, ten minutes late."

Hearing the real Weasel check in for the mission, Cuff—on the interflight channel—directed Swat to go to the predetermined frequency. It was time to get the hell out of there.

As soon as he heard Swat check in, Cuffs said, "Take it down, egress north, EMCOM."

The two aircraft dove to 100 feet at 600 knots, activating their escape plan. Fifty miles north of Baghdad, the two jets turned east and jettisoned their remaining fuel tanks and stores as they screamed for the Iranian border.

———◆◆◆———

The command-and-control center—Kingpin—was chaos. There were no signals of a SAM launch, but the visual description from the on-scene pilots reported the strike on the C-17. A rescue mission was launched to search for survivors and intelligence assets were directed to the scene. The airman on the radio said, "Weasel 31, Kingpin, come in…verify bullseye, repeat last about SAM."

A confused voice replied, "Kingpin, Weasel 31, Bullseye 330/57, 20,000, we're just checking in."

The colonel overseeing the command-and-control center stared at the large monitor displaying a graphical representation of the aircraft in the area and said, "Who were the fighters over Baghdad? Where are they now?"

The airman communicating with the pilots stood and responded, "Sir, Weasel 31 is on station and Weasel 21 is flowing north from Basrah, as we speak."

The colonel ran his hand over his shaved head as he heard the airman's words, but the monitor displayed a different picture. Weasel 21 was fifty miles south of Baghdad and returning to base. Weasel 31 was over Al Assad Air Base in western Iraq, eighty miles from Baghdad; and a C-17 lay burning on the desert floor.

———— ◦ ◦ ◦ ————

Cuffs and Swat flew in the standard line abreast formation sixty miles inside Iranian airspace and, as planned, had not crested one hundred feet. Their cockpits returned to places of peace and tranquility. The explosion of violence they created and the twenty minutes of hell that followed were behind them.

The world once again wrapped around Cuffs and his machine. He began to throttle back and climb. He gave Swat the check-mark hand sign to begin the battle damage check, followed by the drinking hand sign—requesting his remaining fuel. Both planes were low on fuel, and their airfield was fifteen miles away. *Next is our safe passage out,* he thought. *Better be there…and our money.*

Both men were ghosts—the dead meandering among the living, wasting their days away chasing adrenaline rushes, cheap thrills, and loose women. Swat completed his check over Cuffs's airplane. Then it was Cuffs's turn. When he finished, he pulled up alongside his best friend, gave him a thumbs-up, and another *Harrumph!*

———— ◦ ◦ ◦ ————

Thursday, December 15, 2016
Damaged House
Raqqa, Syria

Bart and the three Arabs relocated to Raqqa after the jets took off. In the same abandoned house they had used before, the four sat on the worn rug in the center of the room and ate lunch. The meal consisted of grilled lamb; mashed eggplant with olive oil, tomato, onion, and garlic; fava beans; tomatoes; cucumbers; grape leaves stuffed with rice and a variety of other vegetables; and bread.

Little was said during the meal. The tension was high as they waited on confirmation that the C-17 was shot down and the planes had made a successful landing in Iran. Al-Ghazāli—the first to end his meal—glanced at the others, then motioned with his hand for the young boy to clear the dishes, indicating this course was over. He stood and paused as the others got to their feet, then led them into the next room.

Once the places were cleaned, platters of fresh fruit—bananas, grapes, oranges, and apples—and dishes of dried figs with clotted cream were set for them. The men returned and took their respective places, sitting cross-legged on the carpet. Two of them picked at the fruit and two of them picked up their dishes of figs with clotted cream. Al-Ghazāli's cell phone rang, and the room fell silent as everyone focused their attention on him. He spoke a few brief Arabic words, then ended the call. He looked up at the others, and a broad smile crossed his face. "The C-17 is destroyed," he said.

Al'alim let out a burst of Arabic.

Nassar, smiling, joined him. He looked at Madison and said, "Your plan worked."

Madison relaxed, and a slight smile emerged on his face. "I told you it would. We have one more confirmation."

Within moments, al-Ghazāli's cell phone rang again. All eyes went to him as he answered. After a short exchange in Arabic, he ended the call with a smile. "Both jets are in Iran. The money for the jets has been transferred to our account."

"What about the pilots?" Madison asked.

"Both are well and, as agreed, are on their way out of the country," al-Ghazāli replied. "I will have the money transferred to their accounts in Singapore and South Korea." He punched in a series of numbers into his phone and placed it to his ear. When his call was answered, he spoke a quick phrase, then ended the call. Looking at Madison, he said, "It is done."

Madison gave a quick nod.

Al-Ghazāli turned his head and spoke to the boy standing by the door. Then he motioned with his hand, and the boy disappeared into the next room. "We will now drink to our success." Looking at Madison, he said, "You have done well again. Our brothers are pleased."

"Thank you," Madison replied. "We have one more task."

"Yes, whatever you need."

The boy returned with four short glasses filled with arak—an anise-flavored liqueur similar to raki or ouzo. He served the milky-white drink, first to al-Ghazāli, Al'alim, and Nassar, and then to Madison.

———— ◆ ◆ ◆ ————

Thursday, December 15, 2016
Headquarters, US Special Operations Command
MacDill Air Force Base, Florida

"Approximately six hours ago," Max said to his assembled team, "the C-17 carrying Acting CIA Director Jonathan Wellington was shot down just after takeoff from the Baghdad International Airport en route to Kirkuk. There were no survivors. There's a lot of confusion as to what happened. It was initially reported that his plane was hit by a SAM, but there's no intelligence to confirm that report. The 13th Fighter Squadron flying out of Jordan was deployed from Misawa Air Base, Japan, to MSAB. Two of their F-16s were tasked to provide security, and they checked in fifteen minutes early. Right after the C-17 crashed, another set of F-16s checked in as the same ones tasked to fly the security mission. All aircraft and missiles of the 13th Fighter Squadron have been accounted for."

"Madison," Gail said.

"That's what we believe," Max replied. "We were right all along. He's out for revenge."

"He damn sure is," Gail said. "and he's getting ready for his next move. The Zetas lieutenant is back in the border area. I've requested close surveillance on him."

"Good. I think he might lead us to Madison or the nuke."

"The chatter is up on the internet, but nothing that will lead us to Madison or the nuke," David said. "Al-Baghdadi is boasting more than usual."

"My sources are quiet," Danya said. "That's unusual. I'm leaning on them."

"I believe, and the general agrees, that Madison is about to bring the nuke into the US. Gareth could be his next target," Max said.

# CHAPTER 10

Friday, December 16, 2016
Headquarters, US Special Operations Command
MacDill Air Force Base, Florida

T HE WORKSPACE WAS buzzing with activity as the team sought out intelligence from the incident where Acting CIA Director Jonathan Wellington's plane was shot down the day before. They needed to act fast to gather information that might lead them to Madison or the nuclear warhead. The tactical command-and-control at Muwaffaq Salti Air Base would only offer the information previously supplied. They were conducting an investigation and stated that once the investigation was completed, they would release the details. Max didn't have the luxury to wait that long for information.

"I just finished talking with one of my contacts at DIA," Andy said, sitting opposite Max's desk. "They received a report that two American jets took off from an area south of Palmyra Thursday morning local time. At first, they discounted it, thinking the Syrian informant was attempting to extort money from the US. But after Wellington's plane was shot down, it got a lot of attention. A team was sent to the location and confirmed that jets were stored in an old garage of a vehicle service yard. They found tire tracks from two jets; a map of Syria, Jordan, Iraq, and Iran; and an arming pin from an AIM-120B radar-guided air-to-air missile. Nothing else was found."

"An arming pin?" Max replied. "That's odd that Madison would overlook that kind of evidence. Did the Syrian say anything else?"

"He saw two vehicles leave the service yard not long after the jets took off. They headed north on Route 90. That's it."

Max, followed by Andy, stepped to the large map on the wall, placed his finger on Palmyra, and said, "Shit. They could have gone anywhere. Maybe we were supposed to find the arming pin. While everyone is focused on Wellington's plane being shot down, suppose we are to think Madison is still in Syria and he's trying to draw us over there while he makes his move here. We know he's very good at that kind of deception."

"You're right," Andy replied. "He'd do that."

"I'll contact Danya, and you give Gail and David a heads-up," Max said as he stepped back to his desk.

It was late morning before he was able to connect with Danya. "I met with one of my contacts," she said. "He heard that a shipment is coming into Panama, and it is a big deal. He didn't know where it's entering, and he's heard it isn't drugs. He'll try to find out more."

"That could be it," Max replied. "Let me know as soon as you hear back from him. I'll put a team on standby. I think Madison is trying to lure us back to Syria while he makes his move into the US."

"What makes you think that?"

"We found out the jets that shot down Wellington's plane were stored and took off from Palmyra. Madison's usually pretty good about not leaving any evidence. When the team went in to check the place out, they found tire tracks of the jets, an arming pin from one of the missiles, and a map of the area. It was just too easy."

"That is sloppy for him. Could it be a coincidence or some other bad actor? This big shipment coming into Panama could be counterfeit money, drugs, or even something else."

"You could be right, but I'm betting it's Madison," Max replied.

"You could be right that he is trying to lure us back over there. Is there anything else? I've got a meeting and need to run."

"Be careful," Max said. "I'll call you later. I have a briefing at 1300."

———◆◆◆———

Friday, December 16, 2016
Headquarters, US Special Operations Command
MacDill Air Force Base, Florida

Senator Josh Alexander, Senate Committee on Armed Services, had called for a briefing the previous week by the SOCOM commander on the status of the missing B61 nuclear bomb. He wanted to know the status on recovering it, and what Kenworth was doing. As a result of that meeting, Homeland Security sent its representative, Dawn Blakey, to SOCOM to be briefed by Max and his team.

Dawn had led Homeland Security operations three years ago when Madison plotted an attack on the US. She was acquainted with Max, Gail, and David from that incident. With Dawn was a young action officer, Joel Honeycutt.

Dawn and Joel sat across the walnut conference table from Max, Lieutenant Colonel Johnston, Gail, and David.

"Before you start," Dawn said, her tone condescending, "Senator Alexander has a keen interest in recovering the missing nuclear bomb. He's not happy that the military allowed the terrorists to steal one, let alone six of them. If we have a repeat of Manhattan, heads will roll."

Max took a deep breath and didn't acknowledge her comment. He then gave an introduction and summary of the theft of the nuclear bombs from Incirlik and the subsequent recovery of five of them. "The Muslim Brotherhood had kept one of the nukes hidden until recently," Max said, allowing his gaze to linger on Dawn. "We believe that the Brotherhood and Bart Madison are working together to bring that last nuke into the US."

"Bart Madison?" Dawn said, her eyes wide. "You're mistaken there. The CIA killed him. Senator Alexander didn't mention any of this to me."

"That's what we were supposed to think," Max replied. "We believe they were using him."

"Why would they do that?" Dawn laid her glasses on the table. "The CIA is a US Agency and on our side. Also, we don't have any intelligence that the Muslim Brotherhood is against the US. You're wrong. ISIL, sure, but not the Agency or the Brotherhood."

Max shot a glance to Gail before he continued. He recognized she was already agitated by the young woman and was about to light into her. He motioned with his hand to Gail not to launch across the table at Dawn. Max focused back on Dawn and said, "The CIA has not been forthcoming and blocked all information out of the Middle East. They sent a team to kill Danya and me."

"I don't believe it," Dawn replied. She turned to Joel, "This doesn't make any sense to me. None of it. I think they're wrong about the CIA and Madison. I haven't heard anything about the Muslim Brotherhood being against the US. I want you to check all this out when we get back to DC."

The young man nodded and scribbled on his notepad.

Dawn turned her attention back to Max. "Why haven't I been briefed on this before? I need to get the FBI and Homeland Security briefed and up to speed on this. New York City is the obvious target. What're you doing to stop this? What's your plan?"

Gail's eyes narrowed as she focused on Dawn. "I *am* the FBI."

"Oh…right!"

"I have been working with NYPD since Madison set off the bomb in Manhattan in July," Gail said, using restraint not to reach across the table and punch the young woman. "You don't need to do anything."

Dawn's eyes opened wide, and her mouth gaped. "Manhattan was Madison? I thought it was just some terrorist."

"Yes," Gail said, her tone harsh. "That was Madison. I know you live under a rock. Just stay out of our way and we'll tell you what you need to do or whom to brief. Ya got that?"

"Neither Senator Alexander nor I live under a rock, Gail. My position with Homeland Security is as a liaison between this team and my boss. It appears that neither he nor I have been given the full picture, and if we are going to help, I must insist that all information is shared. I'm certain you would expect no less from us." Dawn folded her arms and sat back in her chair.

"Dawn," Max said, recognizing Gail's anger at the woman, "we have it under control and are trying to recover the nuke before it gets into the US."

"Intelligence reports suggest the nuclear warhead is enroute to the US," Lieutenant Colonel Johnston said.

"The warhead?" Dawn asked. "What about the rest of the bomb?"

"The warhead is the portion containing the nuclear material," Johnston said. "That is the destructive part and what we are worried about."

"What about the rest of the bomb?" Dawn asked.

"Soon after the B-61 bombs were stolen from Incirlik, the terrorists removed the warheads from the rest of the B-61s," Johnston said. "The warhead is the *business end*. The rest is just *throwaway* material."

"Oh," she replied.

Max spent the next twenty-five minutes covering each detail of this briefing. He didn't provide any classified information to Dawn, or any information that wasn't already available to her, if she did the research. He also didn't mention that he believed Madison was out for revenge and that Gareth was a target, or that Madison was working with Los Zetas to bring the nuke into the US. He satisfied the requirements set by Senator Alexander. The senator's interest in SOCOM's operation to recover the nuke—and, specifically, what Max was doing—concerned him.

Max ended his presentation with, "We appreciate any help you can provide. Please emphasize to Senator Alexander and the secretary of Homeland Security that we are doing everything possible to recover the nuclear device before it can reach the US border."

With an air of importance, Dawn leaned forward and said, "Thank you for the update. The secretary of Homeland Security is doing everything possible to keep the borders secure. He assures me they are more secure than they have ever been."

David handed Joel copies of the briefing slides and an information packet as they stood. The two exchanged phone numbers. Max shook their hands and assured Dawn they would keep her informed.

David escorted Dawn and Joel out of the building.

As soon as the two visitors departed, Gail said, "If the US has to depend on her, we've had it. She hasn't changed a bit in the last three years."

"She could be trouble," Max said. "Keep her at arm's length and give her only what is necessary."

"She was a pain in the ass last time we had to work with her and not the brightest bulb on the tree."

—— • • • ——

Saturday, December 17, 2016
Palm Restaurant, InterContinental Hotel
Mexico City, Mexico

Nassar had made arrangements to meet Senator Josh Alexander, although it did take encouragement from Bart Madison for the senator to accept the invitation. Following Madison's instructions, Nassar set the meeting in Mexico City. The chances the senator would be seen there were remote, and Nassar believed the Americans wouldn't be looking for him there.

Nassar reserved a suite for Alexander overlooking the Colonia Polanco, one of the most beautiful and affluent neighborhoods in the city. One could admire the city below through the large picture window. The neighborhood had luxury shopping, the most upscale restaurants, and boasted having one of the most expensive real estate markets in Latin America.

Nassar scheduled an early dinner meeting to be ahead of the crowd and afford the senator the opportunity to visit the neighborhood, if he desired. At five o'clock, Nassar saw the metrosexual senator approach the restaurant entrance and stop in front of the ornate mirror in the hallway. Alexander smiled at his reflection as he remembered that day at Barneys when he snagged this Luca Faloni white linen shirt and Tom Ford sports jacket. He adjusted both and checked his teeth before he turned and approached the maître d'. He remembered to casually place his hand in his pants pocket and scan the room to see if anyone noticed him as he was escorted to the man at the secluded spot toward the back of the room.

Nassar stood and greeted the senator, motioning for him to sit across from him. A waiter followed with an ice bucket and bottle of Sauvignon Blanc. As soon as he set the bucket down, he filled the senator's glass, then Nassar's. He returned the bottle to the bucket and left the table.

"I am glad you could make it, Senator," Nassar said.

Alexander sipped his wine. "Thank you. Nice place."

"It is. I took the liberty of ordering for both of us. I hope you don't mind."

"That's fine. What are we having?"

"We will start with calamari fritti, then a mixed green salad. Our main course is jumbo Nova Scotia lobster and grilled vegetables."

"Sounds delicious."

Nassar was slow in his approach, with light conversation as they sipped the wine. He studied his dinner companion, listening to what he said, what he didn't say, and how he expressed himself. When Alexander's glass was down to a third, Nassar motioned to the maître d'. A few minutes later, a waiter stepped to the table, placed a platter of calamari fritti between the two men, and paused to observe the table to ensure everything was in order. Satisfied, he retrieved the bottle from the bucket, refilled the senator's glass, and topped off Nassar's.

Soon, the lobster was served and the senator's glass refilled. Nassar sensed that Alexander was relaxed, and he guided the conversation to gather intelligence from the senator.

"The meal was delicious," Alexander said. "I can't eat another bite."

"No dessert?" Nassar asked.

"Not for me."

"Join me in a bourbon," Nassar said.

Without waiting for a response, Nassar motioned for the waiter. As soon as he arrived at the table, Nassar said, "Two Blanton's bourbons."

The waiter nodded and stepped to the bar.

Nassar withdrew a bulging envelope from his inside coat pocket and slid it across the table to Alexander. He held his fingertips on the edge of it.

Alexander looked at the envelope for a moment, unsure what was to follow. Then he reached for it.

Nassar kept his index finger on the edge and locked eyes with the young senator. "Bart Madison wanted me to remind you about the intel summary."

"Oh, I know," Alexander said. "I'm sending it Monday." He tried to pull the envelope closer to him. It didn't move.

"I want to know if the US is going to go after the cartels along the southern border," Nassar said. "I want it kept open."

"I haven't heard any mention about the US going after any of the cartels, and the border is open."

"That's good, Senator. I want it kept that way. Do you understand?"

"Not to worry. I understand."

Nassar removed his hand. Alexander grasped the envelope and slid it into the inside pocket of his sport coat.

The waiter returned and set the glasses of bourbon in front of them. The senator gripped his glass and drank half of it before he set it back on the table.

"Keep on SOCOM," Nassar said. "We want to know what Kenworth is planning." He reached for his drink and took a sip.

Alexander nodded. "I understand," he said, then he picked up his glass and downed the remainder. He realized he was in over his head and didn't have a life preserver.

"Cheer up, Senator," Nassar said as he set the glass on the table. "It is not so bad. We will take care of you. There is a beautiful young lady waiting for you in your room. She will cheer you up." Nassar took another sip of his drink, then stood. "Enjoy the rest of your weekend. I will be talking to you soon." He walked out of the restaurant.

# CHAPTER 11

Tuesday, December 20, 2016
Darién Gap
Near the Panamanian-Colombian Border

T HE MUSLIMS, AS agreed, were all too happy to support Madison
in the final phase of his plan after the F-16s landed in Iran. He relocated to the jungle compound once used by the FARC, on the Panama
side of the Darién Gap. On that side of the isthmus, the geography is
mountainous rainforest. The Colombian side is river delta and swampland. No improved roads were in the gap, only primitive jungle trails.
Most of the area was under dense canopy, making detection from overhead very difficult. Madison knew the area well and chose the location
for its seclusion and concealment. The terrain favored him.

The compound had not been used for a couple of years, and the
jungle was trying to reclaim it. Vines were climbing on the few buildings, and grass and bushes grew where none had grown before. When he
arrived, Madison went to work making repairs and planning the security
of the site while he waited for his trusted friend, Franco Trujillo. Madison
worked for Trujillo when he was commander of the Fifty-Seventh Front,
FARC. He expected Trujillo to arrive sometime that day.

At dusk he arrived, accompanied by his girlfriend, an Emberá native.
The evening jungle came alive with the sounds of nocturnal creatures as
they began their normal routine. Madison had prepared a small fire to
cook the fish he had caught that afternoon, and the native girl gathered
fruits, berries, and tubers. The aroma of the fish cooking competed with
the smoke as it rose upward, seeking freedom as it climbed through the
humid air. The dense canopy blocked the view of the night sky and any

breeze. The three ate around the fire, sitting in old chairs Franco had retrieved from the main building.

Franco wiped the sweat on his shaved head with his hand, then dried it on his jungle trousers. "There is a weapons cache not far from here," he said. "We kept it quiet. We didn't go along with the FARC–Colombian peace agreement that was signed last month. One of the things we were supposed to do was turn in all of our weapons. We didn't think that was a good idea. It is well stocked with just about everything you may need."

Bart withdrew a folded piece of paper from his pocket and handed it to him. "This is a list of soldiers and equipment I need. Can we inspect your weapons tomorrow?"

Scanning the list, Franco nodded. "I can get the fighters within two days. The small arms and ammunition are no problem. There are a couple of items I will need to check on. Yes, we will inspect the weapons tomorrow."

Bart stood and stepped to the porch of the main building. Two iguanas darted across his path. Reaching the porch, he stooped and withdrew a bottle of Crown Royal Reserve from his rucksack. He returned to the fire with the bottle in one hand and withdrew his knife from the sheath on his belt with the other hand before he sat. Setting the Crown Royal beside him, he grasped the water bottle Franco drank from and cut it in half. He then filled it with two fingers of whiskey and handed it back to him. Bart motioned with the whiskey bottle to the native girl who sat next to Franco.

She shook her head.

Bart cut his water bottle in half, then poured in the whiskey. He held up his makeshift glass. "To old times, my friend."

Franco held up his whiskey. "And many new ones." He withdrew the cigar pouch from his shirt pocket, took out two Cuban cigars, and handed one to Bart.

"Thank you," Bart said as he took the cigar and placed it in his mouth. He picked up a twig and stuck it in the fire. When it lit, he withdrew it and held it up for Franco to light his cigar. He watched him pull on it, then blow out the smoke. Then he used it to light his own.

The two stared into the fire as it crackled. They sipped the whiskey and smoked their cigars. Franco's girlfriend excused herself and left the men to themselves.

———— • + • ————

Friday, December 23, 2016
Darién Gap
Near the Panamanian-Colombian Border

By the second morning, Franco's fighters began arriving at the compound, and he put them to work improving security. They maintained the undisturbed appearance of the few places where the compound was exposed to overhead observation. Almost all of the fighters were seasoned former FARC soldiers, and none of them supported the peace agreement. They were loyal to Franco. Many of them arrived with their own weapons. In no time the compound came to life. Patrols were established and sentries posted.

After he inspected the weapons cache Wednesday morning, Bart had departed to rendezvous with the Zetas representative to make the final coordination for the delivery of the nuke into the US. Ensuring the route had been reconned and that the Zetas members knew the plan was essential. Madison coordinated for supplies and transportation at specific locations along his route. Although Senator Alexander assured Madison the American border was open and would stay that way, he knew that trusting a politician was futile. Los Zetas had two people positioned to observe the border at the crossing, watching for any change in routine or increased security. Madison worked with the Zetas lieutenant on a deception plan to draw attention away from where he planned to enter the US.

On Saturday afternoon, Madison returned to the compound. Aside from the sentries, he saw three specially equipped Toyota Land Cruisers camouflaged under the canopy. He scanned the compound, looking for any vulnerable areas that needed attention. Not wanting to stay at that location any longer than necessary, he needed time to get the soldiers versed on the operation and locate the stream of migrants heading through the gap. The former FARC soldiers had survived in the jungle for years and knew it well. Their survival had depended on tight security in the past, and they applied it once again.

Madison and Trujillo sat at a makeshift table beneath a large mango tree and planned their onerous route through almost thirty miles of the most inhospitable jungle in the world. Their planning had to be exact and thorough, as the first leg of the route would take them to where everything would kill them. The lawless wilderness posed dangers at every turn, from armed guerrillas and drug traffickers to some of the world's most deadly creatures, the jungle heat, mountainous rainforests, and swampland. In addition to ammunition, they had to carry fresh water, food, and medical supplies. Once out of the dense jungle, they would pick up the Pan-American Highway in the small village of Yaviza. From there, they would proceed to rendezvous with Los Zetas in El Salvador, then on to the American border with planned stops along the way.

Aside from the obvious dangers of the jungle, they had to plan their route to avoid the illegal migrants making their way along the drug routes from Colombia through the gap and north through Panama. These convoys were a magnet for guerrillas, smugglers, and other bad actors looking to make a quick buck from the vulnerable migrants. The SENAFRONT, or National Border Service, a paramilitary police force responsible for border security, flew along the known smuggling routes to track immigrants. That was also a threat Madison had to contend with.

The planning session lasted until nightfall. As the patrols returned, the leaders reported to Franco and provided the intelligence they had collected with notations on their maps. A large migrant flow was identified, and suspected hostile camps were noted on their flanks. The patrols also identified the condition of possible routes through the jungle that the vehicles could traverse and those that should be avoided. The gap was veined with routes. Some were better than others; a few led to traps or nowhere. After the last patrol reported in, a clear picture of the best trail emerged.

Franco's girlfriend, barefoot with a colorful cloth around her waist, had cooked the evening meal for them on the open pit—fish and iguana, served with roots and tubers. Papaya, mango, and pineapple were the dessert.

After their meal, Madison and Trujillo sat around the fire, smoked cigars, sipped whiskey, and listened to the jungle. The raucous sound was welcomed, as silence meant danger. As soon as the native girl cleaned up after the meal, she took her place next to Trujillo.

Late Sunday morning, Madison and Trujillo, with several armed fighters, were camouflaged in the dense vegetation around the landing zone, waiting on the arrival of a helicopter a few kilometers from the compound. The thumping of the rotor blades signaled the approach. The low-flying helicopter circled the landing zone. Madison identified it as the one he expected, then stepped out to direct it to land. He turned around to face where he had stepped out and motioned with his hand. A Land Cruiser arrived with two men inside. The 4 x 4 stopped clear of the rotor blades, then the men got out and approached the helicopter. By the time the vehicle stopped, al-Ghazāli and Nassar were out of the aircraft and greeting Madison. Nassar directed the men to unload the nuke and place it in the Land Cruiser. Within two minutes, Nassar motioned to the pilot, and the blades sped up. The pilot nodded, and the helicopter lifted off. Madison, leading the others and the 4 x 4, disappeared back into the jungle.

———— ✦ ✦ ✦ ————

Monday, December 26, 2016
Gareth Residence
New York, New York

Henry Colby, a senior intelligence officer, had assumed the duties of Jonathan Wellington after he was killed in Iraq. Colby had been Wellington's deputy, and he was well-versed on the Gareths. He knew Jenny had climbed into the bottle after losing the election and that Stew was terrified Madison was going to kill him.

Henry had returned Stew's call, and the two had been on the phone for ten minutes.

Stew pulled on the cigar in his mouth, then set it in the ashtray as he exhaled. "What happened to Wellington?" he asked.

"The Air Force hasn't released any new information. As I told you last week, they found evidence that the C-17 carrying Wellington was hit with an AIM-120 missile. However, all missiles have been accounted for. Reports have surfaced that two American jets took off from an area south of Palmyra the morning the C-17 was shot down. We suspect those jets were responsible for the shootdown."

"Who did it, the Syrians or Iraqis?"

"I don't know. Neither the Syrians nor Iraqis have any F-16s. As I said, the official report hasn't been released yet."

"Damnit man, you've got a pretty good idea. Tell me." Stew stood and paced around his desk as he held the phone to his ear.

Henry took a deep breath and was guarded with his reply. "We're just checking this out. Back in May, when Incirlik Air Base was attacked, two F-16s were used to ferry out the nukes the terrorists stole."

"Yeah, go on."

"The Air Force never found the F-16s. Those jets were probably the ones that shot down Wellington's plane."

"The damn Air Force can't find their jets! It's Madison. Are you going to get that *sonsabitch*? He's coming after me. You're telling me he has two American jets?"

"I didn't say that, Stew. I simply said those were probably the jets that shot Wellington down. We don't know where the jets are or who flew them."

"Hell, man, they're probably in Iran or Russia by now."

"We're searching for 'em and we'll get 'em. If they are in Russia or Iran, we'll destroy them."

"Well, what about Madison? Your people haven't been able to find or kill him. I told Jonathan, and now I'm telling you. He's killed Brock, Fitzgerald, and Wellington. I'm next on his list."

"You've got a good security detail. Just calm down. We don't know if Madison killed them or not. We'll get 'em."

"I been told that before, but it hasn't happened. Do you even know where he is?"

"All the reports we've received lead us to believe he is in Syria. I am confident we're getting close to him."

"When? After he kills me?" Stew terminated the call. Then picked up the smoldering cigar and stuck it in his mouth. He paced and puffed. After several minutes and a glass of Scotch, he sat at his desk. He stared at the phone for a moment, then picked up the receiver and punched in a series of numbers. He received an automated voice telling him to leave a message and his call would be returned. Stew left his name.

Stew looked up as his wife shuffled into the room. She attempted to keep the contents of her tumbler from sloshing onto the rug as she flopped into the chair in front of his desk. She sipped her drink, then sat the glass on a side table.

"I thought we agreed you would lay off that stuff," Stew said, noticing that she was dressed for the first time in two weeks. Although they were wrinkled and stained, she had put on slacks and a decent blouse. She had run a comb through her hair and even applied some foundation. Though it was too heavy, there was eye makeup. The eye shadow was a bit heavy and the mascara was smudged—but again, it was a vast improvement. "You look like you're feeling better," he said as he watched her take another sip of whiskey.

"I am," she replied. "Jonathan Wellington…he was killed last week, right?"

"The week before. Why?"

"Oh, right, right. I liked him. That is such a shame."

"We're about to wind up the same way. It seems Madison has disappeared, and the CIA can't find him. I talked to Henry Colby a little while ago. He said Wellington's plane was shot down by F-16s."

"Americans shot down his plane?" She took a drink.

"No, the CIA thinks it was Madison, and he is somewhere in Syria. They're no help. I'm positive it was Madison."

"What are you going to do?"

"I have an idea. I have a call in to Nassar. Maybe I can work out a deal with him."

"But you wanted the CIA to kill him. Can you trust Nassar?"

"No. If I can get him to help me locate Madison, I'll have Colby hold off on Nassar until they take care of Madison. Then he can have Nassar."

"Might work. But you'll need to have it taken care of before the new administration takes over."

"Let's hope it doesn't take that long."

Jenny wrinkled up the corner of her mouth and nodded, then picked up the tumbler and took a drink. As soon as her hand set the glass on the table, it slid to the TV remote. She picked it up, punched at several numbers, and the TV came to life. "What's going on in the world?" she said, more to herself than Stew.

At that moment the phone on Stew's desk rang. He looked at the phone, then to Jenny. "Mute the TV."

She complied, then shot an inquisitive look to Stew.

"Nassar," he said, and placed the receiver to his ear. "This is Gareth."

"You called," Nassar said. "I haven't heard from you in a while. What do you need?"

"I want to make a deal." Stew cut to the chase without the usual small talk.

Nassar, guarded in his response, listened to each of Stews words and how he said them. "What kind of a deal?"

"I understand the CIA is looking for you, and Madison wants to kill me. I can persuade the CIA to back off of you if you will give me the location to Madison."

"An interesting proposition. How do I know I can trust you? You wanted to double-cross Madison. Now you want me to set him up."

"You can. I'll pay you $25,000 for his location."

"What assurance will I have that you won't double-cross me?"

Stew and Nassar negotiated for several moments, trying to reach an agreement acceptable to both. Both of their lives were on the line, and they knew it. Each suspected the other was trying set a trap, and neither trusted the other.

"Madison is dangerous," Nassar said. "He will kill me if he finds out I made an agreement with you. I will require cash. Fifty thousand dollars, a letter from the acting CIA director, Colby…and a letter from you detailing our arrangement and why."

"Then we have a deal?"

"I will think about it and let you know. If we reach an agreement, I will require payment and the letters in forty-eight hours. The money will be delivered by courier."

"By courier? That will be a bit difficult."

"Those are my terms. I will let you know."

The phone went dead before Stew could reply.

Stew looked to Jenny. "Did you hear all that?"

"Just your side. What did he want?"

"Fifty thousand dollars, a letter from Colby, and a letter from me detailing our arrangement. The money must be delivered to him in forty-eight hours by courier."

"That's a lot of money just for Madison's location. If you put in writing the details of your agreement, that kinda keeps you from having him killed. Otherwise, it puts a noose around your neck. He could even use it against you in the future. What the hell are you thinking?"

"I know. I'll have to figure something out. One step at a time."

Jenny shook her head and upended her Scotch.

# CHAPTER 12

Monday, December 26, 2016
Darién Gap
Near the Panamanian-Colombian Border

T HE DAY HAD been filled with a myriad of activities associated with
Madison's plan. He only had a few days to hone the skills of the
fighters and prepare them for his operation. Patrols scoured the deadly
surroundings, seeking information and keeping track of the migrant
caravan. Each fighter rotated through the rifle range Franco established,
and weapons were cleaned. Madison had detailed specific duties and
rehearsed the soldiers on them. Not everyone could attend the various
training activities at the same time; they had to rotate through as time
permitted.

The sun was hanging low with only a couple of hours of daylight
left. The day's training and preparations had ended. Several Emberá
women, whom Franco's girlfriend had recruited, lit fires and were busy
preparing the evening meal.

Al-Ghazāli and Nassar walked to where Bart, in sweat-stained jungle
fatigues, sat by a small fire in an old wicker chair beneath a mango tree.
He glanced up at the two men as they approached and sat on a log near
him. Without speaking, Bart picked up one of the cups that sat beside
his chair, looked in it, then poured two fingers of Crown Royal Reserve
from the bottle beside his foot. He handed it to al-Ghazāli. Then did the
same for Nassar. He held up his cup to them. "It's been a long day."

Al-Ghazāli and Nassar held up their cups to meet Bart's, then each
took a sip.

Franco walked up and sat next to Bart. As was his habit, he wiped his shaved head with his hand then slid his hand across a dry place on his pants.

Bart poured two fingers of whiskey into a cup and handed it to Franco.

Al-Ghazāli lifted his cup to Franco's. "Your fighters look good. I visited your range today. Most impressive."

"Yes, they are quite good." Franco sipped his whiskey.

Nassar looked to Bart. "I received a call from Gareth."

"What did he have to say?" Bart sipped his Crown Royal.

"He wants to make a deal. I told him I would consider it. Gareth wants me to give him your location. In exchange, he will have the CIA not kill me, give me $50,000 and a letter from the Acting CIA Director Colby…and one from him detailing our arrangement and why. If I accept his offer, he must deliver the letters and money to me in forty-eight hours."

A wide smile emerged on Bart's face. "He's scared. That's good." He sipped the whiskey. "Do not trust him for an instant. He's up to something. Here's what I want you to do. Tell him you agree. Make arrangements to meet him in Mexico City on Thursday."

"You want me to give him your location?" Nassar replied.

Madison shook his head. "No, when you get the money and letters, then tell him I am in Raqqa, Syria. That same bombed house we met in. You will need to give him the location of the house. Tell him I will be there on January third. Tell your people to stage the house and surrounding area to look like there will be a high-level meeting. The CIA will take the bait and send in a team to identify the target. Allow the team in, but keep track of them. Tell them to send several cars to the house, as though they are taking people to a meeting. Then have your people sneak out through the back. The CIA may call in a Predator strike.

"Contact al-Baghdadi and tell him to spread the word the nuke will be taken to Latakia, Syria. It will be placed on a freighter on either the fifth or sixth of January. Tell him to be discreet, to give the story credibility."

Nassar displayed a look of confusion. "I don't understand."

"Gareth will tell the CIA where I am supposed to be. Then the CIA will send a team to assassinate me. With al-Baghdadi spreading the word that the nuke will be put on a freighter on the fifth or sixth, it will give credibility to the claim. I want the US focused on Syria. By the time they discover it was a ruse, I should have the nuke in the US."

Nassar smiled and sipped his whiskey. "I like it. What about Kenworth?"

"He'll pick up on what al-Baghdadi puts out. Hopefully, he will focus on Syria as well." Bart sipped his drink. "It just occurred to me, contact Senator Alexander and tell him the nuke is in Syria about to be loaded on a freighter. Tell him to lean on SOCOM and Kenworth."

Franco withdrew the cigar pouch from his shirt pocket, slid the cover off, and offered one to each of them.

Taking a cigar, al-Ghazāli said, "Thank you." He turned his attention to Madison. "You sound confident that will work. Can we count on it?"

Franco lit a twig, used it to light his cigar, then held it in front of al-Ghazāli for him to light his.

"It's no guarantee," Madison replied, touching a twig to the fire and lighting his cigar. "But the US will still be in holiday mode until after the first of the year. The new administration is looking over the shoulders of the old administration and won't want to take a chance on making the wrong decision. I feel confident they'll take the bait."

Al-Ghazāli nodded as he pulled on the cigar. "Using the senator is a good move."

Franco held the stick in front of Nassar for him to light his cigar.

Madison motioned with his cup to al-Ghazāli. "He will do what he is told. Kenworth will be forced to focus on Syria."

Nassar, holding the cigar between his thumb and index finger, turned to al-Ghazāli and spoke to him in Arabic. Nassar looked to Madison. "We will leave in the morning."

Their conversation lightened and continued for another twenty minutes. Franco tapped Bart on the leg with the back of his hand, then pointed to his girlfriend. She was standing at the fire several feet away, motioning with her hand to come for their food. "Time to eat, gentlemen," Bart said. The four men finished their whiskey, stood, and walked toward the woman.

An hour after their meal, the camp had settled down for the evening and most were preparing to turn in. Bart was sharing a final drink around the fire with Franco, Nassar, and al-Ghazāli. They were going over a few details of Madison's plan. There wouldn't be time in the morning before Nassar and al-Ghazāli departed. They were well-versed on the plan, but al-Ghazāli had requested clarification on several points.

The fire popped and crackled as it began to die down. Their conversation dwindled, and Madison poked at the fire. One of the sentries, carrying an M16 rifle, approached. He stopped near Franco and spoke to him in Spanish.

Franco turned to Madison and in a low voice said, "We have a visitor." He and Franco stood. As a reflex both men touched their sidearms.

Franco leaned toward the sentry and, with a low voice, directed him in Spanish to alert the others. He cautioned him to be as quiet as possible and send four armed men to meet him at the entrance to the camp.

Bart looked to the other two. "Wait here."

The two men scrutinized their surroundings with caution as they walked to the entrance. Approaching the guard post, they saw the second sentry standing relaxed, but holding his M16. Beside him was a man in his mid to early thirties, a scraggly beard resembling that of Che Guevara. His camouflage pants were mud-stained. The unarmed man stood relaxed. His body odor signaled that he had been in the jungle for several days.

"What do you want?" Franco said, stopping a couple of paces in front of the man.

"I know you," the man said as a slight smile appeared on his face. "Franco, isn't it?"

"I am Franco. I seem to remember your face...Cisco "

The man thrust out his hand, "*Sí,* Cisco."

Franco didn't take the man's hand. He studied him for a moment. "It is dangerous to walk in the jungle at night unarmed and alone."

Cisco dropped his hand. "Yes, it can be. But I am not alone. My men are behind me in the tree line. Is the FARC operating again?"

"What do you want, Cisco?" Franco's voice was firm.

"How many men do you have? My men and I would like to join you."

"I have no room for you."

Cisco motioned to Bart. "You must be the American they are looking for."

Bart looked over the man and then the area behind him. He saw two dark figures twenty meters away. "Who's looking for an American and why?"

"They are offering a big reward for the American."

"No one wants me. You are mistaken. I am nobody."

"Be on your way." Franco's voice was firm.

Cisco shrugged, turned, and walked back into the jungle, disappearing in the blackness.

Looking at the sentry, Franco said, "Stay alert. The jungle is full of trouble."

"*¡Sí comandante!*" He returned to his position behind the sandbags of the guard post.

The other sentry returned and stepped behind the sandbags. Four armed soldiers followed. Franco held up his hand for the soldiers to stop and remain quiet. He scanned the area in front of them, then turned to the soldiers. "Follow him. He has at least two men with him. Kill them if you can."

Franco and Bart watched the soldiers disappear into the blackness, then turned and walked back toward the fire. "You know him?" Bart asked.

"He is with the guerrillas. They are into drugs, human trafficking, assassinations, and are known to rob migrants as they try to cross the gap. I do not like him. He is trouble and not to be trusted."

"He was checking us out," Bart said. "We'll move out on Wednesday morning. If our soldiers kill him, that will solve the problem. Otherwise, they'll be watching us, trying to determine our size, then hit us."

"I agree," Franco said. "I will inform the others."

"I'm going to turn in. See you in the morning." Bart and Franco parted.

———— ✦✦✦ ————

Tuesday, December 27, 2016
Gareth Residence
New York, New York

Stew could not get into his usual routine. He poured his third coffee, stepped back to his desk, glanced at the clock, and sat in his chair. The clock displayed 10:06. It had been just seven minutes since the last time he looked at it. He was accustomed to making things happen and calling the shots, but the situation with Madison was out of his hands. He had to wait and depend on others.

Jenny entered the office and walked to the coffee pot on the counter, filled a cup, then took a seat in the wingback chair in front of Stew's desk. She had showered, and her slacks and blouse were clean. The application of her makeup was somewhat improved from yesterday, but it was still haphazard. She sipped her coffee, and just as she lowered the cup, the phone on Stew's desk rang.

He picked up the receiver. "This is Stew."

He recognized Nassar's voice. "Do we have a deal or not?"

"Your offer is acceptable. Meet me in Mexico City on Thursday with the money and letters. I will give his location after I see the letters."

"Why don't we meet in DC or here at the house? I can't get to Mexico City by Thursday. I have several meetings."

"Mexico City on Thursday." Nassar's voice was firm.

"I'm not sure Colby can have the letters in time."

"Do you want Madison's location or not?"

"I do but the logistics are tough."

"You are stalling. Make it happen. Mexico City on Thursday, or no deal."

Stew used great restraint; it was all he could do to control his temper. "I will call you back with my flight details."

Nassar ended the call.

Stew returned the receiver to the cradle, grasped the coffee cup, and lifted it to his lips. "Cold, damn it!" He looked to Jenny. "That *sonsabitch* wants me to take the money and letters to him in Mexico City on Thursday."

"In two days?" Jenny said.

Stew lifted the receiver and punched in the number to Henry Colby.

It was several minutes before Colby came on the line. "Hello, Stew. What's on your mind?"

"I just got a call from Nassar. He wants me to meet him in Mexico City on Thursday with the letters and money. Write the letter we talked about."

"Will they be together? We could get them both and save us a headache."

"I don't know. If they are, good. I'll let you know as soon as I have the location."

It would be nice if we knew about where he'll be. I could have a team nearby. Depending on where they are, it could take a while for them to get there, and we could miss him."

"I'll see if I can get any more out of Nassar. Get me the letter as soon as you can." Stew ended the call.

———— •♦• ————

Wednesday, December 28, 2016
Headquarters, US Special Operations Command
MacDill Air Force Base, Florida

Max was frustrated that very little intelligence regarding Madison or the nuke had surfaced since early December and that most of it had been determined to be rumors. Senator Josh Alexander had contacted the SOCOM commander earlier that morning and wanted to know what Kenworth was doing. He told the commander he received information the nuke was in Syria and was headed for Latakia to be put on a freighter at the end of next week. He accused the general of being asleep. He wanted answers and wanted to be kept informed. The commander sent a note through the J3 to Max with the details of the senator's call. Major General Matherson took the note to Max's office.

Max, surprised at Chugs's unusual visit, stood at the appearance of the general. "Yes, sir."

The general proceeded to tell Max about the phone call from Senator Alexander. "Prepare a response for the commander," he said. "I don't like it, but we have no choice."

"Are you telling me to go to Syria?"

"No. Answer the note. And in the meantime, I'm going to do some checking."

"Yes, sir. You know we don't have any intel indicating the nuke or Madison is still in Syria. The information from Panama leads us to believe the nuke is or is about to be in Panama. My guess is Madison is there close to it. Danya's been pushing her contacts hard. She's keeping us informed. Do you know who gave the info to Alexander?"

"No, he didn't say. I agree with you that it's Panama. Unfortunately, the senator is involved and can make our lives miserable."

"If his info came from the CIA, it would help if we had access. I'll get Andy on it. If it wasn't from the agency, we need to know who. This doesn't feel right to me. We know Madison is good at deception. Probably one of his ploys. If you agree, I'll have Gail check around and see if she comes up with anything on him."

"I was thinking the same thing. Go ahead but keep it low-key." The general turned and walked out of the room.

Max summoned his team to join him at the conference table. As soon as they sat, he went over the note from the commander and what Matherson said.

"There has been no internet traffic to indicate Madison or the nuke is still in Syria," David said. "The information Danya provided points to Panama."

"I know. I want you to search again. Lean on your contacts."

Max looked to Gail. "Check back with Captain Mackenzie. See if he has any new info, and get an update on Gareth. Check out Senator Alexander, but keep it low-key. Something isn't right. Check back with your contacts on the southern border cartels."

"Got it," Gail said. "I'll have a friendly conversation with Dawn Blakey. She'll spill her guts and won't even know it."

"Be nice, Gail," Max replied, then turned his attention to Andy. "Get back with your sources at DIA. And I know it's a dead end, but see if the agency has put out anything. I'll contact Danya. She would have told me, but I'll see if she has anything new."

Max looked at each of them. "I don't want to get caught focused on Syria, and the nuke winds up in the US. I think Syria is a red herring, but we need to check every detail twice to make sure."

# CHAPTER 13

Wednesday, December 28, 2016
Headquarters, US Special Operations Command
MacDill Air Force Base, Florida

MAX WAS COMPLETING the final details of the commander's reply to Senator Alexander. The others on the team had been following his guidance as a result of the senator's note. They were trying to verify the information Alexander provided and its source.

The CIA remained a dead end. Andy's contacts could not find any record that Senator Alexander had been notified within the past five days. If anyone had any information, they were not sharing it. Next, he searched the database and talked with his connections at DIA. Although he came up emptyhanded, they agreed to dedicate time to discovering anything relating to what Alexander provided.

Gail spent over thirty minutes on the phone with Captain Mackenzie updating him with information since the last time they talked. She didn't mention Senator Alexander's call to the SOCOM commander. Mackenzie was a bit distant at first, reminding her that his chief was still unhappy with her. However, she knew how to work Mackenzie, and she soon had him relaxed. "It has been quiet here too," he said. "Mostly the same druggies. Nothing of significance or noteworthy information from the Muslims."

"Are you still watching Gareth?" she asked, ticking off an item on her notepad.

"That's another touchy subject with the chief," he replied. "He is pressuring me. I don't know how much longer we can stay on Gareth. He's pretty much stayed home."

"Keep watching him as long as you can. If I get any more info, I'll let you know. Later, Marion."

"Ok, Summers. Later."

Gail ended the call and took a deep breath before she called Dawn Blakey at Homeland Security. It didn't take long before Gail became annoyed with her and kept the update short. "Dawn, by the way, we were informed that Senator Alexander found out the nuke was in Syria and going to be loaded on a freighter. Do you have any more information on that?"

"Oh, Senator Alexander is so wonderful."

"Yes, he is," Gail replied trying to keep a straight face. "Do you know where or who he got the information from?"

"I don't know. He talks to a lot of people. It could have been from the agency or a dignitary."

"Would you please see if you can find out? We would like to contact whoever it was for more info." It was all Gail could do not to gag.

"I will talk with the senator and let you know."

"Thank you, Dawn." Gail hung up the phone. "Twit," she said to herself. She started to dial Captain Hadley in DC, but then she looked at the clock. *He's gone home for the day. Call him tomorrow,* she thought and hung up the phone.

"Geez!" David exclaimed as he hung up the phone, then stood.

"What is it, Sweet Pea?" Gail said as she looked up at him.

"Al-Baghdadi has released another message to his fighters," David replied as he stepped to her desk. "In his latest speech he tells his followers to be ready. He's said he's sending a bomb to destroy the American infidels. I checked with DIA, and they confirmed it was in his latest speech. I've called NSA and they are checking to see if they captured it as well."

Gail stood and walked to Max's desk, with David on her heels.

"David just found out about another message from al-Baghdadi," she said. "It looks like the nuke is still in Syria."

"I've checked this out with DIA," David said. "I'm waiting on a call back from NSA."

Max took his notes and read the text. "David, get DIA to send us a transcript."

"They're working on it."

"Brief Andy on this, and I'll get in touch with Danya to see if she has anything new," Max said, reaching for the phone.

Gail and David walked to Andy's desk and waited until he finished his phone call.

Max punched in the number to Danya and received her voicemail. He left a message for her to get back with him.

Within ten minutes Danya was on the line. Max didn't take the usual few minutes for cordiality; he got straight to the subject. He brought her up-to-date and gave her the message David intercepted.

"I just got back from a meeting with one of my sources," she replied. "This doesn't sound right to me. Remember about two weeks ago my source told me a shipment is coming into Panama, and it is a big deal? He hasn't found out any more about it, but he heard that one of the ex-FARC commanders was recruiting his former soldiers. I'll dig a little deeper and see what I can come up with."

"OK. But remember your promise. Don't go into the jungle."

"Max! I won't."

They ended the call with their normal I love yous.

———— • ◆ • ————

Thursday, December 29, 2016
Headquarters, US Special Operations Command
MacDill Air Force Base, Florida

The team finished their morning meeting covering the information they had collected over the last twelve hours. Gail had refilled her coffee cup and returned to her desk as her phone rang. "This is Summers," she said as she placed the phone to her ear.

"This is Taner. I've got some info for you."

"Good morning, Marion. Are you calling to make my day?"

"Perhaps. Gareth took a trip this morning. My officer on the stake-out followed him to the airport. Here's where it really gets odd. He left with his security detail and went straight to the FBO at the airport and boarded a private jet. His security did not accompany him on the plane."

"You're making my day. Did your officer find out where he was going?"

"It took a little persuading on his part, but the receptionist told him his flight is to Mexico City, returning tonight."

"That is interesting. We've had another report that the nuke is in Syria and headed for Latakia to be put on a freighter. We're trying to confirm the report, but nothing substantial as of yet. We've received other information to cause us to believe it is or will be in Panama. Keep this close hold for now. I'll let you know when I find out more."

"You damn sure better. I don't want a repeat of Manhattan. You almost cost me my pension."

"Don't worry, Marion. I've got to go. Talk to you later."

"Right." Mackenzie ended the call.

Gail looked toward David's desk. "Sweet Pea, are you over there?"

"Yes, Gail, *dahling*."

"Step over here."

David moved around his cubicle wall and walked to her desk. "What may I do for you?"

"Gareth flew to Mexico City. He ditched his security at the airport and flew alone. He's returning tonight. I find that very curious. Get with NSA and see if they've picked up any communications from, or to, Gareth. Have them look back two weeks."

David spun around on his heels and returned to his desk.

———— ✦ ✦ ✦ ————

Thursday, December 29, 2016
Darién Gap
Near the Panamanian-Colombian Border

On the second morning of the treacherous route through the dense jungle, a heavy rain shower slowed Madison and his fighters. At one point a flash flood and slick mud halted their progress. Although Franco's men knew the jungle well, Mother Nature was still the ruler, and she was often unpredictable. They had traveled almost ten miles the first day and hoped to make at least the same amount of progress on the second.

Despite all the hazards of the gap, Madison believed traveling over land was still the best course of action. Security at the airports and seaports was much tighter than at the border crossings. Besides, those overland ports of entry were easier to circumvent. In his favor was the tremendous number of refugees pouring across the frontier, overwhelming each country. Even the US, with its technology, could not adequately conduct checks and process the people and vehicles flowing into the country. The political pressure to keep the borders open was another plus for him.

Two hours after they began their day, one of the rear guards, his fatigues drenched in sweat, made his way to Franco. He brushed a leafy green limb to the side as he stopped. "We are being followed. I cannot tell how many. Maybe three or four."

"Stay alert and try to identify them. If they get closer, kill them."

The soldier nodded and headed back to his rear position.

Franco made his way to Bart and reported the information to him.

"The guerrillas are gathering intel on us," Madison said. "Pass the word to everyone. Stay alert."

Franco picked a large praying mantis from Madison's shoulder and placed it on a leaf. "Some say these are a symbol of good luck."

"Are you getting superstitious?" Madison asked as he watched him care for the insect.

"No. I just don't want to take any chances."

Madison checked his map for their position and the terrain in front of them. Then he reviewed the notes from the patrols. He motioned to Franco. "About two kilometers ahead is another stream. If the water is up, that'll slow us down and be a good place for an ambush. Send a squad up there to have a look. If it's clear, have them set up and secure a crossing."

Franco wiped the sweat from his face, then looked at the map where Bart pointed. He brushed a beetle from the map. "That could be a problem." He nodded, then stepped toward a nearby soldier. Two mud-splattered Toyota Land Cruisers, their wheels slipping in the mud, passed Franco as he talked with the man. Within a few minutes, that soldier and several others moved ahead of the slow-moving column.

———•♦•———

Thursday, December 29, 2016
Universal Aviation, Toluca International Airport
Toluca, Mexico

The private jet with Stew Gareth aboard pulled to a stop at the FBO, twenty-five miles outside the financial district of Mexico City, at 12:37 p.m. Looking like any of the many executives who passed through, Stew donned the jacket of his Brioni suit and adjusted his tie. With a briefcase in his right hand, he exited the plane and walked into the reception area. Nassar, seated in a chair near the desk, stood and buttoned the center button on his coat as he watched Stew walk in. He extended his hand to greet him. "It is good to see you again." Nassar was catering to the optics, in case anyone should be observing them.

"Right," Stew replied with a smirk.

"I have the conference room reserved," Nassar said. "This way." He motioned with his hand and escorted Stew into the room.

A large-screen TV hung on the wall. A platter of fresh fruit was on the credenza, a tray of pastries, nuts, and chips sitting next to it. Chilled juice, soft drinks, and coffee were on a side table. Nassar picked up the remote and turned on the local news. As a guard against eavesdropping, he adjusted the volume just enough to conceal their conversation.

Stew poured a cup of coffee, then placed his briefcase on the table and sat. Nassar picked up a bottle of juice and sat across from Stew.

"Do you have the letters for me?"

Stew opened his briefcase and withdrew the letters. He glanced at them, then slid them across the table to Nassar.

"Madison's location?" Stew said, holding his glance on him.

Nassar held up his hand. "Allow me to read these."

Stew scanned the room, took a sip of coffee, and checked his watch. Through the glass wall he saw an attractive woman enter the reception area and sit in a chair beside the desk. He turned his attention back to Nassar and watched him read. He raised his arm to check his watch again, then drank the rest of his coffee.

Nassar laid the letters on the table in front of him and sipped his juice. Then he set the bottle down and said, "You have the money?"

Reaching into his briefcase, Stew withdrew five stacks of crisp hundred-dollar bills. Each stack had the distinctive mustard color strap that signified they were stacks of ten thousand dollars. He slid the money across the table. "The location."

Nassar thumbed through each stack before he placed them in a large envelope. After checking them all, he reached inside his coat pocket and retrieved a folded sheet of paper. He unfolded it and looked at it before handing it over.

Stew looked at the paper, then his eyes rolled up to Nassar. "He will be in Raqqa, Syria, on January third?"

"Correct. I believe this concludes our business. Have a pleasant trip home. Please give my regards to your lovely wife."

Stew stood, closed his briefcase, and walked out to the jet.

———— • ✦ • ————

Thursday, December 29, 2016
Headquarters, US Special Operations Command
MacDill Air Force Base, Florida

Phones were ringing and the printers were spitting out paper in the work area. The sun had set, but the absence of windows made it difficult for the team to realize it. David had been on a phone call with NSA for several minutes. "Mexico City? Today? Geez. Send me a copy of the transcripts." He ended the call, stepped to Gail's desk, and waited in the side chair until she was off the phone.

"What is it, Sweet Pea?"

"NSA did capture phone calls between Gareth and Nassar. The two exchanged calls, and then again on the 27th, Nassar and Gareth made a deal. Gareth is to pay Nassar $50,000 and provide him a letter from Acting CIA Director Colby and Gareth about their deal. Then Nassar will give him Madison's location. They were to meet in Mexico City today."

"He met Nassar today." Gail looked at the clock. "He's on his way back now."

"One other thing," David said. "NSA also captured a transmission between Nassar and Senator Alexander. They are sending that transcript as well. Nassar told him to lean on SOCOM."

Gail's eyes widened. "That's how Alexander knew about the nuke in Syria. Get the transcripts. Max needs to see this."

As soon as David received the transcripts, he and Gail sat with Max and Andy at the conference table. They went through both transcripts, studying each to ensure there weren't any cryptic messages. "We know now how Alexander got his info and that the story about the nuke being in Syria was another of Madison's deceptions. It is Panama. Danya was right."

# CHAPTER 14

Friday, December 30, 2016
Mossad Safe House
Balboa, Panama

MAJOR NATAN TOMARI of the elite Israeli force Sayeret Matkal met with Danya and Thaddeus Nussbaum, Chief of Mossad Station, Panama. They had previously briefed him on the current situation, and this was one of his daily updates to them. A large map of the country was displayed on the monitor that hung on the wall, with graphics overlaid on the map indicating their progress.

Thaddeus had requested assistance from the elite unit to help them search for Madison in the vast area between Venezuela, Colombia, and Panama after they learned of Nassar's trip to Bogotá on 30 November. At that time the Israeli Military Intelligence was reluctant to authorize the unit to conduct operations on the isthmus. However, after Danya reported that both Madison and the nuke were on the isthmus, Thaddeus again requested assistance from the Israeli forces, and the soldiers had arrived on 20 December.

Major Tomari, with a laser pointer in his hand, pointed to the map. "As I stated yesterday, one of the two-man reconnaissance teams working the area did locate a column suspected to be that of Madison on 28 December. For two days they followed and tried to determine if, indeed, it was Madison, and if the nuke was with him. From the description and photograph of him, we believe he is leading the column. They suspect the nuke could be in one of the Toyota Land Cruisers, but they have not verified it yet."

"Where are they now?" Thaddeus asked, shooting a glance to Danya.

Major Tomari shined the pointer on the map and looked to him. "Approximately here. That's about sixteen to nineteen kilometers from the end of the worst part of the jungle. They are heading in a northerly direction, probably toward Yaviza. However, they could alter their course and go to the Tuira River, causing us additional problems. The river will be much faster than the jungle."

"How far away from the immigrant convoy are they?" Danya asked as she made a note on her pad.

"It varies. They meander from as close as one kilometer to about two kilometers."

"What about an air strike?" she replied.

"They are smart and sticking to a route with a thick canopy. It is just too thick for overhead detection. We don't have the assets in country for such an attack."

"I was thinking about the Americans," Danya said.

"They will tell you the same. We have another problem." He looked to both Danya and Thaddeus. "We have lost contact with the recon team that was following the column. They missed the last check-in. I have sent one of the other teams to go to their last reported location."

"Keep me updated," Danya said as she stood and left the room.

Ten minutes later Danya punched in the number to Max's secure line at SOCOM. She proceeded to convey the latest update from Major Tomari. "Yes, he is confident that Madison is leading the convoy, but he can't confirm he has the nuke. Tomari has lost contact with his soldiers following the column."

"Madison probably spotted them," Max said. "Send me their last known location."

"Already did."

"I'll see what assets we have nearby. Senator Alexander called the SOCOM commander again this morning. He is pressuring the general and wanted to know if I was headed to Syria. He did try to tell the senator that the intel we had pointed to Panama, but he wouldn't hear of it."

"Are you heading this way?" Danya asked.

"It looks like it, but I don't know when just yet. Hold on while I open your email." Max checked for the classified email Danya sent, opened it, and examined the location. "I'm looking at the location you sent. I agree with Major Tomari; Madison could change directions and go to the river. We've been trying to get time on the satellite, but so far nothing. The canopy is so thick, it wouldn't do us much good anyway. Let me know as soon as Tomari confirms the nuke is with Madison."

Because of the tempo, Max didn't spend the last few minutes with Danya on the phone, as was their custom. It was brief, and Danya closed with their customary closings of affection.

———— • • • ————

Friday, December 30, 2016
Darién Gap
Near the Panamanian-Colombian Border

Two bloody bodies lay on the edge of the trail Madison's column was traveling. Bart, Franco, and one of the rear-guard soldiers searched the pockets and equipment of the dead men but found no valuable intelligence. To Bart's professional eyes, however, the corpses told him a lot.

"Israelis," Bart said as he looked to Franco.

"Are you sure?" he replied and shifted his weight.

"Look at them—their uniforms, weapons—and a dead giveaway is that they aren't wearing unit patches. This concerns me. Let's get back to the column."

Once they returned to their positions, Bart checked his map to determine the terrain ahead. He wiped the sweat from his face, then looked to Franco. "I don't think Kenworth has found us, but those two Israelis were recon. Here is where we crossed the river yesterday. It was a piece of cake, but we won't be so lucky next time. If we stay on this course, we'll lose most of our cover and be in the open here, at the lowlands. No doubt, Kenworth anticipates our direction and will attempt to intercept us about here. We're going to change course and travel northwest to the mountains."

Franco followed as Bart pointed to the map. "That is rough terrain," he said. "I don't think the Toyotas can make it."

"I know. That's a problem. But I don't want to get caught in the open. I need to know where Kenworth is. Send a team to scout out a route to the mountains. Have them look for a good place for us to stay for a day or two that's a good defensive position."

"I remember a cavern here on the east side," Franco said. "About where those two ridges go to the northeast." He put his finger on the location.

"OK, send the recon there. What do you know about this airport, El Real, here?"

"It's not much of an airport. Just an old airstrip, a couple of buildings, and it is located six and a half kilometers southwest of Yaviza. Why?"

"I just had an idea. Send your team out and have them be quick."

————— • ◆ • —————

Friday, December 30, 2016
Gareth Residence
New York, New York

Stew was in much better spirits after returning from his meeting with Nassar the day before, knowing the CIA would soon take care of Madison, and that problem would be eliminated. Energized, he sat back in his chair and smiled as he envisioned the rush brought on by the challenge, excitement, and money of the campaign. The thought of getting out of the house was stimulating. He was now able to focus on getting Jenny's new campaign up and running. He withdrew a legal pad from the desk drawer and began making notes. Money, as noted three times on the pad, was his big concern.

Many of Jenny's big donors had distanced themselves after she climbed into the bottle, and money had dried up. They wanted to see a vibrant candidate, not a drunk has-been. Stew knew not to approach them until Jenny could be seen in the media in a positive light.

A news bulletin popped on the TV and captured his attention. It described a devastating eruption of the San Miguel Volcano and earthquakes in El Salvador. It was an initial report, and the information was sketchy. However, many people had died, and there was extensive damage to the city.

The volcano was eleven kilometers southwest of San Miguel, the country's third most populous city, 115 kilometers southeast of San Salvador, the capital. The Gareth Foundation's mission was to provide humanitarian and disaster support to areas around the world struck by natural disasters. Stew, through the Foundation, had made millions of dollars supporting governments around the world, from Haiti, Argentina, the Philippines, and almost every country in between. Wherever a disaster occurred, the Gareth Foundation was involved. Rumors had surfaced after each event that only a small portion of the money and support actually made it to the affected people. Stew always overcame these reports without legal repercussions, and they died almost as fast as they surfaced. He saw this latest disaster as an opportunity for money and positive media coverage for Jenny.

Stew picked up the phone and dialed his contact at USAID. As he was waiting, Jenny entered his office and sat in the chair in front of his desk. Stew left his name and asked for a return call.

Jenny was pulling herself together. Her clothes were clean and wrinkle-free, and she had just returned from the hairdresser. To Stew's surprise, she wasn't drinking, and she professed not to have had a Scotch in almost three days.

"There was a volcanic eruption and earthquake in El Salvador," he said as he returned the phone to the cradle. "This could be a good opportunity for the Foundation, and you could get some good publicity."

"El Salvador? I haven't heard anything about it."

"I just saw the news bulletin. We'll get all the networks touting how you are helping those poor people. Everyone will see you out there in a positive light and forget about the election."

"I see where you're going with this, but what about Madison? He wants to kill you, and me, remember? El Salvador's a pretty rough place. It might be better to wait a while."

"Colby'll take care of him on the third in Syria. We can't get to El Salvador before then anyway." Stew's arrogance fueled his excitement and overpowered his caution. "Call your press secretary and tell her we're going to help El Salvador with the disaster. Make sure she knows we want lots of coverage. Tell her I'm working on the itinerary now."

"I hope you're right about Colby and Madison being in Syria. Do you want me to start alerting the staff?"

"Yes. We'll take the usual advance party. Tell them to be ready to go as early as next week. Maybe Wednesday or Thursday."

Stew returned his attention to his pad and made several notes. His contact at USAID returned his call, and Stew was promised a contract for humanitarian support, including food, water, blankets, tents, cots, and generators. During the conversation, Stew recognized the easy money and added another tasker for heavy equipment and trucks. Money was flowing like an ATM machine on steroids. The contracts were promised within the next two days.

———— • • • ————

Friday, December 30, 2016
Headquarters, US Special Operations Command
MacDill Air Force Base, Florida

For a little over an hour, Max had been in Chugs's office discussing the current situation. They again reviewed the transcripts between Nassar and Senator Alexander, and the one between Gareth and Nassar. The general had invited the staff attorney to sit in. "Alexander is pushing us to go to Syria, but the intel indicates Panama," Max said as he looked to the attorney. "I recommend Gail go to DC and call on Alexander. She could ask him basic questions, such as who told him, who can verify his information, and things like that. My hunch is that he will contact Nassar or Madison and tell them the FBI is asking questions."

"She should not accuse him, but just question him for background. Nothing threatening," the attorney said. "You may be right that he'll contact Nassar or Madison. Have Gail come see me and I'll tell her exactly what I want her to say and do. We'll get a recording of everything. We have enough evidence to arrest Alexander, but we need to get Madison. I don't want Alexander to lawyer up yet."

Chugs nodded. "That should cause things to happen. I agree that the senator will contact one of them. Then we'll have the correct location and the conversation on tape. Let's do it."

Max nodded as he stood and picked up his notes. "I'll get it planned."

Max returned to his office and assembled the others around the conference table. He relayed Chugs's guidance. "Gail, the attorney is expecting you. He has specific instructions for you."

A slight smile emerged on Gail's face. "Damn! This's going to be fun." She sat back in her chair.

Max looked to Andy. "We must get all of this recorded. Coordinate with NSA and DIA."

Turning his attention to the TV monitor, he addressed Danya. "How confident is Major Tomari that Madison is leading the convoy?"

"He's ninety, ninety-five percent certain," she replied.

"Danya, I need verification the nuke is in one of the vehicles. I don't want to assault the column and the nuke not be there. Alexander will have our heads if we strike them and the nuke turns out to be in Syria. Get with Major Tomari and see if he can get us verification."

"Will do. Another team is headed to the last location we had. They'll try to pick up the trail, if it hasn't washed out. It's raining now."

Max looked at his watch, then back to Gail. "Go meet with the lawyer, then get back here and set your meeting with Alexander for Monday." She grasped her papers as she stood, and marched out of the room.

———— ✦✦✦ ————

Friday, December 30, 2016
Darién Gap
Near the Panamanian-Colombian Border

The rain had stopped and the sky cleared, revealing the evening stars. The recon team guided the column into the dark cavern. A waterfall sounded from deeper inside. Several startled bats flew out of the opening. The vehicles were parked to one side, away from the entrance. Guards were posted, and a patrol was sent out to watch for anyone who might be following them. The remaining soldiers went about their duties in preparing for the night.

Bart and Franco sat by a small fire well inside and out of sight of the opening. Bart studied his map. After several minutes he looked up. "It looks like we have three choices. Each has pluses and minuses and would require us to cross the lowlands. The first is to proceed on to Yaviza. Kenworth probably suspects we are headed there to pick up the highway. The SENAFRONT will be checking there, which we planned for. The second is to go to the Tuira River. There are smugglers, drug traffickers, and SENAFRONT operating along the river we would have to deal with. We would need to travel at night to avoid the SENAFRONT. The last option is to go to El Real Airport and try to get a cargo plane, if one is available. There is also the problem of the SENAFRONT checking the airport."

Franco shifted his position and stretched out his legs. "None of the options will be easy. One of my men is from a village on the river not far from here. He can arrange for boats. We will need to check out the airport. We don't even know if a plane is available."

Bart poked at the small fire. "We don't know if the Israelis or Kenworth is behind us, or how far. I need to think this out."

Franco rose and placed his hand on Bart's shoulder. "See you in the morning."

# CHAPTER 15

Monday, January 2, 2016
Senator Josh Alexander's Residence
Alexandria, Virginia

G AIL HAD MADE arrangements to meet with Senator Alexander at his residence. Although he protested, Gail insisted, and he agreed to meet with her on the last day of the holiday period. She had flown to DC earlier that morning. She grabbed a cup of coffee, then took a cab to the senator's residence in Old Town Alexandria. It was an easy ten-minute ride to the historic district from the airport. The traffic was light, and the pedestrians had not filled the street; otherwise the trip could have been considerably longer. Getting out of the cab, Gail gave the upscale condo a once-over. It was nestled among the historic buildings, art galleries, antique shops, and restaurants along a cobblestone street with a red brick sidewalk. *Just as I pictured where Alexander would live,* she thought.

The senator met her and ushered her in, taking her coat as she slid it from her shoulders. He seated her in the living room, which was bright with warm sunlight. Large windows offered a magnificent view of the Potomac River.

"Thank you, Senator, for seeing me today," she said, turning on her charm. It didn't take her but a few minutes to verify the picture she had of him. "As I mentioned on the phone, this is urgent. I'm just following up on the information you provided the SOCOM commander about the missing B61 nuclear bomb. It's just a few details I need to capture." She spent several minutes in light conversation with him, following the script outlined by the attorney. She confirmed the information Dawn had provided in their meeting at SOCOM, then a few more direct questions, but nothing pointed enough to put him on guard.

Alexander's brow furrowed, and his eyes narrowed. "Where are you from?"

"SOCOM."

"What's the FBI doing with SOCOM? Why the questions about the bomb? Is this an official inquiry?" His face was expressionless. "Oh, you were part of the briefing to my assistant, Dawn Blakey."

"Yes, I was. She's such a dear." Gail could barely keep a straight face. "No, sir. I'm just following up on a few items so we can move forward. Dawn didn't know your source. Can you tell me who gave you the information on the bomb? I need to verify it."

"I gave the information to the commander. Isn't that enough?"

"Well, Senator, it normally would be, but this is a special circumstance. It could have serious international implications."

"Oh, right. I don't know offhand who the person was that told me. I'm sure I have it in my notes at the office. It was probably some staffer from the embassy."

"When were you notified the bomb was in Syria?"

"I immediately passed it on to the commander the same day I received it."

"Did you give it to the CIA or FBI?"

"I think my staff did, or Dawn."

"I see. Why did you give it to the SOCOM commander? I wouldn't have thought of giving it to him."

"I don't know. I guess I knew he was looking for the bomb." Alexander looked at his watch and shifted his weight. "I'm sorry to cut this short, but the president has asked for an update in preparation for his meeting with the Russian ambassador."

"I understand, Senator. Thank you for meeting with me today. I think I have just about everything I need. Please get me the name and contact information of who told you about the nuke. I know you are very busy; you can have Dawn give it to me." Gail smiled and extended her hand.

Alexander shook her hand, helped her on with her coat, then held his gaze on her as she walked to the elevator. As soon as he was sure she was gone, he punched the numbers into his phone for Bart Madison, only to receive the message, *Phone not in service.* Alexander dropped his phone on the coffee table, then paced about the room. He stuck the fingernail of his right forefinger between his teeth and walked to the window. He turned and stepped back to the coffee table. Picking up the phone, he punched in the number for Nassar and heard the short recording, *Leave a message.*

The senator left his name, then returned the phone to the table and paced again. All he could do was wait for the return call. He stopped at the large window and looked out, then went into the kitchen. He filled a glass with water, sipped it, then set it on the counter. He walked back into the living room, sat in an easy chair, and switched on the TV. Nothing interested him. He stood and stepped back to the window. The wait was agonizing. After a half hour passed, the phone rang. Picking it up, he checked for a number, but *Unknown* was in the window. He started to ignore it, then he answered.

"Give your message to the person who arrives at your door in thirty minutes," a voice said. Then the call ended. Alexander looked at the clock, then paced. When the knock at the door sounded, he felt some-what relieved. He would be able to report the visit to Madison and then go about his business. He had no idea what lay ahead.

Alexander opened the door no more than six inches and peeked out. A man in his mid-thirties, dark complexion, short black hair, and wear-ing a heavy, brown coat stood opposite him.

"You have a message for me?"

"Well, ah…I'm not sure. Who are you?"

"My name is not important. You were told to give me your message. What is it?"

"Well, ah, an FBI woman was here. She said she was from SOCOM and asked me a few questions."

"You are to go to San José, Costa Rica. Be there day after tomorrow. I will make your reservations at the hotel you stayed in before. You will be met there."

"I can't go to Costa Rica. We go back to work tomorrow."

"I was told you would say that. I am to tell you to get your ass on a plane and go to Costa Rica. Bart will see you there."

"That's out of the question. I can't just fly off to Costa Rica on a whim. Have him call me."

"Be at the hotel day after tomorrow." The man turned and walked to the elevator.

Alexander felt cold—not from the winter, but from the man's visit. The instructions came from Madison, and he knew it.

———— ·•· ————

Monday, January 2, 2016
Darién Gap
Near the Panamanian-Colombian Border

Franco and Bart had met on the crest of the ridge overlooking their position. The only sounds were those of the jungle. The magnificent view across the valley was a lush jade spectacle. They could not see beneath the canopy, but they knew it harbored dangers of all kinds, one of which was the possibility of soldiers. They had not seen any, neither Israelis nor Americans, since Friday, but they knew they were on their trail. They took a few minutes to relax and admire the beauty.

Bart's SAT phone rang, breaking the tranquility he was enjoying. He checked to see who was calling. Recognizing Nassar's new number, he answered.

"We were contacted by the senator," Nassar said. "He was paid a visit by the FBI. He said it was nothing threatening, and they were following up on some information he provided."

"Yeah, go on."

"The FBI was the woman from SOCOM."

"Kenworth! They're on to Alexander."

"I knew you would want to know. I had the messenger tell him to go to Costa Rica, as we discussed. He will be there day after tomorrow."

"Good. I'm sure he balked."

"He did. I have other news. You need to change your schedule."

"What is it?"

"San Miguel Volcano in El Salvador erupted, and there were earthquakes. I understand there is a lot of damage to the city."

"That shouldn't affect us. It might even be to our benefit," Bart replied.

"No, you don't understand. It is a disaster, and Gareth is going there. He will not be in New York. He has been on the news talking about his Foundation going there to provide assistance. I did some checking around and found out they will arrive there on Wednesday. I am working on getting his itinerary."

"That changes things. I'll have to call you back. I want to think this through, as this requires an adjustment to the plan. I don't want to set up in New York waiting on Gareth to return."

"I understand. What about our agreement to strike the US?"

"Not to worry. I just might not be able to take care of Gareth and New York at the same time."

"I will tell al-Ghazāli. Are you going to meet the senator, or shall I take care of him?"

"I'll call you back."

Bart ended the call and slid the SAT phone back into his pocket. He looked to Franco and said, "We have a change of plans. Gareth is going to El Salvador and will not be in New York. A volcano erupted and there were earthquakes. Gareth's Foundation is providing assistance."

Bart began discussing possible alternatives to his plan. The two went over the pros and cons of each option. One possibility was to remain in the cavern. However, that was discarded as being too risky. They believed the longer they stayed there, the more likely they would be discovered by the Israelis or Americans. They spent over an hour studying the map and discussing their options.

"Here's what we'll do," Bart said, pointing on his map. "We're going to split up. You take fifteen men and go to the village here on the river. Rent a couple of boats and head up the river. Find out what you can from the villagers what the SENAFRONT is doing and about them making checks on the river, and the smugglers. Figure out what all you need, and I'll arrange with Nassar to have it waiting on you. I recommend you take the river north to where it bends back south." He traced the river with his finger.

"That's about forty miles," Franco said. "Depending on what the villagers tell me, I will plan for two days. We will travel mainly at night and close to the bank."

"I'm going to meet the senator in Costa Rica, then Gareth in El Salvador," Bart said. "I'll take six men with me to the El Real Airport and get a cargo plane. The rest of the men will go on as planned and bypass the border at Yaviza. We will meet in El Salvador. Splitting up will slow Kenworth down as he tries to figure out what we have done and who to go after."

"We go tonight."

"Right," Bart said. "You take the nuke with you. I don't want to meet the senator and Gareth while I'm sitting on the nuke."

"No, it would not be wise."

———— · ◆ · ————

Tuesday, January 3, 2016
El Real Airport
Southwest of Yaviza, Panama

Bart and his men crossed the lowlands undetected and began their surveillance of the airport and surrounding area by daylight. The small airport was the closest airstrip to the Darién Gap. It served the roughly 5,000 people who lived in the area and the occasional adventure-seekers destined for the no-man's-land. The airport had a single asphalt runway that could use some maintenance and a couple of metal buildings, one of which doubled as the terminal for the occasional flights. It was debatable whether Mother Nature or those responsible for keeping the vegetation trimmed was succeeding. It was obvious this was not a major airline hub. On the southern end was what appeared to be an airplane salvage yard. Several pieces of airplanes were scattered about the area. A weather-worn sign near the entrance read, Servicio y Suministro de Areo. "That's what we are looking for," Bart said to the soldier beside him as he pointed to the building. "You come with me." Looking to the others, he said, "The rest stay here and keep an eye out."

The two made their way to the unguarded gate and entered. They arrived at the door of the business and saw only two other people on the property, who displayed no interest in them. Bart attempted to open the door, but it was locked. Just as they were about to sit and wait for the proprietor, a man driving an old Willys Jeep pulled to a stop in front of the building. He held his gaze on them before he got out of the Jeep.

The man had a cigar stuck in the corner of his mouth and carried a cup. His jeans were oil-stained, and it was debatable whether his T-shirt was soiled or long past due for the laundry. In Spanish he said, "You boys lost?" He pushed up his faded blue ball cap.

Bart replied in English, "No, I think we are at the right place."

"American?" he replied in English. "Not too many Americans show up on my doorstep. Come inside. What can I do for you?" He displayed a broad smile as he opened the door and held it for his two visitors.

"Have a seat. You want some coffee?" The man seemed gracious and happy to have visitors.

"Coffee sounds good." Bart looked to the soldier next to him.

"Sí. Café."

Bart and the soldier sat in chairs in front of the man's desk.

"It'll be ready in a few minutes." The man turned and picked up the percolator on a table next to his desk. He filled it with water from a bottle, then shoveled four heaping spoons of coffee into it. He replaced the lid, plugged it in, and sat behind his desk.

Pictures of different airplanes decorated the walls of his shop. On one were several photos of him in a US Air Force flight suit standing next to a C-130 Hercules. On an adjacent wall, among other Air Force memorabilia, was a shadow board with patches, unit crests, ribbons, and officer ranks from second lieutenant to lieutenant colonel.

"You were an Air Force pilot?" Bart pointed to the shadow board.

"I was. The good old days. Now I'm just an expat living down here in the jungle. Well, what can I do for ya?" Sensing the two men in front of him were relaxed, the man casually slid open the center drawer of the desk, reached in, and withdrew his hand holding a .45 automatic. "Who are you, and what do ya want?"

"Hold on, mister," Bart said, as he raised his empty hands. "We're friendly. I'm looking to rent a plane."

"You with the government? DEA, CIA, or FBI?"

"Not hardly," Bart replied with a grin. "But if I was, do you think I'd tell you?"

"No, I guess not. You gotta admit, it's not every day that two guys wander in here out of the jungle. Especially, two armed guys looking like you two."

"I guess not. As I said, I want to rent a plane."

The man lowered the .45 and placed it on the desk. "What kind of plane, and where are you going? I have a single-engine Cessna I could let you have."

"I saw an old DC-3 out in your yard. I need to go to Costa Rica, then to El Salvador, and possibly one other place."

"That old DC-3 you are referring to is a workhorse. It may not look like much on the outside, but those engines are pristine. I keep it looking like that on purpose. The authorities don't pay much attention to me and leave me alone. I take her all over Central America to salvage aircraft. A sure way to have the authorities breathing down your neck is to fly around in a sleek, late-model aircraft." The man stood and leaned over to the table. He picked up a mug, looked inside it, then filled it with coffee. He handed it to Bart, then repeated the process and handed it to the soldier. He sat back down.

Bart sipped his coffee. "Can I have a look at it? It sounds like what I'm looking for."

"I gather from that you don't plan on landing at a major airport," the man said. He held his gaze on Bart, knowing what he was asking wasn't on the legal side of the law.

"Correct. I prefer to remain unnoticed. Can I take a look at your plane?"

"Let's go. Bring your mugs, if you want." Eager to show off his plane, the man led them out the back door and into the yard.

The plane had a faded and peeling company logo painted on the side, with Servicio y Suministro de Areo circling the middle. The aluminum skin was dingy with dirt from sitting out in the weather, giving it the appearance of being on its last legs. The pilot grasped the handle of the power cart, pulled it closer to the aircraft, plugged the end of its electric cord to the underside of the plane, then pushed the button to start the auxiliary power unit. It cranked several times, and then it came to life with a sputter. The man looked to Bart and gave a wink and nod. He stepped to the side door of the plane, opened it, and climbed in. Bart and the soldier followed. Ten seats were installed forward; the rest of the cabin space was for cargo. Several oil stains were on the deck.

The pilot entered the cockpit and slid into the captain's seat. He began flipping several switches, opened the cowl flaps, activated the fuel pump booster, and pushed the throttles forward. He turned on the pre-oiler and counted twelve blades as the right propeller spun. Then he flipped another switch, and the Pratt & Whitney engine came to life, belching out gray smoke. He repeated the process to start the left engine. "Whoo! A beautiful sound. Any questions?" He looked up at Bart.

"Sounds good. How long before you're ready to go?"

"Let me shut her down, and we'll go inside and do some paperwork. How many pax? Cargo?"

"Seven pax. Just our equipment."

# CHAPTER 16

Tuesday, January 3, 2017
Headquarters, US Special Operations Command
MacDill Air Force Base, Florida

AFTER MEETING WITH Senator Alexander on Monday, Gail called the office and gave a quick brief to Max and Andy before leaving DC, knowing she would be arriving late in Tampa.

On Tuesday morning Max, Andy, Gail, and David sat at the conference table. Their main focus was Gail's meeting with the senator and their next steps. She placed the small digital recorder on the table and pushed the button to play back the recording she made during her meeting. As soon as it ended, Andy said, "You weren't even out of the building when Alexander made a call. Two, actually. Both were to throwaway phones. The first was not in service. The second told him to leave a message, and he just left his name. He received a call a half hour later telling him to give his message to the person who would arrive at his door in thirty minutes. Madison and Nassar had planned for a possible phone capture on the senator. We don't know who went to his apartment or what was said."

Gail's eyes narrowed, and she pounded the table. "Well, shit! We don't have enough to hold him on, right?"

David jumped when her fist hit the table. "Gail, *dahling*!"

Max shook his head. "Our attorney said we don't have enough to hold him on. We need more. We do have cause for NSA to target him. Andy has made arrangements for a surveillance team. As soon as our attorney is satisfied we have enough to hold him, you can arrest him."

Max turned his attention to the VTC monitor. "Have Major Tomari's men located the column?"

Danya ran her hand through her hair. "They found the two missing soldiers. Both were dead. Rain has washed out the tracks, but they are continuing on the last known course."

Max looked to David. "Has there been anything of significance in the internet traffic?"

"Nothing new," David said. "It has been too quiet. That bothers me."

"I received this image taken over Raqqa, Syria," Andy said. "It appears to show a house being prepared for a big meeting. Note these cars in the courtyard." He handed the image to Max. "It sure seems like something of importance is going on there. Madison was supposed to be there today."

"It's a deception," Danya said. "He can't be in two places at once. I don't believe the nuke is there either."

"I agree that he's in Panama," Andy said. "But it's possible the nuke could be in Syria."

"It's possible," Max said as he tapped the eraser of his pencil on the table. "I just don't think Madison would be in Panama and the nuke in Syria. I'm going to recommend to the commander that we send a team to Yaviza to intercept Madison. Danya, if you get any indication he changes course and heads to the river, let me know right away. Keep pressing your sources."

<hr/>

Tuesday, January 3, 2017
El Real Airport
Southwest of Yaviza, Panama

The pilot escorted the two men back into his office. "There's a shower in the back, if you want to use it," he said as he pointed toward the back of the building.

Bart looked to the soldier. "Signal the others to come in," he said. "Then get cleaned up."

The soldier nodded, then stepped back out the door.

"Have a seat," the pilot told Bart as he sat down behind his desk. He pulled a worn map out of the drawer, unfolded it, and spread it out. "You said you want to go to Costa Rica unnoticed. Where exactly?"

"San José."

"There are about thirty or thirty-five airstrips along the Pacific coast." He put his finger on the map and said, "Here's one. It's about twenty minutes from San José and on private land. I salvaged a twin-engine plane there back in April. I think druggies were either using their own stuff or weren't very good pilots. It should've been an easy landing."

"Are you sure we can get in, and back out unnoticed?" Bart asked.

"Costa Rica has one radar system. It's at the Juan Santamaría International Airport in San José. It's used to monitor commercial flights. I'll come in from the coast at about 500 feet. If you agree, I'll call the owner of the ranch. He'll want a hundred bucks for us to land there, unless it's after dark. Then it's two hundred, because he'll set out smudge pots to light the runway."

Bart studied the man for a moment. "I plan to be there for about twenty-four but no more than thirty-six hours. From there, San Miguel, El Salvador."

The pilot wrinkled up the corner of his mouth. "Hmm, San Miguel," he said. "That could be a challenge. The volcano there erupted and they had earthquakes." He followed the same process in studying the map, then selected a suitable clandestine airstrip that met Bart's requirements.

"Plan on that stop for a couple of days," Bart said. "I may want you to fly me to Mexico after that. I'll let you know."

The man held his gaze on Bart for a moment. "Is there anything else?"

"No, that's it for now."

The man scribbled on a piece of paper, then worked the calculator on his cell phone. He wrote something else, then slid the paper across the desk.

Bart picked it up and raised his eyes to meet the pilot's. "I'll need to make a call. I'll have the money transferred and will need your bank info."

"OK. That price does not include Mexico, if you decide to go there. I've got to get some supplies, top off the plane with fuel, and several other things." He looked to the door as the rest of the soldiers filed in. "Make yourselves at home. I'll be busy for a while."

Bart watched the pilot leave the building. He called Nassar to discuss his itinerary and arranged for a car to pick him up at the airstrip in Costa

Rica. He gave instructions for his meeting with Senator Alexander. Before ending the call, Bart asked about Gareth, and Nassar confirmed El Salvador was still on his schedule.

———— ◆ ◆ ◆ ————

Wednesday, January 4, 2017
InterContinental Costa Rica at Multiplaza Mall
San José, Costa Rica

Senator Alexander finished his breakfast and sipped coffee as the waiter cleared the table. He scanned the room as he reached for the *USA Today* newspaper in front of him. Anxiety built within him with each passing minute. He didn't know what to expect, except that Madison had summoned him. He attempted to read the paper, but he couldn't concentrate; nothing interested him. Glancing to the entrance when a couple entered, he was somewhat relieved that it was not Madison. Rolling his wrist inward, he checked his watch, then looked again to the entrance. Seeing no one, he turned his attention back to the paper, hoping something of interest would occupy his time while he waited.

He began reading an updated story on the disaster in El Salvador when he realized someone had sat at his table. He looked up and was somewhat startled to see a well-groomed man of Latin descent sitting across from him.

"Do I know you?"

"No, but I know you, Senator. You will come with me." The man's voice was cold.

"Wait, who are you? I don't know you."

"My name is not important. I am to take you to Madison."

"OK, let's get this over with," Alexander said as he reached for his wallet.

"I have taken care of your bill," the man said.

Alexander stood, scanned the room to make sure no one was paying attention, then followed the mysterious man through the room toward the entrance. The man's pace was determined as he led Alexander out of the hotel to a Land Rover parked under the portico.

As soon as Alexander closed the door, the Land Rover shot forward and headed out of the parking lot onto the highway leading out of town.

The man never spoke, even as the senator questioned where they were going. About fifteen minutes later they were out of the metropolitan area and had entered the mountainous, tropical jungle. Several more minutes passed before the driver slowed and turned onto a dirt road that wound along the mountain and began to narrow as the jungle thickened. The man turned the vehicle onto what seemed like a seldom-used path. For almost a kilometer, the Land Rover jolted, bucked, and rocked along the trail as the foliage brushed its sides. It stopped abruptly at a small clearing by a stream.

"Where the hell are we?" Alexander asked, his voice full of concern.

The man got out of the vehicle, and Alexander started to follow. "Wait here," he said as he looked back to the senator.

The man disappeared into the dense vegetation. Alexander scanned the area. No one was there. He stepped to the edge of the stream and waited. Without making a sound, Bart Madison stepped up behind him.

"Senator Josh Alexander," Bart said. "We haven't talked in a while. I'm glad you could make it."

Alexander shot around. "Oh, Bart! You scared the shit out of me." His eyes traveled over Bart's fatigues. "Why are we meeting out here?"

A slight smile emerged on Bart's face, but his gaze remained predatory. "Don't you like it out here? I prefer being outside. Look around. It's peaceful here, and we're all alone—so far from all the prying eyes in the city."

The senator began to tense with Bart's words and demeanor. "But why all the way down here?"

"You haven't sent me an intel summary. In fact, you haven't kept me informed at all. I thought we understood each other."

"Bart, I…I can explain."

"I bet you can. You didn't even warn me the Israelis sent a team to Panama to look for me. That disappoints me."

"I don't know anything about the Israelis going to Panama."

"It's your job to know. You are on the Senate Select Committee on Intelligence and the Senate Committee on Armed Services. You are also supposed to be focused on SOCOM."

"I am, but I haven't been briefed on the Israelis and Panama. Even SOCOM has not been forthcoming with information. I did pressure SOCOM to send Kenworth to Syria, just as you instructed."

"Then why isn't he in Syria?"

"I don't know."

"I'll tell you why. Because you didn't try hard enough. I've paid you too much money for you to just make half-ass attempts."

Alexander became defensive and apprehensive. He was in unfamiliar territory, and he was sinking fast.

"What is the status of the US southern border?"

"Well, it's open, as far as I know."

"As far as you know? Senator, you were supposed to ensure it stayed open."

"It is. It is."

"Where is the intel summary for this week, and last week?"

"It was the holidays. I couldn't get much information. Besides, I…"

"You're a terrible liar. You just didn't fucking do it."

Bart reached for the survival knife on his belt, withdrew it, and with a quick thrust shoved the five-and-a-half-inch blade just under Alexander's last rib. The razor-sharp steel slid into his upper abdomen, slicing into the inner chamber of his heart.

The stunned senator fixed his eyes on Bart, and his mouth gaped as his heart stopped. His body dropped to the ground. Bart looked down at the corpse and saw the senator's dead eyes looking up. Bending over, he plunged the knife into the senator's lower abdomen and tugged forward, splitting the body open like a beef carcass so it would attract the scavengers faster. The guts poured out. Bart raised himself and stepped to the stream, where he knelt. Plunging his crimson hands and knife into the cool water, he watched as the blood faded into nothing. The water carried the last essence of Senator Josh Alexander's life away.

Bart stood and motioned with his hand to signal it was time to leave. Within moments, Bart's vehicle emerged, along with the man who had brought Alexander. No one said a word about the corpse. They each knew that by morning it would be stripped clean and the bones scattered. The two vehicles retraced their path out of the jungle and onto the main road. The Land Rover that delivered the senator disappeared along the highway en route to San José. Bart proceeded to the airstrip.

———·✦·———

Wednesday, January 4, 2017
Clandestine Airstrip
Southwest of San José, Costa Rica

Lightning cracked in the black sky as Bart approached the airstrip. Rain poured on the Toyota, making it difficult to drive to the old building where the plane was parked. A thunderclap shook the ground as Bart hustled through the rain and greeted the soldier standing guard by the door.

Bart walked inside, and the pilot stood and walked to him, pushing up his blue ball cap and puffing his cigar as he greeted him.

"I'm ready to depart when you are. I recommend to wait until this thunderstorm passes before we try to take off."

"We can wait."

———·✦·———

Wednesday, January 4, 2017
Headquarters, US Special Operations Command
MacDill Air Force Base, Florida

Danya and Major Tomari had contacted Max with an update from Panama. "I think we found Madison, or where he was," Danya said.

"Our recon began following the course that Madison's column was on," Tomari said. "They discovered he changed course just after our two soldiers were killed. It was difficult for our men to follow because of the rain, but they continued on the trail to a cavern on the northeast side of the mountain." He switched the monitor to display a map of the area, with a tick mark and the grid location of the cavern displayed.

"It appears Madison and his men were here for a couple of days. Madison split his forces into three groups on their departure. It appears that two were on foot and the third had vehicles with them. It looked like there were three vehicles."

"Could you tell where they went?"

"Yes, sir." Tomari switched the monitor again to display the three different routes depicted on a map.

"One group went along this way to the Tuira River." The arrow on the monitor traced the route. "The second went to the El Real Airport." Again, the arrow traced the path. "The third went to Yaviza." The arrow, once again, followed as Tomari spoke. "I don't have the men and resources to follow each route to catch up to them. I figure we are about a day behind them. If I try to check each option, it is a good chance we'll lose them again. What do you want me to do?"

"Max," Danya said, "I could go to the airfield and check that out. Major Tomari could go to the river."

"I'll brief Chugs and see if he can free up a team to help us," Max said. "The other day when I asked, none were available. This sounds like Madison. He split up on purpose to slow us down. He knows we're on his tail. Stand by and I'll get back to you after I discuss this with the general."

Max ended the VTC and stood to go to Major General Matherson's office. Gail stepped to him as he stood.

"Senator Alexander has skipped," she said.

"What do you mean, 'skipped'?"

"The DIA team that was keeping tabs on him said that yesterday, when he left his condo, they thought he was going to his office on Capitol Hill. But he went to the airport."

"Where did he go, and was he alone?"

Andy stepped to Max and Gail as they talked.

"He went to San José, Costa Rica," she said. "He's alone."

"The man that went to Alexander's condo after you left told him to go to San José. Why? Was it to meet with Madison or Nassar?"

"That's what we thought as well," Andy said.

"I checked with the senator's office and they said he was out of the office," Gail said. "They were surprised he went out of town. They didn't have an itinerary or know when he would return. Do you think that bastard decided to disappear?"

"I doubt it," Max replied. "He isn't that smart."

"Gareth is going to El Salvador," Gail said. "Marion called me just a few minutes ago."

"Gareth is on TV now giving a press conference," David said, motioning to the TV on the wall and turning up the volume.

They turned their attention to the TV.

"Is all this a coincidence?" Max asked, more to himself than the others.

"It would be convenient for Gareth to go on to Costa Rica from El Salvador if he was meeting with Nassar or Madison there," Gail said. "I just don't like it that all the players are in motion. Something is up."

Max looked to Andy. "Get ready to go to San José. I'm going to brief Matherson."

# CHAPTER 17

Wednesday, January 4, 2017
Headquarters, US Special Operations Command
MacDill Air Force Base, Florida

RETURNING TO HIS office after meeting with Major General Matherson, Max assembled his team at the conference table with Danya on VTC. Following the general's guidance, Max provided his team with directions. Resources were still tight, but Chugs agreed to send a Special Forces team to search for Madison between the cavern and the El Real Airport. Major Tomari was to pick up the trail of the three vehicles to Yaviza.

Max believed Madison knew he was closing in and split up his forces to throw him off the trail. Unable to cover each route Madison's people took, Max had to choose what he thought was the most logical one. He also believed Madison would take the fastest route with the nuke. The weight of the warhead, approximately two hundred and ninety pounds, required it to be transported by vehicle. That meant either over land to Yaviza and north along the Pan-American Highway, or to the El Real Airport and north by plane.

Max was sending Andy and Gail to San José, Costa Rica, to look for Alexander and determine who he had met with. Max was going to the El Real Airport in Panama. He anticipated the Special Forces team would have completed its search by the time he arrived. With luck, he hoped, the team would pick up Madison's trail. He coordinated with Danya to have Major Tomari meet him in Yaviza. Danya, although she objected, was to stay in Balboa, Panama, and continue working her contacts for any more info on Madison. David was to stay at MacDill to coordinate their activities and continue gathering intelligence.

———  • ◆ •  ———

Thursday, January 5, 2017
El Real Airport
Southwest of Yaviza, Panama

One puffy cloud was in the otherwise clear blue sky as the MH-60 Blackhawk transporting Max from the Tocumen International Airport in Panama City approached the El Real Airport. Visibility was excellent, and there was a slight breeze. The helicopter circled the airstrip before it landed so Max could get a good look at the area, hoping to identify where to start looking for Madison. Spotting a salvage yard on the southern end of the airfield, he directed the pilot to set down near it. At 1637 hours, the Blackhawk touched down.

Two armed soldiers exited the aircraft as soon as the skids touched the tarmac. They scanned the area, looking for any threat. One turned and motioned with his hand toward the helicopter, then Max stepped from it. Satisfied there was no immediate threat, the pilot shut down the two YT706-GE-700 turboshaft engines, and the rotors slowed.

Three figures—two women and a man—emerged from one of the buildings across the field. Two armed soldiers emerged and followed them. One of the soldiers motioned to Max to point out the people approaching. He turned and recognized the woman with short, wavy brown hair as Danya. "They're friendly," he said as he turned back to the soldier. He suppressed his anger at seeing her.

The two soldiers relaxed their position and continued to scan the area for threats.

Danya and Major Tomari flanked a Panamanian woman as they walked. Two Israeli operators joined them, following behind. The woman was dark-haired and attractive, and about the same size as Danya.

When the three stopped in front of Max, Danya said, "Hi, Max! You don't look very happy to see me."

"I am, but you were supposed to stay in Balboa."

Danya kissed him, then said, "This woman and her husband own this salvage yard and company, named Servicio y Suministro de Areo. If Madison flew out of here, I would bet this is where he hired a plane."

Max looked to Major Tomari. "Thanks for meeting me here. Take her inside, I'll be in in a moment. I need to talk to Danya."

The major escorted the woman into the office and the operators followed.

Max turned back to Danya. "I told you to stay in Balboa. What the hell are you doing here? You agreed to…"

"You're being overprotective, Max. I'm a big girl, and this is low threat. I can't stay out of it."

"You're also my wife, and I don't want you hurt."

Danya kissed him again and pressed her body into him. "I love you." She smiled as she locked eyes with him.

Max leaned forward and kissed her lips. "I love you too. I'm not surprised you're here, and I am glad to see you."

"My sources told me that the ex-FARC commander, Franco Trujillo, and his fighters are on their way out of Panama, and an American was with them," Danya said. "There was no need for me to stay in Balboa. I am more valuable out here." She smiled, kissed her husband, and said, "And you need me."

He knew from experience it was no use to argue with her. And she was right, he needed her. "What did you find out from her?"

"Not much," she said. "We haven't been here long. She is playing dumb but knows a lot more than she is letting on."

"Did you and Major Tomari follow the trail into Yaviza?"

"We did but didn't find anything," she replied. "The fighters that took that route were good. They didn't leave many signs, and we lost them near the river."

"Let's see what the woman can tell us." Without waiting for a reply, Max stepped to the entrance of the building, and Danya followed.

Major Tomari had the woman seated in the office area. Max looked around as he entered, and his eyes caught Tomari pointing to a picture on the wall. It was the photo of an American pilot in front of a C-130. Max knew that bit of information would be to his advantage.

"Your husband is a retired Air Force pilot?" Max asked.

The woman dropped her head and remained silent.

"We need your help," he said, his voice sincere. "We are not looking for your husband, but those that may be with him. We need to know where he took them."

"I don't know," the woman said, her voice just above a whisper.

"Several people told us your husband has a twin-engine plane," Tomari said.

"Who are you people?" the woman said. Her voice was harsh.

"I'm Max Kenworth, American, working for USSOCOM. This is my wife, Danya." He pointed to her. "He is Major Tomari of the Israeli Defense Force."

The woman looked to Danya as he pointed to her, then Tomari. Her expression displayed her confusion.

"Major Tomari is assisting us in looking for a group of terrorists. We believe your husband may have flown them out of here. What is your husband's twin-engine plane?"

"Your husband isn't in any trouble that we know about," Danya said as she touched the woman's shoulder. "But he may be in danger. He's with some very bad men."

"Are you people with the CIA?" the woman asked.

"Paulita, isn't it?" Danya said.

The woman nodded as she looked down at her hands.

"We are not CIA, Paulita." Danya said, her voice calm and reassuring. "Max told you who we are and that we are looking for the men your husband may be with. He could be in trouble with them." Danya stepped back, then walked to the refrigerator that sat against the wall across the room. She opened the door and withdrew a bottle of water. She twisted off the cap as she went back to Paulita and handed her the bottle.

The woman took the cool bottle and sipped. "My husband's plane is a DC-3. It's his pride and joy. He taught me to fly it. I usually go with him as his copilot, but not this time. He didn't want me to go. He said he didn't like the looks of the man he contracted with."

"How many men did your husband take on the plane?" Danya asked.

Paulita sipped the water again. "Seven."

"Did they have any cargo? Crates, boxes, or big bundles?" Danya's voice remained calm.

Paulita shook her head. "Just saw rucksacks and rifles. Six of them looked like locals; their leader was American."

Danya continued her questioning for another fifteen minutes, and the woman began to relax as she talked to her. The woman parceled out bits of information: She made meals for all of them to eat on their trip. She packed her husband's bag for several days. They were in a bit of a hurry. They contracted with him, and while he loaded the plane, they showered in the back room. Her husband didn't tell her all the details, just a few things, as he felt the less she knew, the better off she'd be. Although Paulita protested at his reticence, she had little other choice, and she had been down this road before when he did work for other nefarious characters. She didn't pressure him any further when he told her the American wanted to go unnoticed. Paulita knew he was not following the law, and that scared her. "I know he flew to San José, Costa Rica, when he left here," Paulita said. "Other than that, I am not sure how correct his flight plans are, since they were going to clandestine airstrips. San José is correct, as he called me after he landed. He will contact me again when he can."

Learning that Madison did not have the warhead when he flew out puzzled Max. He could only assume the fighters with the vehicles had crossed the river and made it to the Pan-American Highway in the vicinity of Yaviza. Determining that Madison didn't have the nuke with him meant it was either in the vehicles as he had suspected previously, or it was with the group that went on foot to the Tuira River. That was the least likely option, but now it required a more thorough investigation.

The Special Forces team that was searching from the cavern to the Tuira River was past due to check in. "Keep an eye on her," Max said as he stood. "I'm going to see if I can find the team searching the trail to the river. Don't let her talk to anyone."

Danya looked up to Max, then stood. "I'm going with you."

They walked out of the building to where the pilots and crew chief sat in the shade of the helicopter. When they saw Max approaching, they stood. "Let's have a look at your map," he said to the pilot.

The pilot turned, withdrew a map from the cockpit, and handed it to Max.

"I want to locate our team that was searching to Tuira River," Max said. He opened the map and spread it flat to display the area he described. "I want to fly from here, along the river, to about here." As he spoke, Max traced the route, following the river from the airstrip as it meandered from southwest to the northwest for about fifteen miles.

The pilot nodded, then motioned to the crew chiefs to prepare to take off.

Danya climbed in, followed by Max and two soldiers. The General Electric engines began to whine as the rotors turned. Soon after, the helicopter lifted off.

It didn't take long to reach the river. The pilot banked the aircraft and headed along the course Max indicated. At the fourth bend in the river, the pilot banked again and motioned to the left side. "There's your team, sir," the pilot said over the intercom. "I'll circle them again." The helicopter circled to the left and landed in a clearing a short distance away.

The sergeant leading the team met Max in front of the helicopter outside the prop wash and pointed to his map. "We picked up the trail at the cavern and followed it to the river, here," he said, tracing the map with his finger for Max to follow. "It looks like they had three vehicles with them when they started out. They split up here, at the Pirre River. The three vehicles took the trail to the northeast. The others, on foot, crossed the river then headed north to the Tuira River here, where it narrows, not far behind us. A couple of villagers told us that four of the men looked like they were carrying something heavy. They said it was wrapped and looked to be about a meter in length and about thirty centimeters in diameter." He spread his hands to indicate the size, then wiped the sweat from his face.

"That's what we're looking for," Max said. "They rented boats from the villagers and headed north. Go into the settlement and find out all you can about the fighters that rented them. Get what boats you need and head upriver. There's a lot of places upriver where they can hide or exit and take to the land. I'll see if I can get you some better equipment. We're heading back to the airfield. It's going to be dark soon, and we could never spot 'em from the air. I'll be in touch."

"Yes, sir," the sergeant replied. "They've got a pretty big head start on us."

"I know. Do what you can. If you catch up to 'em before I get back to you, keep eyes on 'em and don't lose 'em."

The sergeant saluted Max, then returned to his soldiers. Max stepped back to the helicopter and climbed in. He instructed the pilot to return to the airstrip. As soon as the Blackhawk was airborne, he contacted Chugs via secure SAT phone. He gave the general a quick brief and requested support for the team that he sent up the river.

"Are you sure you have located the fighters with the warhead?" General Matherson asked.

"About as sure as I can be," Max replied. "About a third of the fighters took a plane out of the El Real Airfield. I believe Madison was with them, but according to the pilot's wife, they didn't have any cargo. The rest of them took their vehicles and headed north. The sergeant that tracked the fighters from the cavern believes about another third of the soldiers split off from the three vehicles and headed to the Tuira River with the warhead. They headed northeast to pick up the Pan-American Highway. We need to get the fighters with the warhead before they get to the Bay of San Miguel, if that's where they're headed. By Madison splitting up his forces, I believe only a third of his force is guarding the warhead. He's taking a big chance to throw us off. That's in our favor."

"I'm looking at a map of Panama and Tuira River now," Matherson said. "There are numerous villages along the river and countless places for them to hide or to go back on land. I'll see what support I can get on short notice. I'll need to come up with something to satisfy the politicians. They tend to get a case of the nerves when combat troops cross international borders."

The sun was setting as Max ended his call with Matherson. He sat back in the seat for the final few minutes before they reached the airfield. Danya reached over and grasped his hand. She smiled as he looked to her. The helicopter set down on the tarmac. The pilots shut down the turboshaft engines, and the rotors slowed as the engines whined to a stop.

Standing outside the helicopter, Max waited on Danya to climb out. His SAT phone rang, and he fished it from his pocket. He looked at the number in the display window, recognized it as Andy's, and answered. "Hello, Andy. Whatta ya got for me?"

"Alexander did check in at the InterContinental Costa Rica in San José Tuesday afternoon," Andy said. "He had breakfast in the restaurant Wednesday morning. He was met in the restaurant by a man, and the two left together. The man was not Madison. The waiter that served Alexander remembered him. He said Alexander was nervous and seemed to be on edge. The man paid for Alexander's meal, and the two left together. The waiter had the impression Alexander didn't know the man that met him. No one at the hotel remembers seeing the senator since breakfast yesterday morning. He had a reservation just for the one night, and he never checked out. His overnight bag is still at the hotel."

"Did anyone at the hotel see Madison?" Max asked.

"No, no one. We showed his photo to everyone we talked to."

"Madison chartered a DC-3 and flew to San José late Tuesday afternoon. He could have met with him somewhere."

"Yes, but where? We've checked around but don't know where else to look." Andy's voice was filled with frustration.

"The pilot's wife said that Madison wanted to go unnoticed. There are a number of clandestine airstrips along the Pacific coast in Costa Rica. Take a look at the ones closest to San José."

"Will do," Andy replied.

"Madison didn't have the warhead with him. It looks like they are taking it up the Tuira River. To where, I don't know. Check in with David at headquarters and alert him. Madison has a long way to go and must have some help along the way. Have him keep an eye on all the clandestine airstrips up Central America and into Mexico. Madison could rendezvous somewhere along the route north and load the warhead onto a chartered plane."

# CHAPTER 18

Thursday, January 5, 2017
Damaged Area
San Miguel, El Salvador

T HE SAN MIGUEL volcano had erupted a week ago and continued to belch out toxic gases. Hydrogen sulfide mixed with sulfur
dioxide spread over the area with a rotten-egg and burnt matches odor.
Heavy volcanic ash covered the ground like a blanket of snow. Everyone
was required to wear a respirator mask.

Damage to buildings and property was widespread. Those closest to
the volcano took the brunt of the lava flow as it ignited everything in
its path. The molten rock spewing out of the volcano caused many fires
as it fell back to earth. Most of the structures that weren't burned were
reduced to rubble by the earthquakes. Several bridges were damaged,
and traffic had to be rerouted. Utilities were out and the streets were difficult to navigate; some were closed. People had been evacuated in a
five-kilometer radius of the volcano. However, not all of the residents
left, and the damage reached further into the city than expected. Portable
lights were erected at the worksites, and rescue crews worked around the
clock, meticulously searching for casualties. Some villagers were found
alive, while others were not so lucky. Rescue vehicles and personnel
were ubiquitous in the area. Most of the rescue effort was in the more
densely populated and severely damaged parts of the city.

The DC-3 carrying Bart Madison and his men had landed earlier that
day at a private airstrip on a ranch twenty-four kilometers south of San
Miguel. Nassar had met them at the airstrip with the items Madison had
told him to acquire—change of clothes, construction hats, identification

badges to match the rescue personnel, protective masks, maps, and four-wheel-drive Toyotas.

Madison had directed the men to change into their new clothes as soon as they got off the plane. He wanted the clothes to lose some of their new look, even get a little dirty. New, clean clothes would warrant a second look or appear suspicious. They stored their rifles and rucksacks in the outbuilding the owner had prepared for their sleeping quarters.

At dusk, Madison and his men, in the vehicles, infiltrated into San Miguel. If it had not been for Nassar, it would have been impossible to find Gareth in the 594 square kilometers of the damaged city. In locating him, Nassar counted on the man's penchant for publicity. In this particular case, it was as much for Jenny as for him. True to form, the Foundation's base of operation was well publicized and well lit.

Madison's main mission that night was to reconnoiter the area, discover the best possible routes in and out, and verify the location where Gareth reportedly established his base of operations. He had instructed his men not to talk to anyone, if possible, and to avoid the areas where most of the rescue efforts were concentrated. He wanted to observe the workers and familiarize himself with their actions.

The three vehicles entered the city from the south and went in different directions. The occupants of each vehicle made notes on their maps of what they saw in their respective areas, the condition of the streets, and the concentration of rescue efforts. Nassar had annotated the Foundation's field location on each of the maps along with hospitals, police stations, and military checkpoints.

Following his map, Madison directed his driver to the Walmart on Sur Avenue on the south side of the city, just off the main highway. Little to no damage was sustained to the shopping center or surrounding buildings. A number of other information, rescue, and aid organizations were also set up on the large parking lot. The public relations firm Gareth employed was adjacent to his location. Vehicles entered and departed the complex at a steady pace.

Bart motioned for the driver to park on the far side of the lot. As soon as the Toyota stopped, the three got out and stood at the front. Madison spread out a map on the hood, and the three feigned studying it. They looked over the area and scrutinized the nearby workers and the field location.

The Foundation had erected an inflatable tent complete with air conditioning, a reception area, and three private offices. The Foundation's logos were prominent on the front. Electricity was provided by a portable generator. Madison noted that only a young man and woman, both in their mid-twenties, occupied the tent at that time of the evening.

An ambulance screamed by on the highway behind him with its lights flashing and siren blaring. "Wait here," Madison told the other two men.

He adjusted his mask then strode across the lot to the tent, scanning the area as he approached his target. Halfway across the lot, he paused as a vehicle passed in front of him. Continuing toward his destination, Bart stopped in front of an easel with several notices pinned to it and three plastic pockets at the bottom with information and applications to apply for assistance. One paper pinned to the board listed the areas where representatives from the Foundation would be working the next day. Each location was annotated on a small map. Food and water would be provided to everyone. Another notice was from the weather service giving not only the forecast but the air quality. Madison was sifting through the information and absorbing what he thought was necessary to his mission.

The young man he had spotted earlier stepped out of the shelter, adjusted his mask, and stepped to Madison. "Can I help you?"

"I'm on a break and just wanted to get caught up on the situation."

"Would you like to come inside? The air is filtered."

"Thank you," Madison said. "This foul air gets to ya."

"Yeah, it does. It's supposed to be much better in a couple of days. Almost back to normal."

The young man extended his hand and said, "My name is Jeremy."

"Jimmy," Bart replied, taking Jeremy's hand. "Jimmy Johnson."

The man turned and led Bart into the vestibule. A rush of air greeted them as he opened the door. He paused as the outer door closed, then removed his mask. Madison removed his construction hat, then slid his mask up.

When the young man opened the inner door, the young woman laid her iPhone on the coffee table in front of her and smiled as she stood. It was obvious the two were bored and cherished the opportunity to talk to someone. "Ashley, this is Jimmy Johnson," Jeremy said, looking at the woman, then to Bart. "He's on a break."

"Pleased to meet you Ashley," Bart said as he extended his hand.

"Nice to meet you," she replied, taking his hand.

"Would you like something cold to drink?" Jeremy offered. "We have several different soft drinks and water."

"Water would be great," Madison replied. His eyes roamed over the inside of the tent.

"I'll be right back."

The inside was more like a large, plush office than a tent. Thick foam padding was under the carpet; the sitting area had a couch and three easy chairs. Several side chairs were placed around the room. A flat-screen TV was attached to a tall stand by the sitting area, and there were three desks across the room. The lights were out in the separate office spaces in the back of the tent. Two of the three desks in the main area had laptops on them and a stack of papers. *His and her desks,* Madison thought.

"What area are you working in?" Jeremy asked as he handed Madison the bottle of water.

"About two miles west." He took a long drink of the cool water.

"I understand that area was pretty bad," the woman said.

"Yes. There were a number of casualties, and the area was practically leveled," Madison replied.

"Please, have a seat." Ashley motioned toward a chair.

"Thank you." Bart sat in one of the easy chairs and placed his hat beside the chair. "It's been a long day." He took another drink of water.

The man and woman, eager to talk with someone, sat across from him. *These two preppies don't have a clue as to what is going on,* he thought. *Easy pickings.*

Madison engaged the two in conversation. It was no problem to extract information from them. He talked in general terms and was rewarded with specific information. "Gareth assists all over the world in disasters," Madison said. "I bet it's rewarding working for him."

"Oh, it is," Ashley said. "Mr. Gareth is so wonderful. He does great work helping impoverished people. He's just such a great person. Mrs. Gareth too. They have dedicated themselves to helping others."

"We've only been working for the Foundation for about six months," Jeremy said. "Ashley started just after I did. This is our first overseas trip."

"The Gareths are hosting a news conference and reception tomorrow afternoon at two o'clock," the woman said. "Mr. Gareth would love to have you here, if you are available. He loves any chance to meet and thank rescue and recovery people. It's a casual affair. You could meet him and get to hear about all the good things he and the Foundation are accomplishing for these poor people."

*I bet he'd love to have me here,* Madison thought, suppressing a grin.

"We're the junior crew and get the night shift," the man said. "We miss out on a lot of things, but we get to attend events like this. We're looking forward to it."

"It's all in a day's work," Madison replied, trying to keep a straight face. "It's the job you do. You've made my day, and I thank you for that." Madison's meaning was not the same as the two took it. He continued the conversation for another twenty minutes. He had gotten Gareth's itinerary for the next several days, which was one of his objectives, and even where he was staying. "I thank you for your hospitality," Madison said. "I need to get back to work." He picked up his hat, stood, and started for the door.

"You're welcome," the man said as he escorted him to the door. "We'll be here every night. Come back and relax."

"I will," Madison replied as he pulled down his mask and donned his hat, then pushed the outer door open.

Madison checked his watch as he walked across the lot. He saw the two men he had left at the vehicle get out as he approached. When he reached the vehicle, he leaned over the hood and plotted on the map the places Gareth was supposed to be the next two days. "I want to have a look at these places." Madison said, pointing to the tick marks he had placed on the map.

The three men got into the four-wheel-drive, and Madison directed the driver to the first location.

—— • ♦ • ——

Thursday, January 5, 2017
Servicio y Suministro de Areo
El Real Airport, Panama

Max and the others opted to spend the night at the El Real Airport. If the Special Forces team Max sent up the Tuira River was lucky enough to catch up to the soldiers he suspected had the nuke, he could be at their location in short order.

Paulita, the pilot's wife, and Danya cooked the evening meal on the grill outside the salvage company office building. Paulita provided soft drinks of various kinds, bottled water, and Panama beer. The men sat around the firepit as the evening meal cooked.

Patting out the ground beef, Paulita said, "My husband loves hamburgers cooked on the grill. He likes two slices of cheese. He says you must put mustard on the bottom, then mayonnaise and ketchup on the top. Give it a swirl before you put the top on the meat." She was relaxed with Danya, although worried about her husband. Cooking the burgers made her melancholy. "He fixed me burgers on our first date. We have them all the time."

Danya kept her engaged with small talk, trying to keep her at ease.

After the meal, everyone remained around the firepit, talking and gazing at the stars. When the fire had dwindled to embers and several men left to turn in for the night, Max waited to hear from the Special Forces team on the river. He decided earlier that if there was no word by morning, he would return to Panama City and work out of Danya's office in Balboa. He had coordinated with the pilot to fly him north along the Tuira River as it meanders to the Bay of San Miguel. He hoped to locate the fighters with the nuke.

Danya and Max sat beside the fire and reviewed the details they had, to ensure they hadn't overlooked something that might be of importance. "Wait!" Max said. "What was it Gail said?"

Danya looked at him with a furrowed brow.

"Gail told us Gareth was going to El Salvador to provide assistance," he said. "I want to talk to Paulita again."

Danya stood. "I'll be right back."

She returned shortly with Paulita in tow.

"Please sit," Max said, motioning to the seat next to him. Danya sat on the other side of the woman. A slight breeze caressed the embers, causing them to pop, and bathed the three in their warmth.

"Thank you for the meal," Max said. "The burgers were great. We're worried about your husband."

Tears welled in Paulita's eyes. "I am too."

Danya looped her arm around the woman's.

"Earlier today when we talked," Max said, his voice calm, "you said your husband would contact you when he could."

Paulita nodded.

"Has he contacted you again since he called you from San José?"

Paulita looked to Danya, then back to Max, and nodded. Her eyes fell to her clasped hands.

"When did he call?"

"Not long after you left in the helicopter."

"What did he say?"

"That he was OK, and they landed at an airstrip outside of San Miguel, El Salvador. They are treating him fine and there has been no trouble. He thought he would be there a couple of days and told me not to worry. He's been staying with the plane."

"Did he say where the men went, or who they met with?"

"No, that's about all he said. Oh, he did mention that two men met the plane and gave all of his passengers a change of clothes. He said that six of the men left and one of the soldiers remained behind. He said he would call again when he could."

"When he calls you again, let Danya know right away. Thank you."

Paulita nodded, then stood and walked away.

"We need to be ready when he calls again," Max said to Danya. "Although she didn't say what she told him, I'll bet she told him we were here looking for his passengers. He needs to know we are trying to help and he could be in danger. If she hasn't already told him, I don't want her telling her husband that we're here looking for them. We need to know their exact location and if they have set up a routine."

"I'll coordinate this with Paulita," Danya said.

"Madison went to El Salvador, but is it to meet with Gareth for something or take out his revenge?"

"Good question. My guess is it is the latter."

"We're going to El Salvador," Max said.

He looked at his watch. "Shit. It's too late tonight to get anything done. I'm calling Gail." He retrieved his phone from his pocket and punched in Gail's number. Her voicemail answered and gave the customary greeting and instructions. Hearing the tone, Max spoke, "Gail, call me as soon as you get this. Max."

He punched in Andy's number, and his voicemail answered as well. He left the same message and ended the call. All he could do was wait and hope they would catch up to Madison soon.

# CHAPTER 19

Friday, January 6, 2017
Headquarters, US Special Operations Command
MacDill Air Force Base, Florida

A LTHOUGH DAVID WAS left behind, he was busy seeking information on the clandestine airstrips in Central America as well as keeping up with the intelligence as it came in from his sources. The tempo in the office was much slower than when the entire team was there, but it seemed like he had created as much as three people. The phones rang and the printer spat out intelligence-related notes and reports at a steady pace.

While he took a moment for his morning snack—a jelly donut and coffee—David's phone rang. Recognizing the number as his contact in Key West, he swallowed, wiped his mouth, and said, "Hey Mitch, what's going on?"

"Hello, David. I've got something for ya."

"Yeah, whatta you got? Oh, geez. Can you hold on for a minute? I'm the only one in the office and one of the other phones is ringing."

"Sure, go ahead."

David returned to the phone within a few moments. "OK, Mitch. What's going on in Key West?"

"One of our contractors flying out of Panama spotted a DC-3, and it could be the one you are looking for."

"That's terrific, dear boy! Where is it?"

"It's at a private airstrip on a ranch twenty-four kilometers south of San Miguel. The cartels use the strip occasionally."

"That sounds like what we're looking for. Do you have the coordinates?"

"I do. I'll send them now, along with a copy of the imagery taken from an air-breather."

"That's wonderful, Mitch! Thank you," David replied, then ended the call. He turned his attention to his computer and waited for the information. He fidgeted with anticipation, knowing the plane images would show more detail than satellite images. Within moments of ending the call, an email arrived with the documents. He opened the file and examined the image of the plane, then plotted the coordinates on the map. *Oh my God! That's it,* he thought. Then he sent it to Max via the secure satellite link.

Lifting the receiver, he punched in the numbers to Max.

As soon as Max answered the call, David said with excitement, "I got him!"

"Slow down, David," Max replied. "What do you have?"

"I just got an email from Mitch at JIATF-South in Key West. I contacted him earlier this morning. He knows all kinds of people in the narco-trafficking arena, and I think he found Madison's plane. I just sent you the info with grid coordinates for the DC-3 in El Salvador."

The Joint Interagency Task Force South (JIATF-South), Headquartered at Naval Air Station Key West, Florida, is a multiservice, multiagency task force that conducts interagency and international detection and monitoring operations. It facilitates the interdiction of illicit trafficking and other narco-terrorist threats in support of national and partner-nation security.

"Thank you, David. Good work. Now, find out all you can about Gareth's operation in San Miguel. Where his field headquarters is located, his schedule, where he's staying. Everything."

"Yes, sir," David replied.

"Get us clearance to go into El Salvador. Don't mention the warhead or terrorists. If the government wants to provide troops, decline it as not needed."

"Just keep it low-key in dealing with the embassy, correct?"

"That's correct, David. Get busy on the clearance, as we will be on our way. It'll take a bit for us to get there. I'll send you a text with our arrival details after I talk with the pilot." Max ended the call and alerted the others.

———— ◆ ◆ ◆ ————

Friday, January 6, 2017
Damaged Area
San Miguel, El Salvador

The sun was high in the clear blue sky. It seemed like a perfect day in the tropics, except for the odor of hydrogen sulfide gas that danced about. That was a constant reminder of the destruction twenty-four kilometers to the north.

Bart Madison reviewed the plan he had developed the night before, after learning of Gareth's itinerary. The press conference with reception was a bonus he had not anticipated. That was the primary target location; the alternate was Gareth's second scheduled location that day.

Prior to leaving the airstrip, Madison rehearsed the plan with his men. He instructed everyone to dirty their clothes to look like they had been working in the rubble. Once he was satisfied with their appearance, he sent one vehicle with a driver and two men to the alternate location to begin surveillance. Madison led the other vehicle to a position next to a toppled building close enough to observe the front of Gareth's inflatable tent. He spaced out the others in the debris to look as though they were searching for survivors. One man at each location nestled himself in the rubble, where he could observe the target. Everyone was in position an hour before the scheduled start of the press conference.

Soon, two vans arrived with Perla's Events painted on the sides. A woman wearing a mask emerged from the tent and held the doors open while four men, wearing black T-shirts with the pink logo of the company on the front, unloaded the vehicles. Another woman exited the public relations tent next to Gareth's. She stopped at the first van, looked inside, then stepped to the other one. She had a short conversation with one of the men as he returned to the van. *Supplies and refreshments for the conference and reception,* Madison thought.

Another vehicle arrived, and a man in uniform got out and led a dog into the tent. *Bomb dog,* Madison thought. *Probably only a two-man security detail inside, and whatever dignitaries show up will have their own security.* Soon the two catering vans departed, and the dog handler and the dog left a few moments later. Madison continued to watch and wait.

Vehicles arrived at the entrance of the tent and discharged their passengers. Madison checked his watch. *The little people first,* he thought. The woman he saw a few minutes earlier holding the door open and a young man, their faces covered by masks, held the doors open and greeted the people as they entered. Seeing several mannerisms the two displayed, their build, and the color of their hair, he guessed it was the man and woman from the night before. It all appeared orchestrated, with people arriving in stages so they could each make their entrance. Not knowing who was who, Madison determined their seniority by the entourage of the arriving dignitaries and their arrival times. He checked his watch again as the last car arrived. *1400 hours,* he thought. *That's who we watch for to leave.*

Madison stepped back to the Toyota and checked his appearance in one of the mirrors. He picked up a handful of dirt and smudged his clothes a bit more. Next, he added a little more dirt to his trousers and a little to the fringes of his beard to ensure it looked soiled. He was satisfied.

Twenty minutes had elapsed when the senior person, who had arrived at 1400 hours, left with his straphangers. The same two held the doors open as the people departed. Soon, others departed. *About time for the reception to start,* Madison thought. *Probably just the lesser important and money people from the US Ashley mentioned.* He looked to the fighter on his right. "Stay alert. If anyone chases me out, take 'em out. Remember, if this goes to hell and they take me out, get everyone back to the airstrip and contact Franco."

The man nodded.

Madison stood and adjusted his construction hat and mask. He negotiated the rubble as he made his way to the asphalt parking lot. He was relaxed in his stride as he ambled toward the tent. As he neared the entrance, the doors opened again. A couple emerged and stood at the front as a car approached and stopped in front of them. As soon as the couple closed the car doors, it drove away.

Madison raised his hand to greet the woman at the door as she held her gaze on him.

Holding the door open as he approached, she spoke to the man across from her. He focused his attention on the man as he neared. She looked back to Madison and spoke, her voice muffled by the mask. "I'm so glad you could make it. Mr. Gareth just finished the press conference."

"Come in," the young man said, his voice muffled.

The air rushing out of the tent washed over the three as they entered the vestibule and the doors closed behind them. Ashley and the other man removed their masks. Madison removed his hat then pushed up his mask. He bent over and dusted his trousers; a cloud of dust appeared as his hands patted at the clothes. He rose and continued dusting. He ensured his performance captured the attention of Jeremy and Ashley.

"Sorry about the dust," Madison said. "It's dirty work out there." He brushed at his face and beard. "You said it was casual and come as you are. I can't stay too long."

"You're fine," Ashley replied. "Mr. Gareth expects the workers to be dirty. I'll introduce you to him. I'm sorry, but I forgot your name."

"Jimmy. Jimmy Johnson," Madison replied as he held up his badge. Looking at the young man, he asked, "You're Jeremy, right?"

"Yes, Jeremy," he said, then opened the door. "Would you like something to drink?"

"Water would be great." Madison's eyes roamed the interior of the tent. *About thirty people,* he thought. *There're three more token rescue workers for Gareth to use as props.* He didn't recognize anyone in the room and was confident no one would recognize him. He wasn't expected to be there, and these people were there to donate to the Gareth Foundation. Madison, self-assured in his disguise, continued his performance as a rescue worker.

"Would you like something stronger than water?" Jeremy asked.

"Not right now. Thank you."

Jeremy left to get the water, and Ashley remained next to Madison. Her hesitation was a signal for him to walk through the metal detector in front of them.

Madison looked to the lone security man at the detector and took note of his demeanor. *He's bored,* he thought. Without hesitation, he placed his hat on the small table and started to step through. The security man motioned to his head, indicating for Madison to remove his mask. It was obvious that was a common occurrence. He reached up, removed the mask, and laid it beside his hat. The machine remained silent as he stepped through.

"Mr. Gareth is talking to someone right now," Ashley said as soon as he cleared the detector. "You can put your hat and mask in one of the cubbyholes over there." She pointed to a rack of storage spaces next to the wall where other masks were placed. "As soon as he's free, I'll introduce you to him. There are cookies, pastries, and fruit on the table over there. If you decide you would like to have a beer or something stronger, the bar is there." She indicated the table of desserts, then the bar on the far side of the room. "I'll check on you in a few minutes. I need to see how everyone is doing with refreshments."

"Certainly," Madison said. "I'm already enjoying the fresh air." He smiled and placed his hat and mask in one of the compartments.

Jeremy returned with a bottle of water and handed it to Madison. "Make yourself at home. I need to give Ashley a hand."

"No problem. I'm fine."

Most of the people were in the back half of the tent, hoping to get to speak with Gareth. Madison made his way around the room, appearing to be friendly and sipping the water. He had identified one security man at the metal detector and another one eating a cookie and nursing a drink in the crowd around Gareth. He saw Jenny standing to the side, talking to the same woman he'd seen earlier coming out of the public relations tent. One of the rescue workers was talking to the two women. The other two rescue workers were on the side by the refreshments, talking with several guests. Stew, well into the throng of people and about the center of the room, was engaged by a middle-aged couple, and several more stood nearby, drinking cocktails and waiting their turn to talk with him. As Madison ambled about the room, he began to identify the Foundation statters. They were, for the most part, younger than the crowd, and they catered to whomever they talked with. He stayed aware of both Ashley and Jeremy. They stayed busy supplying cocktails to the guests.

Madison held his focus on Gareth, studying him. He finished his drink and called to Jeremy as the young man neared. "Jeremy," Gareth said, "the Sullivans need another drink." Jeremy's jaw tightened, displaying strain. It was obvious Gareth was ending the conversation with the couple and moving to the next. "I'll have another too," he added.

Recognizing the opportunity to strike, Madison moved to intercept Jeremy on his way to get more drinks and said, "Let me give you a hand."

"Thank you," Jeremy replied, somewhat relieved to get some help. "These people are sucking it down faster than we can pour it."

"What's Mr. Gareth drinking?"

"Scotch. His bottle is under the table on the far end."

Madison, with his hand in his pocket, walked around the table, glanced over the room, withdrew his hand, then bent down and retrieved the bottle of Scotch. He looked around the room again. No one was paying any attention to him. He completed his task, then put the bottle back under the table.

Madison walked back to Jeremy, held the drink out, and said, "Here you go."

"Oh, thank you," Jeremy said as he topped off the second of four glasses of water.

"You take the boss his drink, and I'll take care of these," Madison said. He took the bottle of water and began filling the other two glasses. Madison couldn't have been any more affable.

Nodding in the direction of Jenny Gareth, Jeremy said, "Do you mind taking these drinks to that group of people talking to Mrs. Gareth?"

Madison delivered the tray of glasses to the group. As he stopped, four arms reached for the drinks.

"Would anyone else like anything?" he asked.

The others in the small group shook their heads. None of them took the time to notice that the man delivering their drinks was wearing dust-covered work clothes. None of them cared. Madison stepped back to the refreshments table and set the tray down.

Ashley stepped in next to him. "Thank you for giving us a hand," she said. "Jeremy tends to get a little stressed out."

Madison smiled and nodded. "I picked up on that." He watched Gareth take a drink of the Scotch Jeremy handed him. He engaged Ashley for a moment and watched Gareth take a second sip of his drink. "I need to get back to work," Madison said. "Mr. Gareth is busy. I'll try to get back later and meet him."

"You must leave so soon? I'm sorry you won't get to meet him. Perhaps next time."

With a smile, he said, "Thank you again for inviting me," and he shook the woman's hand. He stepped to the storage space where he had placed his hat and mask in one of the cubbyholes.

Madison checked his watch. Without rushing, he picked up his hat and mask. He looked around the room. No one seemed to notice his departure. He stepped to the door of the vestibule and entered. A commotion inside the tent behind him was the signal he anticipated. He donned his mask, adjusted it, then put on his hat. Pressing on the outer door, the rush of air seemed to push him out. With an easy stride he made his way across the parking lot to where his men waited. No one called after him or followed him.

Taking his position as before, next to his fighter, he settled in to watch the tent. "We will wait for a few minutes," he said to the soldier.

Fifteen minutes later, they heard an ambulance approaching on the highway. Madison looked to the entrance of the parking lot and saw the vehicle, its lights flashing, turn in and stop in front of the Gareth Foundation tent. Two paramedics got out of the vehicle and rushed inside. Ashley held the door open as they entered. Minutes later, the paramedics returned to the ambulance and retrieved their gurney.

Madison motioned to his men. "Let's go. Take your time."

———— • • • ————

Abbigale Martin, the public relations contractor for the Gareth Foundation, took Jenny by the arm and helped her stand. She thought Jenny was grieving, but, in fact, she was pissed. She escorted Jenny into one of the offices in the back of the tent and sat her in an easy chair

Abbigale recognized that the situation in the tent had evolved into chaos. Her first chore as the new face of the Foundation was to get Jenny under control. After all, her job depended on its success. She needed to demonstrate to the world that the Foundation was still viable and would carry on as though Stew Gareth was still in charge. What she didn't know was that Jenny wasn't about to let her be in charge.

"Tell Jeremy to bring me a drink," Jenny said as she flopped into the chair.

Abbigale handed Jenny a box of tissues and patted her on the shoulder.

Jenny batted the box away.

Abbigale set the tissues on the desk, then stepped into the main room. As she entered, Jeremy was escorting Ashley, who was sobbing, into the office opposite Jenny. "As soon as you take care of her," Abbigale said, "get Jenny a drink." She didn't wait for a response.

Abbigale stepped to the center of the room to address the guests. "Thank you all for coming. In light of the current tragedy, we are closing for the day. Jenny has asked that you continue your support for the Foundation and the wonderful people of El Salvador. Jenny knows that you would like to express your condolences but has asked to be alone. I will be publishing updates on the arrangements for Stew and when Jenny will receive visitors. Thank you again for coming." She moved toward the door to politely encourage the guests to leave.

Jeremy returned to Jenny with a glass of water, handed it to her, and asked, "Is there anything else I get for your, Mrs. Gareth?"

"What the fuck is this?"

"You asked for a drink," he replied as a chill spread over him.

"Bring me that bottle of Scotch. And shut up that bimbo in the next room."

"Yes, ma'am." The rattled young man stiffened and marched out.

Jenny looked around the office where Stew usually sat and saw that her world had exploded. She caught her reflection in the glass of a picture on the desk. Her hair was a mess, and her makeup had slid down her cheeks like mud down a mountain.

The efficient Abbigale was coordinating with the rest of the staff to clean up the office in anticipation of meeting with the press later that evening. She saw Jeremy carrying the bottle to the back office. *This is going to be a challenge,* she thought. She intercepted Jeremy just before he turned into the office, and she grasped the bottle. "I'll take care of this," she said. "You go in and console Ashley." She stepped into the office, set the bottle on the desk, and reached for a glass.

"Just give me the damn bottle," Jenny said.

"Would you like a glass with ice?" Abbigale replied.

"Just the bottle." Her tone was as hard as her heart.

She handed the bottle to Jenny, who grabbed it, opened it, and gulped it down almost before Abbigale could withdraw her hand.

"Is there anything else I can get you, ma'am?"

"Abby, for Christ's sakes, stop hovering. Get me some lipstick and a goddamn hairbrush. I need to work this out. I need to think. Oh, get me another bottle of Scotch; this one is about empty. Then get the hell out."

Jenny leaned back as Abbigale left the room. Her mind raced. *What the hell am I gonna do now?* she thought. She lifted the bottle to her lips again and gulped, then rested it between her thighs. She pulled out a tissue and blew her nose. *You son of a bitch, Stew. You had to come down to this godforsaken hellhole to help me get elected. Well, I gotta do it myself now.*

She wasn't sad, she was pissed. *You die in a tent in some Third World goddamn Walmart parking lot, you sorry son of a bitch. You couldn't even die with dignity.* A slight smile crept onto her face. *I can turn this into my advantage. I'll do what Jackie Kennedy did—quietly distraught, head down.* "Abby, come in here!" Jenny shouted.

Abbigale took a deep breath, rolled her eyes, and stepped into the office where Jenny sat. "Yes, ma'am." She set another bottle of Scotch on the desk. "I've sent for someone to come help with your makeup and hair."

"Here's what I want you to do," Jenny said with a stern look. "I'm going to the hospital after a while. Alert the press and get pictures of me arriving. Then tell them that I'll give a press conference tomorrow at ten."

"That's good, Mrs. Gareth." Abbigale replied. "I don't think you should say anything this evening. Just wait until tomorrow. I have a few ideas how we can turn this situation to your benefit, I'll work on a few details and make some calls."

"I don't need a fucking snowflake to tell me how to handle the press. I was managing those bastards when you were still in diapers. Now get the fuck outta my office and go make your phone calls. I'm not to be disturbed. I'll call you if I need you."

"Yes, ma'am. I'll be in the main room if you need me." Abbigale turned to leave, narrowed her eyes, and whispered, "Your royal bitchiness." She stepped into the next room.

The sun began to set as the limousine with Jenny and Abbigale in the back pulled into the hospital and stopped by the front door. As Jenny had orchestrated, photos of her were snapped with her head down. Abbigale, her arm around Jenny, escorted her inside. Her excellent performance was that of a grief-stricken widow. No one noticed she had difficulty walking.

———————•♦•———————

Friday, January 6, 2017
Headquarters, US Special Operations Command
MacDill Air Force Base, Florida

David had obtained the clearance for Max and the others with him. An officer from the US Embassy in San Salvador, Office of the Defense Attaché Lieutenant Colonel Greg Matthews, met Max's helicopter at El Papalon Airport, three miles southeast of the city. David did as he was instructed and said it was not necessary for him to accompany Max, but Matthews insisted. Since Stew Gareth, considered an important person, was providing humanitarian support to the country as a result of the earthquake, the defense attaché was concerned. If trouble should erupt, he wanted a representative there to coordinate with authorities. That was a condition for the clearance. Matthews provided protective masks for Max and the others and informed them the air quality was improving, as the wind had shifted toward the west.

Max, Danya, and the two soldiers, in a Toyota SUV, followed Matthews's Toyota to the Walmart parking lot. Major Tomari and his two Israeli operators had returned to Balboa when Max departed. At 1537 hours the two Toyotas stopped in front of the Gareth Foundation tent. Lieutenant Colonel Matthews entered the tent. Max and the others exited their vehicle, and the two soldiers stood by the entrance. Max and Danya scanned the area, looking for any signs of Madison.

Within a few moments, Matthews stepped from the vestibule, followed by a woman. "This is Ms. Abbigale Martin," Matthews said. "She is the public relations person for the Foundation. Stew Gareth has suffered a heart attack. She is going to put out a statement about Mr. Gareth."

"I'm sorry to hear that," Max said. "We're looking for a man that might have been here." He handed her a photo of Bart Madison. "Have you seen this man?"

Abbigale held a lingering, inquiring gaze on him. "No, I can't say as I have. We had political representatives here, a number of financial contributors, and that was about it. Well, we did have several rescue workers at the reception. Four, I believe. Ashley and Jeremy had more contact with them than I did. They're inside, I'll get them for you." She turned and disappeared into the tent. Within a few minutes, she returned with the two young people.

"This is Ashley," Abbigale said as she motioned to the young woman. "This is Jeremy." She indicated the man.

"I'm Max and this is Danya." Max, seeing Ashley's red eyes and tear-streaked cheeks, glanced to Danya.

Taking the cue Danya took Ashley's hand and led her several steps away.

Max shook Jeremy's hand, showed him a photo of Madison, and said, "We're looking for this man."

"Why are you looking for him?" Jeremy asked.

"It's a matter of national importance," Max replied. "He might have a beard."

"Well...he kinda looks like one of the rescue workers that stopped by. Jimmy Johnson was his name. Nice guy." Jeremy shrugged and handed the photo back to Max. "I couldn't swear to it that that was him."

"How long was he here? Did he say anything? Was anyone with him? Do you know where we could find him?"

"No, he just visited and rested last night. He came by again today. Both times he was alone, and I don't think he was here for more than thirty minutes. I don't know where he's working. I think he said last night he was working about two miles west of here. That's all I know."

"Thank you, Jeremy," Max said, then looked at Danya as she approached with Ashley. "Thank you both," Max said. "That's all we need."

They turned and walked into the vestibule.

"Madison was here," Max said as he looked to Danya. "He came by last night. Probably doing a recon. Then he was here this afternoon for about thirty minutes."

"The girl is crushed," Danya said. "She sobbed the entire time I tried to talk to her, and I didn't get much out of her." She picked up a rock and threw it at a pile of rubble. "It looks like Madison saved the US taxpayers the cost of trying Gareth," she said. "Too bad you probably won't be able to prove Madison did it."

"Let's go see if the DC-3 is still at the airstrip," Max said, heading for the Toyota.

———— ✦✦✦ ————

Friday, January 6, 2017
Private Airstrip
San Miguel, El Salvador

Madison led the two other vehicles back to the ranch and onto the airstrip. He had given instructions to the fighters with him to get the plane loaded as soon as they could. Just after they entered, Madison held up his hand for the driver to stop. The fighter he left at the airstrip was on guard, and he approached the Toyota.

"Any activity here?" Madison asked.

"No, comandante. Esta tranquilo," he replied.

"We are leaving right away. We'll signal when we are ready to go. Stay alert."

"Sí, comandante."

As soon as the vehicle pulled away, the man returned to his concealed position.

When they arrived at the plane, there was a flurry of activity for several minutes as the fighters loaded their equipment. Madison took the opportunity to talk to the pilot.

"I want to leave here as soon as possible," he said. He glanced to his soldiers, then back to the pilot. "I want to make a short hop over to El Tamarindo to pick up a few more passengers. Do you know it?"

"I know it," the pilot replied. "It's about fifteen miles southeast of here, on the Gulf of Fonseca."

"That's it," Madison replied.

"Low profile, I assume."

"Correct."

"Where do you want to go from there? You had mentioned Mexico earlier."

Madison held his steely eyes on the man.

Sensing he'd crossed the line; the pilot shifted his stance. "I need to think about fuel."

"I'll arrange to have fuel available at the airstrip. How much do you need?"

"About 600 gallons. I'll be ready to go in a few minutes. I need to make a few checks."

Madison nodded. "I'll be waiting." He took out his phone and punched in a phone number. When the phone was answered, he spoke into it. "Arrange to have 600 gallons of 100LL aviation gasoline for us when we land," he said. Then he ended the call.

When the men finished loading their equipment onto the plane, they climbed aboard. Before the last man boarded, he signaled to the guard, who then double-timed to the plane. Each one of them made themselves comfortable in their seat as they waited. Soon, the pilot entered, closed the door behind him, and began to climb the long-sloped cabin to the cockpit. He stopped beside Madison and asked, "Would you like to sit up front?"

Madison stood, signaling his acceptance of the invitation. He followed the pilot and sat in the seat next to him, on his right.

The pilot went to work. He checked to ensure the propellers were clear, then began flipping switches. He spun the propeller as he counted the blades, and then the engine came to life, belching out gray smoke. He repeated the process for the other engine. As soon as it belched smoke, a wide grin emerged on his face, satisfied at the sound of the engines.

He nudged the throttles forward, and the vintage aircraft seemed to moan and groan as it began to move. A few audible squeaks and creaks caused Madison to look at the unconcerned pilot. He steered the plane to the end of the strip, then moved the throttles full forward and watched the RPMs and manifold pressure increase. The DC-3 picked up speed as it raced toward the end of the airstrip, and soon became a graceful creature of the sky.

<hr />

Not knowing what to expect at the clandestine airstrip, Lieutenant Colonel Matthews followed Max's Toyota. In the vehicle with Max were Danya and the two soldiers. They headed out of the Walmart parking lot and entered the highway to the ranch, twenty-four kilometers south of San Miguel. They stopped a short distance from the ranch. Max had identified a trail off the main road that appeared to lead to a small hill. The Toyota bounced and rocked as Max steered it onto the old trail. Then he pulled to a stop at a clearing just below the crest of the hill. The two soldiers exited the vehicle and led the others to the top. The dense foliage provided good concealment. From their vantage point, they could see most of the airstrip and one outbuilding. Max didn't want to drive onto the property without knowing the situation.

Using binoculars, Max searched the area. Then he lowered them and studied the image David sent him. "The plane's not there," he said, more to himself than to Danya.

She took the binoculars and looked through them. "Are you sure we're at the right place?" she asked. She lowered the binoculars.

Pointing to the image, Max said, "This is the same outbuilding and airstrip. We're at the right grid location. Just the wrong time." Max withdrew his phone and punched in David's number. When he was on the line, Max told him they were at the location he gave them. "The plane is gone. We missed him."

"Well, *sheet!*" he replied. "I thought we had him."

"Get back with your contact at JIATF-South. Tell him the plane is gone. Ask him to keep searching the airstrips. Madison could be heading north into Mexico or possibly somewhere in between. If he stops somewhere, it could be to pick up the nuke. Stay on this. We're not far behind him."

"Will do," David replied. "Anything else?"

"Gareth is dead," Max said. "His PR person said it was a heart attack, but I don't think so. However, he wasn't exactly the model for health, and it seems unlikely he would just keel over like that. My instincts tell me it was Madison. I don't know how he did it, but he was there. The PR person could be putting out a cover story for what happened. See what you can find out and if someone is doing an autopsy."

"I'm on it," David replied.

# CHAPTER 20

Friday, January 6, 2017
Clandestine Airstrip
El Tamarindo, El Salvador

THE OLD DC-3 carrying Madison and his men touched the grass airstrip as gently as a bird could. Once it was on the ground, it was obvious the plane didn't land on an improved runway. The bouncing and vibration ended as the DC-3 rolled to a stop. Madison took a few minutes to scan the area, looking for trouble or a friendly face.

Looking over his shoulder, Madison released his seatbelt and moved to the cabin. "We'll be here just long enough to refuel. Establish security, and give Franco and the others a hand in loading." He moved out of the aisle so the pilot could pass, then stepped in behind him.

The pilot swung the door open and climbed out of the plane. He looked around, stepped down, walked around the plane, and climbed onto the starboard wing to prepare for the fuel. He glanced up and saw a 1988 Mack DM686 truck with a fuel pod approaching. He scanned the area but didn't see anyone else. As the truck neared, he saw two men in the front. Then it pulled to a stop in front of the plane. The man on the passenger side got out of the cab and went to the rear. Without speaking, he withdrew the hose and handed it to the pilot. When the pilot signaled he was ready, the fuel man signaled to the driver, and the fuel began to pump into the plane.

Madison had climbed out of the plane and was met by Franco. "Good to see you," Franco said as he shook Bart's hand.

"Any trouble?" Bart asked as he held his grip.

"We were followed by soldiers up the Tuira River. We managed to lose them. I believe they were Americans. Will we be here long? I have two men on an OP."

"It was probably Kenworth's men that followed you."

"That is what I thought. But we haven't seen anyone for a long time," Franco said.

"Get the plane loaded, we'll leave as soon as we get fueled up."

———— • ♦ • ————

When the pilot began fueling the tank on the port wing, he looked over his shoulder and saw the fighters loading the plane with their gear. His curiosity peaked when he saw the four men carrying the wrapped bundle to the plane. He suspected it could mean trouble. When he saw the men struggling, he knew he needed to be aware of the weight.

Standing behind the wing, Bart looked up to the pilot. "How much longer?"

"Almost finished. About a minute or so."

Max turned to Franco. "Pull your OPs in. Let's go."

Franco stepped to one of his men who was standing by the tail and told him to signal the OPs to come in.

Bart saw the pilot hand the fuel hose to the fuel man before he climbed off the wing.

"That bundle your men loaded, how much does it weigh?" the pilot asked.

Bart held his eyes on the man, suspecting he was a little too curious.

The pilot, sensing Madison's sensitivity, added, "I need to do weight and balance."

"Two hundred and ninety pounds," Bart replied.

"Get your men loaded. I need to figure out the weight distribution to maintain the center of gravity. I may need to shuffle them around," the pilot said.

"We're waiting on two men," Bart replied. "They'll be here in just a few minutes. Get the plane started."

———— • ♦ • ————

Friday, January 6, 2017
Headquarters, US Special Operations Command
MacDill Air Force Base, Florida

Gail, David, and Andy were working their contacts, and Max had kept them updated on his progress in El Salvador. The intelligence to date led them to believe that Madison was making his way to the US with the nuke. Gail kept in close contact with Captain Mackenzie in New York, as well as her contacts on the southern border. So far, no new information had surfaced from anyone. With each phone call Gail made to Mackenzie, he seemed more and more anxious.

Andy's contacts at DIA had little to add, and he seemed to provide them with more than he received. The CIA didn't provide anything either. The unusual silence from the Muslim Brotherhood and ISIL was frustrating. Often in their exuberance, bits of intelligence leaked out, giving Andy clues as to their intentions.

David's contacts at JIATF-South provided the most information. Mitch and David talked several times during the day. The landing strips along the known drug routes of Los Zetas were included in the contractor flights after he identified the DC-3 south of San Miguel. David and Andy limited their focus to Los Zetas' routes through Central America and into Mexico. The plane's range of 1,580 miles made predicting the stop impossible, as they could reach well into Mexico or the southern border of Texas, depending on their route.

When Andy's phone rang, he recognized Max's number in the display. After a brief round of cordialities, Max got down to business. "I was just notified by JTF-Bravo in Honduras that a twin-engine aircraft took off from the vicinity of El Tamarindo, El Salvador. The observer was on the Bay of Fonseca." JTF-Bravo was a subordinate command of US Southern Command, headquartered at Soto Cano Air Base, Honduras. It was responsible for the joint operations area in the seven Central American countries.

"Madison, right?"

"I'm certain it was," Max replied. "The intel report didn't contain a tail number. El Tamarindo is on the Zetas drug route. My guess is that he picked up the nuke and his men and are headed north to enter the US."

"That makes sense to me too," Andy said. "Are you heading back to Tampa?"

"Yes. There's not much else I can do from here."

———— • ✦ • ————

Saturday, January 7, 2017
Clandestine Airstrip
Cuajinicuilapa, Mexico

Just after midnight, the DC-3 approached the Pacific coast of Southwest Mexico. Madison withdrew his SAT phone and punched in a phone number. As soon as his call was answered, he said, "We're approaching. Turn 'em on." Then he ended the call. From the dark cockpit he pointed to the faint stretch of lights that popped on, indicating the runway five miles to their front. It wasn't difficult to see the airstrip, as the surrounding rural area had a scant population and artificial light was nonexistent. It was two miles south of the Ometepec River and sixteen miles west of Cuajinicuilapa.

The plane eased down onto the grass strip and rolled to a stop. Two pair of lights left their position on the airstrip, circled, and advanced toward the aircraft. They stopped with their lights illuminating the side of the plane. The soldiers filed out of the plane and assumed a defensive posture as they awaited recognition of the occupants of the vehicles as they stepped in front of the lights. Nassar shouted his name. Four more pair of headlights approached and stopped next to the others.

Madison, stepping down from the plane and to the front of the fighters, said, "He's friendly! It's Nassar." He shook his hand. "So far, so good. We have the nuke."

"The vehicles are here and ready for you. Al-Ghazāli will be pleased when I tell him. I have a place for you and the fighters to stay. It is a few kilometers from here."

"Good. I want to leave here as soon as possible."

The pilot leaned against the door and waited anxiously for his next instructions. He was unsure of what might be coming next, but he feared the worst. He said a prayer to himself. Those talking to Madsion spoke in low, soft voices. He strained to hear the men talking but could only pick up a few words.

"What about the pilot and plane?" Nassar asked.

"He hasn't been any trouble. I'm going to let him go."

Franco stepped to Madison and said, "We are loaded. Do you want me to take care of the pilot and plane?"

"No, I'm going to let him go. He hasn't been any trouble."

"He knows where we are," Franco replied in protest.

"That's all he knows," Bart replied. "The plane can't stay here, and you can't burn it. Besides, we may need to use him again sometime. I'll send him on his way." Bart turned and stepped to the door of the plane where the pilot was standing. "You're free to go."

"Thank you." He sighed with relief and touched the brim of his ball cap. He closed the door. Within a few minutes one engine, then the other, belched smoke, and sped up. The vintage aircraft began to move. In no time, the bird took to flight and disappeared into the sky.

———◆◆◆———

The vehicles stopped in front of an old ranch house. "The rancher who owns this place lives in the village now," Nassar said as he stopped the SUV. "You can stay here as long as necessary."

Franco was out of his SUV by the time Bart and Nassar got out of theirs. Nassar led the others into the house.

"This'll do fine," Bart said as he turned to Franco. "Have your men put the warhead by the wall." He pointed across the room. "Get everyone settled, then let's turn in."

"A nightcap?" Nassar said as he looked to Bart, then Franco.

"I could use one," Bart replied.

"Pour me one," Franco said. "I'll be right back. I need to give instructions to the men."

———◆◆◆———

When the DC-3 leveled off, the pilot set the autopilot, retrieved his cell phone, and switched it on. When it came to life, he punched in Paulita's number and wrote:

I'm OK, airborne, and on my way home. No pax or cargo. I just left the southwest coast of Mexico.

He checked his watch and settled back, not expecting to hear from his wife. Within a few minutes he received a text back. It read:

Thank God! I have been very worried. I couldn't sleep. Please be careful. I want you home.

# CHAPTER 21

Saturday, January 7, 2017
Headquarters, US Special Operations Command
MacDill Air Force Base, Florida

A NDY AND GAIL had just returned from lunch. Gail had brought a hamburger and fries back to the office for David. "Sweet Pea, are you here?" Gail said as she entered.

Cupping his hand over the mouthpiece, he replied, "Yes, Gail dahling. I'm on the phone."

She walked to his desk to deliver the sack containing his lunch. "Cheeseburger and fries," she said in a low voice.

David mouthed, "Thank you."

The phone on Gail's desk rang just as she sat. "This is Gail," she said.

"Gail, this is Max. Danya received a message from Paulita, the pilot's wife. The pilot took Madison to Mexico. The message said he was leaving Southwest Mexico and returning home without any pax or cargo."

"Madison has the warhead in Mexico?" she replied. "I'll get back with my sources on the southern border. Did she provide a location?"

"She just said it was southwestern Mexico. Big area, I know. Danya has been trying to get back in touch with her, but so far, nothing. I have no idea where he'll enter the US, and Los Zetas has a lot of experience crossing the southern border. They could enter anywhere."

"David talked to JIATF-South this morning, but they didn't have anything new," Gail said.

"Has he found out anything on Gareth's death?"

"No autopsy has been done yet," she replied. "They don't work on the weekends and told him that it may take four or five days or more to do it. They're backed up because of the volcano."

"Tell Andy to call Lieutenant Colonel Greg Matthews at the US Embassy in San Salvador. He might be able to expedite the autopsy," Max replied. "We'll be back in Tampa tonight."

———————— ♦ ♦ ♦ ————————

Wednesday, January 11, 2017
Headquarters, US Special Operations Command
MacDill Air Force Base, Florida

Since his return to SOCOM, Max was under great pressure to locate Madison and the warhead. The fear was that he would cross the border with the device and detonate it. So far, he had been able to stay ahead of Max's team and exact his revenge unabated. He didn't know just how close Max was behind him in El Salvador, nor did he know how far he was able to get ahead of Max when he reached Mexico. Madison knew Max was on his trail and he couldn't afford to waste time.

Max made the decision to send Danya and Andy to the El Real Airport to question the pilot and his wife, Paulita. Danya's phone calls to them had not been returned. Since the pilot had spent time with Madison, Max suspected he might be able to provide evidence on his destination and intentions. He thought the pilot might have overheard something, or Madison might have said something that would be a vital clue.

The team at SOCOM had been reviewing the data it had received, making sure it hadn't missed anything of importance as well as scratching for new material. Anticipating Los Zetas would bring the warhead into the US, it made the cartel its main focus. Any tidbit of data was thoroughly checked out.

Gail had just hung up the phone from her conversation with Captain Mackenzie. He wanted an update on the nuke, and his phone calls had increased to three times a week. Each conversation yielded little new material, except that Madison was making steady progress toward the US, which always lit Mackenzie's fuse. There was little Gail could do except suffer through his calls. She had always been able to appease him, but that no longer seemed to be the case.

As she was about to go for a walk to calm down, her phone rang again. She answered the phone, not paying attention to the number, and identified herself, "Special Agent Summers."

"Hi, Gail. This is Dawn Blakey, Homeland Security," said the chipper voice.

Gail took a deep breath and rolled her eyes before she replied. "Hello, Dawn. What's Homeland Security doing?" She tried to be reasonably friendly and not too sarcastic.

"I report to *the* secretary of Homeland Security now."

"How nice for you. Is this an invitation to your party?"

"Ha! Ha! Gail, you're so funny. I am coming down to SOCOM for you to brief me on Friday. It's been a couple of weeks since we last talked."

Already annoyed at the young woman, Gail replied. "It's customary to request a meeting, Dawn."

"Oh, ha! You know what I mean. Can I come down there for an update?"

"We're quite busy right now. As you know, we're trying to prevent a terrorist from bringing a nuke into the US."

"Yes, Gail. I know that. That's what I need an update on. *The* secretary is very concerned about the status. He feels that DC and New York City are the likely targets. He's frustrated that you haven't recovered the nuke and captured Madison."

Gail opened her calendar, checked her Friday schedule, and said, "OK, Dawn, I can give you an hour. How about ten o'clock?"

"OK, ten o'clock, Friday morning. I'll bring Joel Honeycutt with me. Max and Lieutenant Colonel Johnston will be there as well?"

"Yes, Max will be here, but Lieutenant Colonel Johnston will be on travel."

"Thank you, Gail. I'll let *the* secretary know."

"You do that, Dawn."

"See you Friday."

"Right."

Gail hung up the phone, then sat back and sighed. She looked up and saw Max step away from Andy. "Max," she said, "I just got a call from Dawn Blakey. She wants to come down on Friday morning for an update."

He took a deep breath, and the corner of his mouth tightened. "OK."

"Homeland Security was created as a result of the 9/11 terrorist attack on the US, to coordinate the security efforts for the homeland," Gail said. "That means antiterrorism and border security. As powerful and foreboding as the name implies, bureaucracy and politics have hampered the concept of the organization. Dawn Blakey exemplifies those of the staff."

"Be nice, Gail," Max replied, although he silently agreed with her.

"Competency isn't a prerequisite either," she said, then leaned forward and entered the date and time of the meeting. She labeled it *Homeland InSecurity*, then sent invitations to the team.

Dawn Blakey was a bureaucrat, low on intelligence and high on self-importance. Gail didn't care for the young woman, but she had to put up with her. Her visit would be a distraction for the team. Dawn was like the pesky fly. She didn't contribute anything to their mission and was annoying. Aside from that, they had to be careful with her, as they knew that after the briefing, she would confuse the information as she reported it back to her superiors.

Late that same afternoon, Andy received a call from Lieutenant Colonel Greg Matthews at the embassy in San Salvador. "It took a little finesse," Matthews said, "but I got the coroner to expedite the autopsy on Gareth. I'm sending you a copy."

"Thank you," Andy replied. "What's the bottom line?"

"As you suspected, it wasn't a heart attack. He had a lethal concentration of fentanyl in his system. The coroner is advising the police. But since it's been several days. I doubt they'll find anything."

"Well, we know it was Madison. We just can't prove he did it. Thanks for your help."

Friday morning rolled around before the team was ready for it. However, they had somehow found time to prepare for the meeting. It had been several days since they had gained any intelligence on Madison, and they suspected he was near the border or had already crossed into the US.

Danya had sent a text to Max notifying him that she and Andy had arrived at the El Real airfield.

When it was time to start the meeting, Max sat at the head of the conference table with Gail and David to his left. Dawn and Joel sat to his right. David had passed out copies of the presentation to each of them. Max, from his previous experience with Dawn, knew what to expect and kept the meeting unclassified. However, he stated at the start that should the need arise to discuss anything classified, he would do so, and he would forward copies of that information to them, if they desired.

Max started with the events since Dawn's last meeting with them in December. "We have tracked Madison from the Darién Gap, up through Central America, and we believe he is now in Mexico. We're all but certain Madison is working with the Muslim Brotherhood and Los Zetas to bring the warhead into the US.

"With the aid of the Brotherhood, Madison was responsible for shooting down the C-17 carrying Acting Director Wellington on 15 December. We're confident he's also responsible for Senator Alexander's disappearance on 3 January. Then he was tracked to San Miguel, El Salvador, where, coincidently, Stew Gareth was given a lethal dose of fentanyl."

"Wait," Dawn said, her face revealing she didn't comprehend what Max had said. "I wasn't aware of any of this." She shot a look to Joel.

He shook his head and shrugged his shoulders.

"Haven't you read any of the reports we've submitted?" Gail asked, her eyebrows furrowed.

Dawn returned a look of bewilderment. Her mouth hung open.

"Why do we bother to send you information if you don't bother to read it?"

Gail flipped her pen onto the table and sat back. She was already frustrated with the young woman.

"Well…I…we read reports all the time," Dawn replied. "I guess I missed those."

"I guess you did," Gail said. "It's your job to read the reports and be informed."

"Tell me how Madison is responsible for the senator's disappearance," Dawn said.

"Senator Alexander was receiving money from the Muslim Brotherhood, and we believe he provided information to them," Gail said. "We think that he became a liability, and Madison or the Brotherhood killed him when he went to Costa Rica."

"I don't believe it," Dawn said. "You must be mistaken about Senator Alexander." Her complexion turned pale.

"Yes, Dawn," Max said. "Here is a copy of the report that was sent to DIA and your office." He slid a folder across the table to her.

"Los Zetas is the cartel in Mexico, correct?" Dawn asked.

"Correct," Max replied.

"How do you know Madison is working with the Brotherhood and Los Zetas?"

"Nassar is a representative of the Brotherhood, and he has met several times with him and Senator Alexander. We have copies of the transcripts, if you would like to read them. Madison used Los Zetas before, and Danya has seen Madison meeting with their representative."

Max continued with his briefing, providing Dawn with the latest intelligence. Watching her body language, he believed she had trouble comprehending all of it. He was fulfilling the objective for the meeting. He was well aware that if he didn't provide her the latest accurate information, the commander of SOCOM would receive a blistering call from the secretary of Homeland Security. That would require devoting time to answering an irate Cabinet secretary.

Max followed his briefing outline and hoped Dawn would refer to the copy of briefing slides when she reported back to her headquarters. He continued with his PowerPoint presentation, running forty minutes over their scheduled time.

"With the help of Los Zetas, Madison is getting ready to cross the border into the US," Dawn said, leaning forward in her chair. "The Zetas are going to enter the country in Otay Mesa in California. I need to get Customs and Border Patrol up to speed on this. I think the California National Guard should be put on alert too."

Max motioned to Gail to remain calm. "Dawn, what intel do you have that indicates they will enter in Otay Mesa?" Max asked.

"We know they have constructed several tunnels there and have moved big shipments of drugs through that area. We even prevented

Madison from bringing that bomb into the US through one of those tunnels three years ago."

Max took a deep breath. "Yes, several drug tunnels have been constructed in the area, but by the Sinaloa Federation, not Los Zetas. Madison never intended to bring the bomb into the US through one of the tunnels three years ago. It was a ruse. The two cartels don't generally get along and stay in their respective areas. However, I do agree that things do change."

"Dawn," Gail said, her voice calm and cold, "we know Madison and how he operates. We've been after him for some time. If you have any actionable intelligence indicating he or Los Zetas plan to enter the US with the warhead in California, please share it with us. We do not have any such intelligence."

"Well…No, I don't have any intelligence," Dawn replied. "I just assumed he would. Why wouldn't he cross there?"

David chuckled at her response of not having any intelligence.

Gail covered her grin with her hand and glanced at David. She, too, was amused at the young woman's response.

"Madison is smart and cunning," Max said. "It is unlikely he'll cross into California, because he's using Los Zetas to bring it into the US, and they'll use one of their routes in their area. With no other intel to go on, if I had to bet, it would be South Texas. We're trying to get that intelligence now. So, please, don't jump to any conclusion."

Dawn sat back in her chair. It was obvious she was thinking over the last few minutes, trying to process everything. "Well, I hope you are right, but I still think California."

"OK, Dawn," Gail said as she laid her glasses on the table. "You think that. In the meantime, read the reports we have submitted. You have been given the most up-to-date data we have. If you want to help, get the CIA to share information with us."

———— ✦ ————

Thursday, January 12, 2017
Staging Area
Piedritas, Coahuila, Mexico

The convoy, led by the Zetas lieutenant, Carlos, arrived just after midnight at the old ranch five miles north of the small village of Piedritas, about ten miles south of the Texas border. The poor village of 115 people, without computers, seemed to have been skipped over by time. It was rustic and in the middle of nowhere. It was the perfect place for Madison to stage before crossing the US border.

He wanted to rest his men for several days after the arduous journey from Panama. The trip ahead would be rugged and about as dangerous as the previous one. He also needed time to train his men. The Zetas were experienced with the route into the US and would be teaching the Panamanians every aspect of the journey.

As soon as the men were settled in for the night, Max, Franco, and Carlos sat around a small fire. Franco passed out cigars, and Bart opened a bottle of Crown Royal Reserve. He poured each of them two fingers of the whiskey into soda cups. "Franco, Carlos, you have done well," Bart said as he held up his cup to salute them.

They each sipped their drink.

"Tomorrow, we rest," Bart said. "Let the men sleep in."

"We can use the rest," Franco replied, then knocked back his drink. "The fire and whiskey are nice, but I am about to go to sleep. See you in the morning."

"I am retiring as well," Carlos said, then ended his drink.

Bart held up his cup to the two as they stood. He watched them as they disappeared into the darkness.

# CHAPTER 22

Friday, January 13, 2017
Servicio y Suministro de Areo
El Real Airport, Panama

D ANYA AND LIEUTENANT Colonel Andy Johnston went straight to the office of Servicio y Suministro de Areo. The old Willys Jeep was parked outside, and the pilot, Dennis, was inside, alone, filling out paperwork at his desk. The cool air greeted Andy as soon as he opened the door. He introduced himself then turned and motioned to Danya. "This is Danya, a member of our team."

Dennis nodded in acknowledgment, then his eyes shot to Danya. "You were with the others that came down here while I was gone. My wife told me about your visit." His eyes shifted back to Andy. "Your people scared my wife, and I don't appreciate it. What do you want?"

"Dennis, isn't it?" Andy held his gaze on him.

"Yeah."

"We want to talk to you about your trip. Where's your wife?"

"She's not here."

The door opened and Paulita stepped in.

"Hello, Paulita," Danya said. "This is Lieutenant Colonel Andy Johnston."

Paulita stood motionless and looked to her husband, then to Andy.

Taking Paulita by the arm, Danya said, "Let's take a walk outside. Andy wants to talk to your husband."

She glanced back to her husband; her eyes were full of fear.

"It's OK, Paulita," Dennis said. "Don't worry, everything is fine."

She followed Danya's direction into the warm sun and soft breeze.

As soon as the door closed, Andy slid a chair forward and said, "Slide your chair around the desk."

Dennis looked puzzled.

"I don't want you to get nervous and do something dumb, like pulling your .45 out of the center drawer."

Dennis's expression was unchanged. "What makes you think I have a .45 in my desk drawer?"

He didn't blink. "I'd have one."

Andy sat as Dennis rolled his chair to the front of the desk. He began by telling Dennis they knew about his charter with Bart Madison. He outlined the trip and went over each stop at the clandestine airstrips, laying out the information to show Dennis they knew who he took on the flight and where they went.

Andy was sending a subtle signal to Dennis not to lie to him. He had set the stage well. Taking his time, he spent fifteen minutes recapping their trip.

"That's all correct," Dennis said. "Why are you telling me all this if you know all about my charter?"

"I want to know what you and Madison talked about. Also, about anything you might have overheard the others say."

"Nothing. The passengers sat in the back, and I flew the plane. I couldn't hear anything over the sound of the engines."

"You were with them for about six days, and you didn't hear anything?" Andy's tone was stern.

For over twenty minutes the two sparred back and forth with questions and few answers. Dennis remained committed to his denial. Andy, a seasoned military intelligence officer, suspected Dennis was concealing something. He continued his questioning, asking in different ways.

— ◆ ◆ ◆ —

Danya engaged Paulita in easy conversation, leading her to the spot where they had enjoyed the evening cooking burgers "Let's sit here in the shade," Danya said. It was a comfortable and pleasurable place where Paulita and her husband had cooked out many times. Danya was slow and gentle in her questions. She had gained Paulita's confidence before, and she continued to build on it.

"I am frightened," Paulita said as tears welled in her eyes.

"I know," Danya said with empathy. "That's why we are here. Andy and I want to help you and keep anything from happening, but we need some information to do that. What did your husband tell you about his trip?"

"Nothing," she said, sniffling. "He just said it was long, and the plane was fine."

"He didn't say anything else?"

"No. All he said was it was fine. What is going on?"

"We want to protect you, but you must tell me everything you know. Even the smallest thing might be important. Those men your husband took in his plane are bad. The American is a traitor and international terrorist. The others are former members of the FARC. They are meeting up with Los Zetas and are planning an attack on the US. We think they may come back for your husband for what he knows. That puts you at risk too."

Paulita began to tremble, then she burst out crying. "But I don't know anything."

"I know. But they think you do because of your husband."

"He doesn't know anything either!" she protested through her tears and runny nose.

Danya continued her gentle approach. They talked for another fifteen minutes. Paulita finally confided that her husband was worried, and she suspected he knew more than he had told her.

"That is all I know," Paulita said. Then she pulled out her handkerchief and blew her nose. "Honest. Dennis didn't tell me any specifics, but I know he knows something. He thinks he is protecting me by not telling me."

Danya gave her a hug. "I need you to tell your husband to tell us everything. Let's go back inside."

The two stood, and Paulita followed Danya's lead.

———— ◆ ◆ ◆ ————

Dennis looked to the door as it opened, and Paulita stepped in, followed by Danya. He saw Paulita's red eyes and knew Danya's questions had been hard for her.

Danya slid two chairs close to the two men. She seated Paulita in one and took the other.

"Dennis, please tell them what you know," Paulita said, then blew her nose.

Danya grasped Paulita's hand in support.

Dennis looked down into his hands, then raised his head. "I did pick up more passengers in El Tamarindo, El Salvador. The leader of that bunch was a big, stocky man in his mid-forties. His name was Franco. They loaded a large bundle onto the plane. Madison told me it weighed two hundred and ninety pounds."

"Why did he tell you that?" Andy asked.

"When I saw that it took four men to carry it, I asked him how much it weighed. I told him I needed to worry about weight and balance."

"Go on," Andy said. "From there?"

"We flew to Cuajinicuilapa, Mexico, on the Pacific southwest coast. We landed two miles south of the Ometepec River and sixteen miles west of Cuajinicuilapa." He paused and looked to Paulita, then back to Andy.

"Go on," Andy said.

"We were met by about six vehicles. They lit the landing strip when we approached. I heard Madison say the man's name that met us was Nassar." His eyes went to Paulita again, then dropped to his hands.

"Madison told him they had the nuke. I swear to God, I didn't know what they were going to do! If I had known they were going to put a nuke on my plane, I wouldn't have flown them. Honest to God, I didn't know anything about it."

"Those men, aside from Nassar, were Los Zetas," Andy said.

"Shit! What's going on?" Dennis asked.

"I think you know the answer to that. Show me on the map where you dropped 'em off."

Dennis stood, stepped around his desk, then pulled out the map of Mexico he had used. "Here is where I dropped them off," he said, placing his finger on the map.

Andy, then Danya, looked at the location on the map. They returned to their seats.

"Did Madison or anyone else mention where they were going from that location?" Andy asked.

Dennis shook his head. "No, nothing was mentioned. When they unloaded that bundle, I just wanted to get away from there."

"Dennis, you know too much," Andy said. "Madison doesn't leave loose ends. There must be something else you haven't told us." He held his gaze on the man.

"Know too much?" Dennis replied in exasperation. He raised his hands and said, "I don't know shit."

"You know where you dropped off Madison and the others," Andy replied. "You know he picked up a nuke and offloaded it in Mexico. Need I go on? I think that's enough for Madison. What else?"

"After I dropped them off, I overheard Nassar and Franco tell Madison they wanted to kill me. Madison disagreed and told them the plane couldn't stay there, and they couldn't burn it. That's when I knew I was in deep shit."

Andy nodded and kept his eyes locked on Dennis's.

"Go on. It doesn't make sense that he let you go. Why did he?"

Dennis held his eyes on Andy momentarily, then dropped his head. "Before we landed at Cuajinicuilapa, Madison told me he wanted me to fly him to South America. He said it would be about ten days, more or less. I am to be ready when he notifies me. He told me not to say anything to anyone."

"That's why he didn't kill you," Andy said. "Where're you to pick him up and drop him off?"

"He didn't say. He said he would tell me when he notifies me. I'm afraid if I take him, I won't return. I could have just ended my life for telling you all this."

"That's Madison's way," Andy replied. "I believe that if you don't fly him to South America, he'll pay you a visit. You need to trust us."

Paulita burst out crying in fear. Danya squeezed her hand.

"Either way, I'm screwed," Dennis said. "What are we supposed to do?"

"You can work with us and do as we say," Andy replied.

"Hell, we're out here in the jungle and a long way from help," Dennis said. "What're we supposed to do if Madison shows up on our doorstep again? We can't just leave. From what you said, that's not an option."

Andy spent the next few moments trying to relieve the couple's anxiety and instructed both of them what to do. They both objected several times and pointed out their vulnerability.

"I'm going to see what I can do about getting you some protection," Andy replied. "Just stay put for now, and don't go anywhere without notifying me or Danya. Be armed at all times. One of us will be back in touch with you with more instructions."

"Sooner rather than later," Dennis replied. His tone was harsh. "Just remember, we are out here all alone."

Andy nodded. "I know. If Madison should contact you, notify us immediately."

Andy and Danya returned to headquarters with the information Dennis had supplied. It confirmed their suspicion that Madison was at or near the southern US border and was preparing to cross it. Although Dennis provided the location of where he took Madison, the US border is long, and he could choose to cross anywhere. However, Max and his team had kept their primary focus on the Los Zetas drug routes into the US.

En route, Andy had called Max to give him the information Dennis had provided. "They are both scared," Andy said. "I suggest several soldiers be sent down to protect them. It appears to me that Madison has his escape plan worked out, and he plans to go to South America. If we help Dennis lead Madison into thinking Dennis is flying him to South America, that could be another place where we could get him. We could use the soldiers we send down to protect Dennis and his wife in getting Madison."

"I agree," Max replied. "I'll include this in my report to the general. Let's hope we get Madison before he has a chance to execute any of his plans."

"How was the meeting with Homeland Security?" Andy asked.

"About like you probably suspected. She didn't provide any information."

"Figures."

"She believes Madison will enter through California."

"Did she provide any intelligence to support her belief?"

"None."

"We'll be back in Tampa tomorrow evening."

"Have a safe trip."

Max ended the call and went to work preparing his report to General Matherson. The lives of Dennis and Paulita were on the line, and Max was not about to let Madison slip away this time. He had already instructed Gail and David to tighten up their focus on the Zetas' routes into the US, and he hoped to stop him at the border. His biggest problem was that Senator Alexander had been successful in keeping the US southern border open, and it appeared the current administration had no intention of closing it. Homeland Security, the department responsible for the borders, was no help. Other commitments by the military forced Max to operate with scarce resources, and he had to practically beg for additional assets when the situation dictated. It was impossible for him to adequately cover the entire border.

The memory of three years ago was never out of his mind. Madison proved he was an able adversary then, and Max knew he wouldn't make mistakes this time either. Knowing Madison, Max suspected he would not likely repeat the same scenario as before. He suspected Madison would choose an unsuspected or unlikely entry point.

# CHAPTER 23

Sunday, January 15, 2017
US Customs and Border Protection, Hidalgo Command Center
Pharr, Texas

O N FRIDAY, GAIL had received a call from one of her contacts, Special Agent Tony Chavez at the Border Patrol in South Texas. He informed her that a man arrived at the Port of Entry claiming to have vital information regarding Bart Madison. Gail confirmed that she and David would meet him at the center as soon as possible. She requested Agent Chavez begin interviewing the man.

Gail and David arrived at the Command Center at 10:30 a.m. Even on a Sunday, the center was a busy place. Several agents were at their computers observing the security cameras tracking the steady stream of vehicles and pedestrians crossing the border. Others escorted detainees to the holding facility and conducted inspections. Radios cracked with communications to and from the agents in the field. The tempo was nonstop.

The two were met by Agent Chavez as they were processed into the center. "Tony, this is David Elsworth," Gail said as she clipped her visitor's badge to a lanyard, then slipped it around her neck.

David took the man's outstretched hand. "Pleasure to meet you, Tony."

Tony held his gaze on David for a brief moment. He started to comment on David's choice of shirts—neon, light magenta.

Gail noticed his hesitation and said, "He's OK, Tony. He always dresses like that."

Tony suppressed a grin and handed David his visitor's badge.

"I've got our man in an interview room," he said, handing Gail a folder. "This is a copy of the interview update from last night and this morning. His English is good. I was a bit surprised."

"Thanks. I read your notes from his previous interviews. Is there anything new?"

"Not really," Tony replied. "Just basic info stuff. His name is Chico Espinoza, and he says he's a member of Los Zetas. We're checking that out. He wants to talk to a senior person in charge of looking for Bart Madison, and the reward."

Gail looked up from the folder with raised eyebrows. "Member of Los Zetas? The reward. Of course he does. OK, let's have a talk with him."

Tony turned and led them through the security doors and down the hall. A guard, standing by a door, opened it and allowed the three to enter. Tony, Gail, and David took seats at the table opposite a slender man in his early thirties, wearing dingy blue jeans, a faded black T-shirt, and old sneakers. He had short dark hair. Tattoos covered his arms and neck.

"Hey, man," Chico said as his eyes locked onto David. "Nice shirt. I dig it."

"Thanks," David replied as he pressed the record button on his camera.

Gail looked over the man before speaking. "I'm FBI Special Agent Gail Summers. You're Chico Espinoza. Right?"

His entire body moved with his nodding head. "Yeah, Chico. You are not a bad looking bitch. I want the reward for the information on Bart Madison. Then you can help me spend it."

Gail leaned into the table. Her eyes narrowed. "You haven't seen bitch...yet!"

David hid his smile. He knew what was coming.

"I'm not going to put up with your bullshit. I want straight, truthful answers. Otherwise, we'll throw your ass outside and you won't get shit! And we'll let Los Zetas know you were an informant. Got that?"

The startled man, his eyes opened wide, replied, "Yeah."

"You haven't told Agent Chavez much of anything. I want to know everything you know about Bart Madison. Let's start from the beginning."

"I've told Agent Chavez everything."

"You haven't told him anything," Gail said, holding her gaze on him. "I want details. When and where did you come in contact with him?"

"OK. At an airstrip sixteen miles west of Cuajinicuilapa, last Sunday."

"Who else was there?"

"Some were Los Zetas, some FARC, a man called Nassar, and Bart Madison."

"How do you know about the reward?" Gail asked.

"Everyone knows about the reward." His demeanor was smug.

Her eyes narrowed. "Los Zetas or Madison will come looking for you."

He shrugged and wrinkled his mouth. "It is a lot of money you are offering for Madison. I can disappear and live well on it. I am not worried."

Concealing her emotions and her lack of patience, Gail continued her questioning for another hour without gaining much more than she already knew. He was coy, and guarded with his answers. She used many forms of questions looking for inconsistency. However, his answers were the same as he had given over the last two days of questioning. She'd had enough, and her tolerance for the man was exhausted.

Gail slammed her fist on the table, startling the others. "I'm tired of you wasting my time. Do you want the reward or just play games?"

"You are exciting me, mama," he replied, holding his narrow eyes on her in defiance. "I think we should go get something to drink, and smoke some *doña Juanita*. Have you ever smoked any? What do you say?"

"Knock it off. Do you have information on Bart Madison or not?" Her tone was harsh. "So far, all you have done is feed me a lot of bullshit. If you've got anything on Madison, I want it, and now! No bullshit and straight answers! Otherwise, I'll ship your ass to Guantanamo."

Gail began her interrogation again, starting with pointed questions. Her mood had turned foul. "Tell me what you know, or no reward, and the interview is over. What's Madison planning to do?"

"I dunno."

"Interview is over." Gail said as she stood and closed her folder. "Take him out of here. David, Tony, let's go."

Chico sat back, and his eyes roamed the room.

Gail, leading the others, reached for the doorknob.

"OK, bitch. He is going to take a bomb across the border."

"When?"

"Thursday."

"Where's he going to cross?"

"Laredo. Now can I have my money?"

"Look, asshole, I'll tell you if, and when, you'll get the reward. Just answer my damn questions. What's his plan to cross the border?"

"Cross at night, northwest of the city."

For the next forty-five minutes Chico was forthcoming with information. He answered Gail's questions without his previous insolence and haughtiness. Special Agent Chavez began to relax with confidence, as it seemed Gail was getting somewhere with Chico. Gail was suspicious of Chico and suspected his story was a deception, but she persisted. She continued to extract information for fifteen more minutes.

Chico interrupted her. "I want a drink, and I need to piss."

Gail looked to Tony, then to David. "We'll take a break."

David stopped the recording and stood.

Tony opened the door and spoke to the guard, giving him instructions.

Gail's eyes landed on Dawn Blakey walking toward her as she stepped out of the room. She turned to Tony and said, "What the hell is she doing here? Get her out of here."

"Hi Gail!" She ignored Tony. "I got here as quick as I could. I'm so glad he came forward and this is about over. What has he had to say? Are you finished questioning him? Is this where Madison is going to try and cross? I've told everyone to be ready. I have the press coming."

Gail raised her hand and said, "Hold on, Dawn. First of all, you are not supposed to be in here. Secondly, the interview isn't over. I'll let you know when the interview is over and I have answers. We're just taking a break. No press." She continued walking down the hall.

Dawn picked up her pace to catch up with Gail. "I'd like to sit in on the interview when you resume."

"No," Gail replied. "There're three of us in there now. You'll be briefed when and where I say."

"*The* secretary wants me to keep him informed," Dawn replied in protest.

"Leave, now, or I'll have two of these officers drag your ass out. One of your Louboutins could lose a heel."

Gail pressed her chin. "This isn't a sideshow." It was all she could do not to coldcock the twit. "Go to the breakroom, get a coffee, polish your nails, or watch TV. I need to go to the bathroom, and you're not invited."

————— · ✦ · —————

As soon as Gail was out of sight, Dawn had garnered the agent in charge of the center and his deputy. She was her usual self, speaking with authority, and emphasizing *the secretary*, to give the impression she had power. She started her excited approach to the men by emphasizing the threat to the border by terrorists.

By observing the two agents, anyone—except Dawn—could tell they didn't respect her and they thought of her as another bureaucrat seeking publicity. They were more interested in doing their jobs than listening to Dawn. She told them she was meeting with the press and wanted them to prepare for their arrival. Before she had gone much further, Gail appeared and marched up to her, having overheard her mention the press briefing.

"Dawn," Gail said. "In here, NOW!"

Seeing their opportunity to escape from Dawn, the men stepped away.

"Yes, Gail."

As soon as the men left the room, Gail said, "What the hell are you doing? I said no press. I told you I would provide you with a briefing."

"Oh, Gail, I thought it would be good to show off the border security and show the American people we are on top of things. The secretary will appreciate us keeping the people updated."

"Why don't you just pick up the phone, call Madison, and spill your guts to him?"

"Ha! Ha! Gail, you are so funny. Why would I do that?"

"Dawn, if you brief the press, Madison'll see it, and he'll know what we're doing. He'll change his plans and we'll be back to square one, trying to catch up. He's not stupid. If no one has told you, this is all classified."

"Oh, I didn't think of that," Dawn said, and harrumphed.

"Now, cancel the fucking press and keep your damn mouth shut." Gail's tone was caustic. "From now on, you check with me before you do anything."

"OK."

Gail looked up to see Tony approaching. "Are you ready to continue?" he asked.

"Yes, put him in the room."

Once back in the room, David resumed recording.

"Chico," Gail began. "Before the break you said that Madison was going to cross the border on Thursday with a bomb at Laredo. Is this correct?"

"Yeah, that is right. Can I have the reward now? I want to get out of here."

"No! Where's Madison now?"

"I dunno. We spent a couple of days at an old ranch house not too far from the landing strip. Then I left."

"You just left? They let you fucking leave?" Now Gail was more than suspicious. This reeked of a setup.

"Yes. Well…I didn't want to do what they were planning. I wasn't offered any more money, then I had a disagreement with Franco. So I was sent away. I was to go back to Anáhuac. That's when I decided to get the reward."

"What were they planning that made you not want to go along with them?" Gail asked.

"Carry the bomb across the border."

"Where's Madison going with the bomb after he crosses the border?" Tony asked.

"I dunno. He never said."

The interview continued for another thirty-five minutes. Gail asked several questions again for clarification. Chico was true to his previous story, giving the same answers. "OK, we're done. Get him out of here," Gail said, sweeping her notes into the folder.

"Can I have my reward now?"

"I've already told you. Don't ask me again. You're going to stay with us while we check your story."

Tony stood, stepped to the door and spoke to the guard. He returned to his chair as the guard took Chico by the arm and led him out.

"What do you think?" Tony asked.

"It doesn't feel right," Gail replied. "I think it's shit. Start checking out his story. First thing, see if you can locate any place that looks like it has been prepped for a crossing. See if there are any drainage pipes, aqueducts, anything that Madison could use to get to the river unnoticed. Small boats too. Try to use drones. I don't want Madison to get any idea we are there. I'm going to review the recording."

"It'll take a while to do a thorough search. There's a lot of places they could hide a small boat. He would pick one of the busiest crossings in the US. Do you want me to alert Laredo?"

"I know. That's one of the things that bothers me. No, don't alert Laredo yet."

---

Sunday, January 15, 2017
Staging Area
Piedritas, Coahuila, Mexico

Inside the old ranch house, seated at the rickety table, Bart was holding his regular status meeting. Franco and Carlos slid out chairs, sat at the table, and unzipped their jackets. Bart spread out a map of the area.

"Tell me about the men," Bart said. "Are they ready?"

"They are doing well," Carlos replied. "They have been good students. A few bumps and bruises, but in a couple of days they will be fine. We have provided them a lot of information about the trail. They should do well."

"I agree," Franco said. "My men are still adjusting to the cooler temperatures, but they are OK."

"Good," Bart replied. "As I said earlier, we will do a recon this evening. We will leave just after sundown. I want to see the trail and determine how long it will take to get to the border, then cross. Did you send word to your two men watching the border that we were coming tonight?"

"I did," Carlos replied. "They are expecting us. There has been no change since they have been there."

Bart nodded. "Chico should have been interviewed by now."

"Do you think the Americans will believe his story?" Franco asked.

"It'll depend on who conducted the interview," Bart said. "I doubt Kenworth would do it, but it could have been one of his people. If they did it, it's iffy. Franco, send two of your men to watch the border where Chico told them we will cross. Any increase in patrols and helicopter traffic could indicate they are searching for the crossing. Look for anything. It won't take them long after they start searching to determine that it is a ruse. I just don't want anyone to make that determination until after Wednesday. Tell them to pick a spot with plenty of vegetation and trees for the false crossing. Make the area look like someone tried to camouflage the site. Have them leave early in the morning, and remind them not to use the phones except to contact you, and to keep the conversations short. I want them to be in position by noon."

Franco nodded, "I will have them leave at 05:00. They will know what to do."

Bart looked to Carlos and twisted the map. "Show me the trail."

Carlos leaned over and, with a pencil, indicated their current position, then traced the route as it snaked through a canyon. "My men are on this ridge, on the north end of the finger," he said. "The altitude is about a thousand meters. They are about a kilometer from the border and have good visibility all across the front. It's going to be cold."

Bart looked up and glanced to Franco, then Carlos. "This is our final step. If all goes well, we'll depart on Wednesday as planned. Any questions?"

Carlos and Franco shook their heads.

# CHAPTER 24

Monday, January 16, 2017
Headquarters, US Special Operations Command
MacDill Air Force Base, Florida

M AX READ THE note confirming the soldiers were en route to the El Real Airport in Panama to provide security for Dennis and Paulita. He added the contact information of the team sergeant into his phone. Just as he finished, the phone rang and Gail's number appeared.

Gail had finished her summary of the interview with Chico Espinoza and sent copies to Max and to Dawn Blakey. She placed the call to Max since she knew that as soon as Dawn had her copy in hand, she would create chaos for them.

"I just sent you a copy of the interview summary with the informant," Gail said.

"I just pulled it up," he replied. "What do you think?"

"He's feeding us bullshit," she replied. "He had a lot of factual stuff in his statement to make his story believable, but a few things just didn't add up. He said Madison was going to cross the border northwest of Laredo on Thursday night."

"On Thursday night, northwest of Laredo?"

"That's what he said. I've got people searching the area, looking for any boats in the area and signs that might indicate the location. I just think he's a ruse. You'll see in his statement that he had a disagreement with Franco, and they sent him away. He was supposed to go back to Anáhuac but decided to seek the reward instead. It just doesn't seem right that Los Zetas would let him go like that."

"I agree. One of Madison's deceptions. The Zetas wouldn't let someone just walk away. Andy received word from one of his contacts that the Zetas are planning a big shipment to cross into the US at Amistad Reservoir. That seems a lot more plausible to me."

"Dawn Blakey was down here and has a copy of the interview. She was poking her nose in, trying to make herself relevant. Even though I told her that I thought the informant was a con, she believes that's where Madison will cross."

"Thanks for the heads-up. I'd better get this to the general before DHS calls him."

Max hung up the phone and looked up to see Andy enter the office. "That was Gail," he said. "The informant she interviewed seems to be a part of Madison's deception. I believe he is about to make his move."

"That sounds like it, but where?" Andy replied. "I've requested surveillance flights along the border from Presidio to Del Rio. I requested satellite coverage along the entire border, again, but that looks doubtful. I'm in contact with the Texas National Guard. They've established observation posts in the mountains along the southern Texas border."

———— ⋅ ◆ ⋅ ————

Monday, January 16, 2017
Staging Area
Piedritas, Coahuila, Mexico

Bart, Franco, and Carlos completed the recon and returned to the ranch house late in the afternoon without incident. The border, as seen from their observation post on the ridge, appeared unchanged, and the men had not seen anyone or any aircraft since they had arrived at their location. Carlos had assured Bart that their planned route would not be used by Los Zetas. However, they faced dangers from the inhospitable terrain and its inhabitants along their route.

The terrain was considered a natural barrier along the border. It was remote, rugged, and many things in it would kill you. The area was populated with black bears, mountain lions, javelinas (collared peccaries, medium-sized animals similar to wild boars), and poisonous snakes. In addition to the dangerous wildlife, the treacherous landscape was filled with steep inclines, sheer drop-offs, deep canyons, unstable footings, and the diverse Chihuahuan Desert. Only three of the horses had made the trip once before. Bart chose this route, at the suggestion of Carlos, precisely because of the dangerous conditions and because it was least patrolled by Border Protection.

Just as the sun set on Wednesday, Carlos led the men, on horseback, north along the trail to the Rio Grande. Bart had sent two scouts ahead of them. Their route would take them to the river south of Chisos Mountains and just west of Mariscal Canyon. The column would travel in darkness, without lights, until they crossed the river and entered the rugged and dangerous mountains. Then they would switch on their lanterns as they made their way through the terrain.

After the first mile, the men were settled into the trip. The only sound was the gentle crunch of the horses' hooves on the sandy Chihuahuan Desert trail. Most of the Los Zetas men Cisco had chosen were experienced horsemen. The FARC members had just gained their horsemanship at the ranch over the last few days. Carlos paired each one of his men with Franco's to ensure they paid attention to their horse and terrain. The landscape ahead was unforgiving and required the riders to be attentive at all times.

———— • ♦ • ————

Wednesday, January 18, 2017
US Customs and Border Protection, Hidalgo Command Center
Pharr, Texas

Dawn had been avoiding Gail and disregarded her summation of the interview, which stated that the informant was a deception, and her instructions and advice. Unbeknown to Gail, Dawn focused the resources of Border Protection on the area northwest of Laredo in anticipation of Madison's crossing there. She had invited the press to be there, and she also encouraged the secretary of Homeland Security to call the governor of Texas to add additional National Guard troops to patrol the Amistad Reservoir as a secondary precaution. In her communications with the secretary, Dawn had requested a Blackhawk helicopter to be on standby for her if it was determined that Madison was crossing via the reservoir. In typical bureaucratic fashion, she had created a *dog 'n' pony show* that no one could miss. Aside from impressing her boss, she was intent on showing the world how secure the US southern border was.

Preparations for Dawn's show were falling into place, and by late Wednesday afternoon media trucks from several TV stations had arrived, as well as the helicopter she had requested. The resulting chaos slowed down the busy border operations. Inspections ground to a trickle, and traffic crossing into the US slowed. Dawn had directed everyone to be ready for Madison's capture by 8:00 a.m. Although she didn't have details about an expected time, she wanted everyone ready and standing by.

The general received a call from Homeland Security and then met with Max, seeking an update. Both the commander and J3 were frustrated by his uncharacteristic failure to keep them informed, so Max placed a call to Gail. He got her voicemail, but she returned his call a few minutes later. "What's going on down there?" Max asked. "Homeland Security says Madison is crossing there tomorrow and has ramped up."

"That's news to me," Gail replied, her voice full of surprise. "I haven't found out anything new since I talked to you about the informant. Where did that come from?"

"The general got a call from Homeland Security and wanted answers."

"Dawn Blakey!" Fury filled Gail's tone. "It'll take me about twenty minutes to get back to the center. Maybe I can calm down enough that I won't kill her. I told her not to do anything, that this is a deception."

"I want to make sure you don't have anything new about Madison crossing there tomorrow. Is that correct?"

"That is correct. I don't have anything new. I'll call you back after I have a talk with Dawn, if I'm not in jail."

Gail ended the call and sped up as she headed to the center. As she approached, she saw the spectacle Dawn had created. The parking lot was blocked off for the media trucks. She pulled to a stop, put her identification badge around her neck, and got out of the car. After a quick look around the area, she marched into the building. Dawn stepped around the corner of an adjoining hall. Gail intercepted her. "What the hell's going on?"

"Hi Gail," Dawn said with a smile. "We're preparing for Madison's capture."

"Dawn, Madison isn't going to cross here. I told you it was a deception. I also told you no press."

"Oh, Gail, the secretary thought it would be a good idea to show his capture."

"Why don't you have a big sign out near the river that flashes, 'Cross here, Bart'?"

"Why would I do that?"

"Get rid of the press and let these agents get on with their jobs. What does it take to convince you the informant was a ruse? You do know what deception means, don't you?"

"I just want to be ready."

"Even if he was going to cross here, he sure as hell isn't going to now. He's probably sitting across the river laughing his ass off at you."

"I didn't see anyone over there."

"Hell, I give up."

Gail turned and stepped away. She went to Tony's desk and sat in the chair next to his.

"Have a seat," Tony said with a smile. He could tell by her demeanor that Gail was not happy.

"I'm going back to Tampa in the morning," Gail said. "I was afraid Dawn was going to turn this into a circus. Madison won't be within a hundred miles of this place."

Tony shook his head and wrinkled up the corner of his mouth. "I know. I'm expecting an intel update in a few minutes. Are you going to stick around?"

"Not unless you need me. I'm going for a drink. If there is anything in the report I need to know about, call me. You're welcome to join me." She stood and walked out.

Back in her car, Gail withdrew her phone and called Max. "Just as I suspected, Dawn has created a circus here. There is no new intel indicating he is crossing in this area. That twit just took it upon herself to get everyone spun up. She has it in her head that this is the place."

"I figured as much. Thank you."

"There's nothing else I can do here. I have a flight back to Tampa in the morning."

———— ◆ ◆ ◆ ————

Wednesday, January 18, 2017
Rio Grande
US-Mexico Border

The column had been snaking along in a ravine along a ridgeline. Their course led them along a meandering path down from 600 meters. A short distance beyond the river, the terrain began to climb again. The night was a cool forty degrees, with clear skies. There was no light pollution, which provided a beautiful view of the stars, which looked like diamonds. It seemed as though you could reach up and touch them. The darkness prevented them from seeing the stunning limestone cliffs of the canyon, but that didn't matter, as they were not there for sightseeing.

Carlos stopped them a kilometer from the border to wait for the two scouts. Within a half hour, they arrived. After talking with Carlos for several minutes, they turned their horses and headed back toward the river.

Carlos briefed Bart on the report from the two men. "It is clear, no one is in the area. The water is low. No problems. The scouts are going to check the site where we will stop for the day. It is a few hours from here." It was common for no one to be in the area at that hour. Darkness added to the dangers of the terrain, so hikers and tourists retreated to their camps by nightfall.

Two javelinas darted out of the brush, spooking the horses. Two of them became unruly, and their riders struggled to keep them under control. The horses were turning and fighting against their reins, their hooves kicking up dust. Those who could withdrew their rifles or pistols, but no one could get a clear shot at the attacking animals. Bart, after controlling his horse, saw the drawn weapons, waved his hand, and shouted, "No, don't shoot! Don't shoot!"

Carlos, also waving, shouted, "¡No *dispares!* ¡No *dispares!*"

One rider was thrown against the rocks at the onset. Another man fought with his horse but lost the battle after several bucks and twists. He was thrown to the ground in the path of the attacking collared peccary. The other men were able to control their horses and scattered from the battleground.

The commotion jolted everyone and heightened their senses. The commotion was only a moment in duration, but it seemed like an eternity. It, in fact, turned out to be an eternity for the two men. The first rider struck his head on a rock and died. The second man was killed by the vicious javelina. The first frightened horse bolted and disappeared in the darkness. The second horse was caught by one of the other men. Carlos directed the men to dismount and calm the horses. He led his horse to the man holding the reins of the second horse. As he approached, he saw the animal favoring and holding up his right leg. Patting him, he ran his hand down the injured leg. Blood covered his hand. He looked up as Bart approached. "The javelina ripped open his leg. He is bleeding to death."

"Damn, two men and two horses lost."

Carlos handed his reins to Bart and said, "I'll take care of this one." He led the limping horse away from the others to a spot out of sight. Patting the horse's neck again, he withdrew his knife from the sheath on his belt. With a quick thrust and withdrawal, the horse's neck was sliced. The animal went down.

Carlos returned to the others, stepping around the bodies, and stopped in front of Bart. "Done." He took the reins from Bart and commanded, "We will continue." The others, hearing him, mounted their horses and formed back into a column as he led them to the river.

———— ◆ ◆ ◆ ————

Thursday, January 19, 2017
Headquarters, US Special Operations Command
MacDill Air Force Base, Florida

The office was buzzing with activity by the time Andy arrived. Danya and Max were responding to several messages about the possibility of Madison crossing the border that day. Dawn Blakey's actions, based on her belief that Madison planned to cross the border northwest of Laredo, had generated concern at Homeland Security, the FBI, the Intelligence community, and no telling what other agencies that hadn't contacted them. Each one started with: *A terrorist is bringing a nuclear bomb into the US.* Dawn had created a firestorm with her misinformation.

Max, explaining on the phone that the information was incorrect, motioned for Andy to step to his desk. Max handed him a phone message slip, cupped the phone, and said in a low voice, "He wants you to call him."

Andy looked at the paper and stepped to his desk. It was from Captain Dan Rowe, Texas National Guard. Sitting at his desk, Andy placed the call to the captain.

Once he was on the line, Captain Rowe said, "Is this line secure?"

"Yes, go ahead."

"We talked a few days ago and you asked me to call you if we saw anything suspicious."

"Whatta got?" Andy replied.

"From one of our OPs in the Chisos Mountains: 'We spotted a column of men on horseback cross the river into Texas just west of Mariscal Canyon.' It was about midnight, and we counted twenty lanterns. They're making their way through the terrain and avoiding the park trails. We've seen the drug cartel do this several times. Our orders are just to observe and report. I thought you would want to know about this."

"Thanks, Captain. It is exactly what I was wanting to know. Can I reach you at this number?"

"Yes, I'll be at this number."

Andy ended the call and stepped to Max's desk. As soon as Max ended his call, Andy laid a map of Texas on the desk and briefed him on his call with Captain Rowe.

"From the sound of his report," Andy said, "it could be Madison. The only thing they could see was the column with lights. The cartels have used the same route on horses before." He placed his finger on the location and said, "Here's where they crossed."

"It could be him," Max replied. "That's the best lead we've had in a while. Get back in touch with the captain and have him keep eyes on the column, but not to get close to them. I want to know their route and places where they rest. I want to know everything about them. I'll give Chugs a heads-up and ask him to call the Texas Military Department for coordination and assistance from Captain Rowe."

"I thought that's what you would say."

# CHAPTER 25

Thursday, January 19, 2017
Headquarters, US Special Operations Command
MacDill Air Force Base, Florida

B ETWEEN PHONE CALLS, Max called Chugs to brief him on the situation and ask him to call the Texas Military Department. Helen, the general's secretary, took the call and informed Max that General Matherson was in with the commander, and she would give him the message when he got out of the meeting. "Oh, Max," she said, "I'm not all that sure what's going on, but the phones have been ringing off the wall. Neither the commander nor General Matherson are in a very good mood. Watch out."

"Thank you, Helen."

Max hung up and continued with his preparation to intercept Madison in Texas. Before he could execute his plan, he needed confirmation that the column on horseback was, indeed, Madison and his men. General Matherson had approved Max's Warning Order for a platoon-size unit to prepare to deploy to West Texas. The phones continued ringing nonstop, leaving Max little time for his preparation.

Andy had talked with Captain Rowe twice. He was willing to help, but was waiting on orders from his headquarters and couldn't do anything until then. Gail and David returned to the office after lunch, and as the three of them sat at the conference table, Andy said, "Now that you are back in the office, let me get you up to speed. Max is trying to arrange for assets to assist us in Texas. I've talked to Captain Rowe twice, and he is keeping eyes on the men that crossed the border on horseback. They're headed northwest toward a ghost town, Terlingua, a former mining town."

David's eyes opened wide, and his mouth gaped when Andy said "ghost town."

"Max wants to leave tomorrow, if possible," Andy said. "He's been trying to brief Chugs, but he's been with the commander almost all day. The town is approximately ten miles north of the border, and it has a population of about eighty people. Tourists keep the town alive."

David leaned toward Gail and said, "I don't do ghosts."

"I doubt there're any ghosts there. At least I'm pretty sure," she whispered with a smile.

Danya approached the table and sat. "I just got off the phone with Thaddeus. Agents in Colombia identified a man they believe is Nassar and are tailing him. He is using an alias and traveling on a false passport. The man is booked on a flight to San Antonio."

"San Antonio?" Andy said. "He's going to meet Madison. OK, find out if San Antonio is his final destination. I want to know if he meets anyone. Check with the car rental companies for a reservation. Find out all you can. I'll make arrangements to have him followed from the airport."

Gail looked up to the large monitor on the wall to see the news report. She grasped the remote and turned off the mute. A news reporter was presenting a breaking report, and Dawn Blakey was standing beside him. The man reported that the US had information that an international terrorist with a nuclear bomb was attempting to cross the border. He turned to ask Dawn a question.

"Max, are you on the phone?" Gail said in a loud voice and pointed at the monitor for them to see the breaking news. "Look at the news flash."

Max stepped from his desk and sat with the others. The reporter began interviewing Dawn. "That is correct," Dawn said. "We have reason to believe an international terrorist is planning to cross the border just to the northwest of Laredo. We have located a place on the Rio Grande we believe he has prepared for his river crossing. We're ready to apprehend him."

"That damn woman is a nitwit!" Gail said. "I should have shot her before I left Laredo."

"That's what's causing all the excitement," Max said as he stood. "Shit, I'd better get to Chugs's office. Gail, get in touch with Dawn and shut her down. She may have just set us back."

"Maybe she gave us an unexpected gift." David said. "Madison is probably watching for a news story like this. He could relax a little, thinking we are looking for him in Laredo."

"It's possible," Max replied. "No, I don't think so. Madison is too good to make that kind of mistake." Max took a step from the table just as Major General Matherson walked in.

"I was on my way to your office, General," Max said. "We just saw the news flash from the border."

Matherson pointed to the monitor. "That woman has caused us a big problem. The commander has been on the phone with the secretary of Homeland Security, SecDef, the chairman of SSCI, and a host of others."

"I told her all this is classified," Gail said.

"Didn't you tell Blakey the informant was a deception?" Matherson asked, holding his gaze on her.

"Yes, sir," she replied. "I told her it was a ruse, and there was to be no press."

"The commander is getting a lot of pressure on this," Matherson said. "The secretary of Homeland Security is pushing hard. He wants you and your team to get down to Laredo too."

"General," Max said, "we believe Madison has already crossed the border. Andy has talked to Captain Dan Rowe, Texas National Guard, several times. They have OPs established on the mountains overlooking the border, and they spotted a column of about twenty men on horseback last night crossing into Texas. They're headed northwest toward Terlingua. He can only observe and report. We believe this is Madison."

"How confident are you it's Madison?" Matherson said. "Everyone else thinks he's near Laredo."

"Yes, sir," Max replied. "I'm 90 percent certain. Blakey is leading them in the wrong direction."

"We need Captain Rowe to stay on the target until we can get into position, but he can't help us without authorization from the Texas Military Department," Andy said. "Can you get us approval to use Captain Rowe?"

"I'll see what I can do," Chugs replied. "I was hoping to keep to a minimum the number of people knowledgeable about Madison and the nuke. We don't have any choice now but to get the Texas Military Department involved. If they are, and we have Gail, there shouldn't be a problem with the Posse Comitatus Act. I'll need to get this cleared with the lawyers."

"We're preparing to leave in the morning to go to Terlingua," Max said. "Madison'll have vehicles waiting for him to switch to as soon as he gets out of the rugged terrain in the vicinity of Terlingua, and I plan to intercept him before he can get to them."

"Stand by," Chugs said. "I came in here to send you to Laredo. I'll get with the commander and give him an update. He's trying to put out the firestorm Blakey created."

"We need to get there ahead of Madison," Max said, his tone full of urgency.

"I know," Matherson replied. "The firestorm first."

"I request the soldiers we have alerted be ordered to deploy in the vicinity of Terlingua," Max said. "They can be in position and develop some intel by the time I get there. They can contain them if Madison arrives before we do. I don't want to miss him. I'll coordinate with the platoon leader. They'll land under cover of darkness at least thirty kilometers from the town. I'm sure Madison has scouts out, and I don't want us to be seen. We'll infiltrate in, hopefully remain undetected by any of the civilians or Madison's men. I'll need to coordinate with the pilots on the best place to land."

"OK, send them," Matherson replied. "But you and your team stand by." He locked eyes with Gail and said, "Call Blakey and shut her down."

"Yes, sir," she replied and marched back to her desk. She took a deep breath and grasped the phone before she sat. When Dawn answered, Gail didn't exchange pleasantries. "God dammit, Dawn. What the hell are you doing?"

"Hi, Gail," she replied. "What do you mean?"

"I told you all this about Madison and the terrorists crossing the border is classified and there was to be no news media. I just saw you on TV spilling your guts about the terrorists crossing the river. I told you before, the river crossing at Laredo was a deception. Knock it off and cancel the news. Do you understand? Keep your fucking mouth shut, and stay out of the way."

"Gail, *the secretary* thinks this is important. The people should know. And I have a clearance."

"You won't, if you don't do as I say and get rid of the news. You say one more word about this and I'll be on you like flies on shit and throw your ass in jail before the sun sets."

"OK…OK…OK. I'll do it," Dawn cowed.

———— ◆ ◆ ◆ ————

Thursday, January 19, 2017
Somewhere
Southeast of Terlingua, Texas

About an hour before sunset, Carlos began alerting the men to prepare for their night's journey. They had found shelter from the sun in the shadows of the rocky outcrops along their path. They had time to eat a cold breakfast, then prepare their horses. As he left the last man's position, Carlos turned and saw one of the men step to a ledge, then disappear. Sprinting to where he last saw the man, he was joined by Bart, followed by Franco. They stopped at the edge and saw the motionless body about 100 meters below.

Madison, looking down, saw the fresh break in the rock ledge. "It gave way as he stepped close to the edge," he said. "Warn the men again."

Carlos, recognizing the man as one of his, said, "I will check on him."

Bart and Franco stood motionless and watched Carlos work his way down the rocky cliff. Soon they were joined by most of the others, seeking to know what had happened. Within a few moments, Carlos reached the injured man and checked him. He looked up to Bart and shook his head. The man was dead. Carlos began checking the man's pockets to ensure he wasn't carrying any incriminating evidence. His tattoos would reveal he was a member of the Zetas, but that didn't matter. They would be clear of the area before his body was found, if the predators didn't find him first. Satisfied the man's pockets were empty, Carlos adjusted his footing, then made his way back up the cliff. As he neared the top, Bart extended his hand to help him the last few feet.

"That's three men we've lost," Bart said. "We should make it to Terlingua tomorrow. We'll wait until dark before we switch to the vehicles. Caution the men again. I don't want to lose anyone else." Bart shot a glance to both Carlos and Franco. "We'll leave at sunset. Remind your men, no fires."

Franco and Carlos both nodded, then stepped away.

Bart walked back to his position and sat. He withdrew his map and compared it to the terrain. Then he scanned the area with his binoculars for any signs of life. Nothing but tarantulas moved, but his close proximity to the border meant he had to stay alert. As far as he was concerned, he was in enemy territory. Although the US was playing a crazy game of security with the borders, he didn't want to take any chances. He had managed to stay ahead of Kenworth since Panama, and reaching the vehicles in Terlingua was a critical transition point. He would be stationary and out in the open. He planned to minimize his exposure and get on the road as fast as possible. The place he had selected for the transfer was away from the inhabitants, in a canyon two kilometers south of the town.

Carlos stepped to Bart and sat beside him. "My scouts will leave in a few minutes."

"Good," replied Bart. "Tell them to be extra vigilant tonight. About two kilometers south of Terlingua, there is a ridgeline." He pointed to the position on the map for Carlos to see. "Have your scouts occupy a position there and be vigilant. Wait there for us, and do not go into the town. If they see anything suspicious, get back to us, but don't use phones. What about the rear security?"

"They're leaving as well. Should we add a couple more men?"

"No, those two will be enough. Just tell them to stay alert. I don't want anyone coming up behind us."

Carlos nodded. "I understand." He stood and walked away.

When darkness fell, Bart signaled to Franco, then Carlos. In silence, the men mounted their horses. Bart looked around to see that everyone was ready. Satisfied, he motioned to Carlos to head out. The only sound was the soft crunch of the horses' hooves.

—— • ◆ • ——

Friday, January 20, 2017
Texas Highway 118
Terlingua, Texas

A mighty MC-130J Commando II appeared out of the darkness like a giant owl focused on its prey. It moved with grace and precision as it made its penetration descent to deliver the platoon of Rangers, equipment, and civilian SUVs. At 0247 hours, the first aircraft of the two-ship sortie touched down on Texas Highway 118, forty-eight kilometers from Terlingua. The moon and stars normally provided the only light on the rural road. However, on this night, the sky was overcast, making the entire area blacked out—no stars, no moon, just blackness. As a safety precaution, the Highway Patrol had established roadblocks on either end of the stretch of road where the planes landed. The dark and desolate stretch of highway was not a heavily traveled road, and at that time of the early morning no one was on it.

The rear ramp lowered as the aircraft rolled to a stop, and the cool night air greeted the soldiers as they began to disembark with their gear. The four Rolls-Royce turboprop engines continued to idle as the bird waited to get into the air again. The plane's interior lighting provided illumination for the crew and soldiers. The ominous glow highlighted the soldiers' silhouettes as they emerged from the plane.

The rear ramp was raised as soon as the last man stepped off. When the plane took off, the second MC-130J appeared and made its tactical arrival. It rolled to a stop near the soldiers, and the crew chief lowered the ramp for the vehicles. Everyone worked in synchronization, off-loading the vehicles in an orchestrated manner. Once the last vehicle rolled off, the ramp was raised and the turboprop engines raced. The aircraft roared down the highway and took to the air, disappearing into the darkness just as it had arrived.

The convoy of Rangers, following the Hercules, headed south to the staging area near Terlingua.

———— ✦ ✦ ✦ ————

Friday, January 20, 2017
Headquarters, US Special Operations Command
MacDill Air Force Base, Florida

Max and Danya met the others at the headquarters first thing in the morning. Danya made coffee as they waited on Chugs's authorization to proceed to West Texas. The phones rang with anxious political officials wanting to know if the terrorist had been apprehended. Each caller was told the terrorist did not attempt to cross in Laredo and had not been captured there.

Gail was just about to sip her coffee when her phone rang. When she saw Dawn Blakey's number on the caller ID, she slammed her cup down hard, and the coffee sloshed onto the desk. She strained to keep her voice civil but stern. "Hello Dawn."

"Hi Gail." Her chipper voice elevated Gail's annoyance. "Well, Madison didn't try to cross the border yesterday."

"No, shit. I believe I told you it was all a deception. What do you want now?"

"Are you coming back down here?" Dawn asked.

"Why?"

"Well, you know I have a helicopter, and I have an idea."

Not wanting to talk to her any longer but her curiosity piqued just enough, Gail said, "Oh? What is it?"

"I thought I would search along the border and see if I can find him. I know the Border Patrol could use the help. I can meet you here."

"Dawn…" Gail said, then took a deep breath. "I think the Border Patrol can handle it. I suggest you send the helicopter home, and get yourself to a safe place too."

"Oh, Gail. This will be so exciting. The secretary thought it was a good idea."

"I'm sure he did. What are you going to do if you see Madison?"

"Uhm… Call the Operations Center to have him picked up."

Gail closed her eyes and dropped her head. "Don't plan on me being there, I'm tied up here. If you go, I suggest you search the area from Laredo to Amistad Reservoir. Remember, the intel report said the Zetas were planning a big shipment there, and you wanted the guard to patrol the reservoir."

"Oh, that's right! Good idea. Thank you, Gail."

"Sure. Have a good trip." Gail tried to suppress her sarcasm. She hung up the phone and sipped her coffee. It was cold, but that didn't faze her. She stood and walked toward Max when she saw him step to the coffee pot. "I just had a call from Blakey."

"Now what?" he asked.

"She wanted to know if I was going back down there. She has a helicopter and wants me to go with her to search for Madison along the border. She thought it would be exciting."

"Damn! She's going to alert him."

"I told the nitwit to search the area from Laredo down to Amistad Reservoir. Maybe that will keep her out of our hair."

A smile appeared on Max's face as he nodded. "Hope so."

General Matherson entered the room and was greeted by Max as the others looked on with concern. "Max, you and your team are cleared to proceed. The Texas Military Department is on board and will help. They are offering up guardsmen, if you need them."

"Thank you, sir. Yes, I would like to use them. I'd like to have some soldiers come in behind Madison and a few to meet us in the vicinity of the town for reinforcements. Also, I'd like the guardsmen and state troopers to establish roadblocks on the roads leading out of Terlingua, just in case Madison is able to evade us. There's not that many improved roads heading north. He'll try to get to Interstate 10. I just hope we're not too late and already missed him. He'll put up a fight."

Chugs nodded. "I know. I'll request the support from Texas and forward you the contact information. Good luck, Max."

Max smiled and nodded as the general left the room, then he looked to Andy. "Get in touch with Captain Rowe. I want him up to speed right away. While you're doing that, I need to study the map." He turned to Danya and said, "What's the latest on Nassar?"

"He did fly to San Antonio. There were no reservations for rental cars in his name, and no one matching his description rented a car."

"Max," David said as he stepped from his desk, "Nassar probably went to the FBO and boarded a private jet as soon as he got to San Antonio. I'm trying to find out where he went."

"Thanks, David," Max replied. "As soon as you find out, let me know."

"He's flying to somewhere in the vicinity of Terlingua and will pick up vehicles there," Gail said. "I'll start searching for airfields in the nearby towns that can handle a private jet and that have rental vehicles. If we can find out where and be there in time, do you want me to pick him up?"

"No, don't pick him up. Follow him." Max looked back to Andy and said, "Have you received the latest updates on the surveillance flights or satellite coverage?"

"I just got 'em," he replied. He handed Max the image and pointed to the horses. "Here are the riders on horses Captain Rowe told us about."

"It could be Madison or the Zetas. Damn, we need a positive ID. When you talk to Captain Rowe, find out if he can get pictures of the men. But I don't want him to get close to them until we get there."

# CHAPTER 26

Saturday, January 21, 2017
Gareth Residence
New York, New York

S TEW GARETH'S BODY had arrived on Thursday. Abbigale Martin, the public relations contractor for the Gareth Foundation, had assumed additional Foundation duties and become the campaign chairman of Jenny's new election effort. She had brought Jeremy and Ashley with her to help chaperone Jenny and take care of the funeral arrangements for Stew.

In the two weeks since Stew's death, Abbigale had closed out the operation in San Miguel, El Salvador, planned fundraisers, conducted several publicity campaigns, and organized events for Jenny to attend. Ashley worked to get the body returned and coordinated the service and viewing at the funeral home. At Jenny's insistence, she had arranged a big media event for the viewing and upcoming funeral. It was a production that rivaled a state event. The police had held up the return of Stew's body because of their ongoing investigation into his death. Lieutenant Colonel Gregg Matthews was able to cut through the bureaucracy and expedite the return of the body, which would have taken much longer otherwise. Jeremy looked after Jenny and tried, in vain, to restrict her booze consumption. Bottles of Scotch seemed to magically appear. It was a full-time job for him to keep space between Jenny and the liquor.

Abbigale rented office space. She avoided going to the Gareths' residence as it was too time-consuming and frustrating dealing with Jenny. The first few times she went to the residence after their return from San Miguel, Jenny was almost more than she could tolerate. However, the money was a great inducement for her to stay on the campaign.

Jeremy had the hardest task of all, babysitting Jenny. He tried to keep her from the bottle. His reprieves came when she passed out for long periods of time. He called Abbigale several times a day reporting on Jenny. Knowing what Jeremy was going through, Abbigale increased his salary to keep him on.

As part of Jenny's strategy for the campaign, she had determined that scheduling a viewing of Stew's body at the funeral home would be good publicity. Abbigale coordinated with the news media to cover the arrival of the great man's grieving widow. Ashley was dispatched to assist Jeremy in getting Jenny ready for her appearance. Jenny was to arrive at three o'clock, greeted by the media's cameras. It was to be her second *Jackie Kennedy* performance.

Ashley arrived at the residence at ten o'clock to find Jeremy frustrated and sitting beside the pool. It was a partly cloudy, cool day. The high would be a chilly forty-five degrees.

Ashley approach Jeremy and said, "What the hell are you doing out here? We've got to get Jenny ready for this afternoon."

He stood. "I'm glad you're here. She's passed out in a chair in the office. I couldn't wake her."

When he led Ashley into the office and flicked on the light, a foul odor greeted them. A Scotch bottle and a tumbler lay on the floor. Jenny appeared to have slept in the chair and hadn't bathed in a couple of days.

"You were supposed to get her to shower and eat yesterday," Ashley said, her voice conveying her frustration. "Abby is going to have a fit."

"I tried. She wouldn't eat anything I fixed and kept demanding to have a Scotch."

"She's had more than a drink of Scotch. She's had the whole damn bottle. We've got to get her sober and cleaned up in time to get to the funeral home. Go make some coffee and something for her to eat. We're going to need a lot of coffee. I'll try to get her into the kitchen."

Jeremy went to the kitchen to work on breakfast and coffee while Ashley stood next to the chair. She paused for a moment to consider her options, then stooped and touched the dingy muumuu, giving Jenny a gentle shake. "Jenny, wake up. Wake up, Jenny. Wake up, Jenny. You need to take a shower."

Jenny waved a limp hand. "Go away."

"Jenny, wake up. Jeremy has some breakfast for you."

She mumbled and slurred her words. "Fuck off. I don't want any."

"Jenny, wake up. We need to get ready for the press."

She rolled her head sideways, and her heavy eyelids began to raise.

"Come on, Jenny. Get up. Time to eat."

With Ashley's help, she struggled and managed to stand. Ashley placed Jenny's arm around her neck, and her body odor was almost too much. As soon as she was sure Jenny wasn't going to fall, she led her into the kitchen. Within a few minutes of her sitting, Jeremy set a large mug of coffee on the table in front of her. With the back of her hand, Jenny slid the cup away. She folded her arms on the table and rested her head on them. In no time she was snoring.

Moments later Jeremy set a plate of two fried eggs, toast, and bacon on the table. He shook her shoulder. "Jenny, wake up. Here's your breakfast." As soon as she raised her head, he slid the plate in front of her.

Holding her head between her hands, Jenny stared at the plate. "What the hell is this?"

With a stern voice, Ashley said, "It's breakfast. Abby said you need to eat, then take a shower."

"Is she my mother now? Fix me a damn Scotch."

"We're going to the funeral home to be with Stew. The press will be there."

"Oh."

Jenny grasped her fork and began feeding herself like a three-year-old. When she worked the fork to load it for the third bite, she dropped the contents on her muumuu. Looking down, she located the egg that plopped on her breast. With an unsteady hand using the fork, she scraped the mess from her garment, then guided the utensil into her mouth. Setting the fork down, she reached for the toast, and it broke, falling onto her lap. She guided an unsure hand to the toast, then shoved it into her mouth.

As soon as Jenny finished breakfast, Ashley and Jeremy helped her get up the stairs. Jeremy returned downstairs as Ashley guided Jenny to the shower. When she finished and was dressed, Ashley helped her to a chair and worked on her hair.

Ashley escorted Jenny back downstairs to the office as she began to sober up. An hour before they were to depart. Jenny started her demands. "Jeremy, get me a drink."

He looked to her and then to Ashley, who nodded.

Jeremy took a deep breath; he knew what would follow. "Abby said no drinks. You're meeting the press and need to be sober."

"I know what I need, a fucking drink! God damn it, a drink."

"Not until after we go to the funeral home." He went to the kitchen and poured her another mug of coffee. Returning to the office, he set the mug beside her.

A scowl covered Jenny's face. Then she sat in silence, plotting her next move. She would get that next drink.

Ashley was able to get Jenny presentable, dressed in a black dress with matching large hat and a veil. So far, Ashley had managed to keep her away from the bottle while pouring coffee down her throat. Thirty minutes before they were to depart, the limousine arrived, and Jeremy admitted the driver into the house.

"I need to go to the bathroom," Jenny said. Ashley escorted her, and as soon as the door latched, Ashley went to the other bathroom. When she returned, Jeremy and the driver were sitting in the living room. Jenny was still in the bathroom. Ashley tapped on the door but received no response. She opened the door and saw Jenny gulping something from a shampoo bottle.

"No!" Ashley shouted. "You've got to be sober." She wrestled the bottle from Jenny's hand. "We need to go." She sniffed the contents. *Scotch,* she thought.

"Jeremy," Ashley said, her voice stern. "Come help me. She's put some Scotch in a shampoo bottle."

As Jeremy appeared at the bathroom door, he was met with Ashley's scathing look. "You were to search everywhere for booze."

"I did, but I didn't think to look in the damn shampoo bottle," he replied in astonishment.

It took both of them to walk Jenny to the car. Ashley called Abbigale to alert her of Jenny's condition. Abbigale was not a happy camper.

When the limousine arrived, cameras flashed, and the lights focused on the grieving widow. Jeremy was on one side of Jenny and Ashley was on the other, propping the large woman up. Abbigale, adding to the charade, gave Jenny a hanky and leaned close to her. "Clutch this close to your face as though you are crying," she told her. "You smell like a Scotch bottle. Do not talk to anyone."

The flashing lights jolted Jenny's instincts. She stood more upright but depended on her escorts to keep her steady. A question was shouted out to her. She lifted her veil and sniffed, using her hanky. Nothing but dignity was in her face. After all, she intended to be the next president. Everyone needed to see what a strong, determined widow she was. Jenny lowered her veil without speaking. *I'll give them a performance that'll rival that of Jackie's,* she thought.

She sat in the first row in silence, flanked by her two escorts. She raised her veil as a prayer was given and occasionally sniffed for effect. No one realized Jenny's real condition. They all assumed she was a grieving widow. Abbigale was always there, shielding the drunk from the press.

At the conclusion of the viewing, Abbigale gave apologies to the press that Jenny was too distraught to say anything, and Jeremy and Ashley assisted Jenny to the waiting car.

After they arrived back at the residence, Jenny had pulled herself together. Abbigale ensured that Jenny was settled, and, of course, that no more bottles of booze were in the house. "I'm fine, Abby," Jenny said. "I'm going to be the next president. No more booze. Sober from now on."

Abbigale smiled, "Good. We're on the campaign." *She sounds sincere enough*, she thought.

— ♦ ♦ ♦ —

Sunday, January 22, 2017
Gareth Residence
New York, New York

Jeremy arrived at the residence a little after nine o'clock in the morning. The house was dark as he entered, and no one answered when he announced his arrival. The staff was off for the weekend. He sighed, relieved that Jenny was not up yet. He just wanted a cup of coffee and to sit for a few minutes. A half hour passed, and he still hadn't heard Jenny upstairs. He stood and walked into the office. *Maybe I didn't see her when I came in,* he thought. *I hope she didn't sleep in the chair again.* Not seeing her in the office, he turned and looked through the rest of the downstairs. *Not down here.* He walked back to the kitchen and stopped when his eyes caught something outside. He stepped closer to the window and peered out. A chill ran through his body, and his hand shook as he reached for the doorknob. It was unlocked. He jerked open the door and bolted to the pool. A large woman in a black dress was floating face down in the water. "Oh my God," he said. "Jenny!" He retrieved the safety hook, stood on the edge of the pool, and slid the body close to the side. *It's her.* He withdrew his cell phone and punched in the number for Abbigale.

"Abby, its Jeremy," he said, his voice trembling. "She's in the pool."

"What do you mean, she's in the pool? Is she already drunk?"

"Abby, she's dead. She drowned."

"She's dead?" The following pause was deafening. "Call the police and report it. I'm on my way over."

By the time Abbigale arrived, the ambulance and police were there. Captain M. Taner Mackenzie, NYPD, arrived just after Abbigale. Abbigale went straight to Jeremy, who was sitting at the kitchen table, and he told her what he knew.

One of the policemen briefed Captain Mackenzie on the situation. "It looks like she was drunk and fell in the pool sometime last night." He held up a Scotch bottle in an evidence bag. "It was in the laundry room. I thought it was odd to have a bow around the bottle."

"Was there a card or anything attached to it?" Mackenzie asked.

"No, sir. That's it. That's why I bagged it. I didn't see any wounds or bruising on the body. She smells of alcohol. No witnesses. The young man at the table found her this morning about 9:30. He said the security alarm was off and the house was dark when he arrived. That's about it."

Mackenzie stepped into the kitchen. He introduced himself and began interviewing Jeremy. Shaken by the event, Abbigale consoled Jeremy as he told the captain everything he did upon arriving at the house.

"I need you to make a written statement," Mackenzie said. He nodded to the policeman standing in the door, indicating for him to take the statement. Mackenzie stepped outside and walked to where the para-medics had laid the body beside the pool. He knelt beside the corpse and methodically inspected it. When he was finished, he stood and returned to the kitchen.

Looking at Abbigale and Jeremy, Mackenzie said, "I want to get your fingerprints to eliminate you. Please, show me her room."

Abbigale looked up at the captain. "Why are you taking fingerprints? I thought it was just an accident."

"A few things don't seem right."

"You mean she was killed?" she replied with a horrified look.

"I didn't say that. I want to check a few things. The autopsy will pro-vide more information. For now, I am listing her death as suspicious."

Abbigale nodded and stood. Mackenzie's words sent a chill through her. She led him upstairs to Jenny's room.

# CHAPTER 27

Saturday, January 21, 2017
Vicinity Texas Highway FM 170 and Terlingua Creek
Terlingua, Texas

T HE RANGERS, FROM the 75th Ranger Regiment, had arrived
before sunup and occupied a staging area in the vicinity of Terlingua
Creek, five-and-a-half kilometers east of town. To the casual observer,
they looked like hikers and tourists—complete with SUVs and civilian
attire. Their weapons were kept concealed but were readily accessible, if
needed. Starting at 0900 hours, and continuing every two hours, two to
four of the soldiers went into town, acting as tourists while they surveyed
the area and collected intelligence. They visited the few shops, places to
eat, and ruins. It was not the best day for tourists, with the temperature
going from fifty-two degrees to sixty-two degrees, with rain at noon and
wind gusts from twenty to thirty miles per hour. But the soldiers were
not there as tourists.

Anticipating that Nassar was already in the area or would be soon,
they needed to identify him and the vehicles he would have. Once he
was identified, they would keep eyes on him and watch for anyone who
might contact him. It was imperative they control the situation and plan
where and when to attack Madison.

Max and his team arrived as it started to rain. He coordinated with
Lieutenant Barron, the platoon leader, and the five of them were briefed
on the current situation. As soon as the lieutenant finished, he and Max
reconned the area, followed by Danya, Gail, and David, going in a different direction. Andy left to meet with Captain Rowe. One of Max's
top priorities was avoiding civilian contact and collateral damage. The
rain proved to be a benefit. It camouflaged their identities and kept the

tourists off the streets. The mud splashed onto their SUVs, providing additional coverage. But it was slippery and made their exit difficult.

Within five minutes Max had circled the small town as the lieutenant navigated. They made a brief stop at the old cemetery. Orienting his map so Max could see it and observe the area to the south, the lieutenant said, "There aren't many buildings but quite a few ruins. Lots of cover."

"Terlingua is an old mining town," Max said as he looked to the lieutenant.

"Mining town?" Barron replied. "What did they mine?"

"Cinnabar," Max said. "That's where mercury comes from. It was discovered here in the mid-1880s. Miners came to the area, which created the town of about 2,000 people. When the demand for mercury dropped, the miners walked off. What you see are the remnants of their stone and stucco houses, shops, and various buildings."

"They just walked off and Mother Nature did the rest," Barron replied. "Sad."

"We'll take Madison in the flat area," Max said. "I believe he'll switch to vehicles south of FM 170." He tapped the location on the map with his finger.

"Nassar will probably have several vehicles," he continued. "We need to identify him and the vehicles as soon as he gets here. Madison'll transfer to the vehicles after dark in an isolated place."

"I've studied the map and there are many gulleys and ravines in the area," Barron replied.

"This is the reported route we believe Madison has taken so far. My guess is they'll continue following this draw coming from the southeast." Max traced the map. "Lieutenant Colonel Johnston is meeting with Captain Rowe as we speak. He'll give us an update on the route and their current location."

"I recommend an OP with two men on the hill in the front of the staging area," Barron said, tapping the hill on the map. "A two-man OP south of FM 170 on the ridge east of the low area, and two men on the ridgeline south of FM 170 on the west side of the low area. That's high ground, and they have an interlocking line of sight into the lower terrain leading to the draw." He touched the map on the two positions.

"I agree," Max replied. "The OPs can alert us if they spot any SUVs entering the area from either side of the town. I want you to put a squad of men on this ridge west of the town on FM 170, and a second squad ready to block FM 170 in front of the staging area." Max tapped each position with his finger. "Deploy a squad in this ravine south of the highway, about in the center of the low area." He traced the ravine. "Captain Rowe and his men are going to circle behind Madison and block his escape to the rear. He'll stay protected in the low areas on each flank until I give him the word to block a retreat. Caution your men, as I don't want Rowe's men shot by mistake. This could be a very dangerous situation."

"I know. We've done this a couple of times," the lieutenant replied.

"Continue rotating your people into the town and have them watch for SUVs. As they return, put them in uniform." Max headed his vehicle back to the staging area.

— ✦ ✦ ✦ —

Lieutenant Colonel Johnston met Captain Rowe on Rainbow Mine Road, eight kilometers west of the staging area. In accordance with Johnston's instructions, Captain Rowe, in civilian clothes, arrived at the location first and waited in his 4 x 4.

Within minutes, Johnston arrived. As soon as his vehicle stopped, he got out, stepped to the other vehicle, and identified Captain Rowe. "I've got us a pizza and a couple of beers in my vehicle," Johnston said. He turned and stepped back to his 4 x 4.

Captain Rowe followed Johnston and got in the passenger side. He gave him a quick brief on his situation. Because of the rain, few tourists were out, and no one found their way along the dirt road. Johnston picked up the pizza carton, opened it, and offered it to Rowe. Next, he handed him a beer. "My treat."

"This beats the hell out of MREs," Captain Rowe said as he took a bite of pizza.

Andy picked up a slice of pizza and took a bite as he scanned the terrain in front of them. He then withdrew a map from inside his shirt. "We're in a staging area in the vicinity of Terlingua Creek off FM 170, east of town." He placed his finger on the location.

"After I talked to you, I sent two men to get some pictures," Rowe said as he sipped his beer. "They were able to circle the column of riders. I'm certain they weren't seen." He placed his laptop on his lap and booted it up. He bit off a piece of pizza as he waited on the machine. As soon as the laptop came to life, he turned it so Andy could see the photos. "Here're the pictures they got. They're not the best."

Johnston clicked through them, pausing on several of the images. "That looks like our target, Madison. Where's he now?"

"They're set up eleven kilometers southeast of Terlingua, in a protected area on the west side of Rattlesnake Mountain in a small canyon." Rowe made a small circle on the map of the location. "If he stays on the same route, he'll follow this ravine northwest into town." Rowe traced the map between the two ridges.

"The Rangers will head him off to the north in the low area just south of FM 170, here," Johnston said, placing his finger on the map. "Your men are to occupy these two ridges to the south."

Johnston circled the ridges. "This is dangerous, and we don't want you to get shot by friendly fire. Stay down, and we'll tell you when to get up. As soon as your men get into position, send their grid locations to Lieutenant Barron, the Ranger lieutenant. He'll give you his locations." He retrieved a paper from his pocket and handed it to Captain Rowe. "Here's his frequency and call sign. The tricky part will be which side of this ridge Madison will choose to take. Don't let him see your men."

Rowe took the paper, looked at it, then placed it in his pocket. He leaned forward and took a closer look at the map. "I know that area. My guess is he'll choose the west side of the ridge." Rowe tapped the ravine on the west of the ridge. "He has more cover, and it is easier to negotiate."

"Good point," Johnston replied as he examined the map. "He could stop in this small canyon, where the dry riverbed makes an S curve. That's about a kilometer from FM 170. That dirt trail passes right by that curve. It's low, and it would block the view of his vehicles from FM 170." He tapped the canyon.

"We won't be able to see them from the position you want us to occupy," Rowe said.

"Rangers will be on this large ridge to the west," Andy said, tracing the ridgeline. "They'll also be on the ridge to the east." He circled the areas.

The two discussed the plan for several minutes and finished off the pizza. "Get your men into position as soon as you can," Andy said. "Any questions?" He lifted his beer to take a drink.

"No, doesn't seem too difficult. I'll contact you when we are in position." He picked up his slice of pizza, took the last bite, and washed it down with the last of his beer.

"Good. Stay in contact and keep your heads down," Johnston replied as he finished his pizza.

The rain had stopped. Rowe glanced to the sky and said, "This muck will dry out quick if the wind keeps blowing. Thanks for the pizza and beer. Talk to you soon."

"No problem. Be careful. Remember, these guys are smart and tough. Expect anything."

"Will do. See you soon."

———— • ✦ • ————

Saturday, January 21, 2017
Staging Area
Terlingua, Texas

David was set up in one of the large civilian camping tents that had become the command post. He sat on a folding camp stool at a small portable table and was working on his second hot chocolate. Internet and communications were established back to SOCOM, Captain Rowe, and Lieutenant Barron. He sipped his hot chocolate as Gail entered the tent.

"I'm freezing," he said. "I thought Texas was supposed to be hot."

"It's winter, Sweet Pea," Gail said. "Get up and move around. Did you get the latest imagery of the area yet?"

He opened a file and retrieved the image. "Here you go, dahling."

"Are there any new intel updates? How are you doing on the car rental agencies?"

"Nothing new since the one I gave you this morning," he replied. "I'm waiting on a callback from a rental company in Alpine."

Max, followed by Andy, entered the tent, and Gail handed him the latest image of the area. Taking the image, he shared it with Andy. "Not the best image, but that verifies what Captain Rowe reported," Andy said.

"Now, everyone needs to be in position, without being seen," Max said. Then his eyes went to David. "Lieutenant Barron and Captain Rowe are to notify us as soon as their men are in position. Let me know immediately when they do."

"Yes, sir," he replied as his SAT phone rang. He immediately answered the call.

Lieutenant Barron entered and stepped to Max. "The OPs and squads on either end of the town on FM 170 are in position. The soldiers are en route to the OPs on the east and west ridgelines. The squad in the center of the low area is also en route. They're making their way along the dry riverbed."

"Thank you, Lieutenant. Keep me posted," Max replied.

"Max," David said as he set his phone on the table, "that was the car rental company in Alpine. They've only rented one SUV and one car this morning."

"One SUV and one car?" Max asked. "That's odd. He'll need more than that for the twenty men he has, the nuke, and any equipment. Keep checking around. Others could be rented from somewhere else."

Max looked to Danya. "Give David a hand in checking with the car rental companies."

"Andy, check with NSA and see if they've captured any traffic on the numbers we have for Madison and Nassar."

"Yes, sir," Andy said. "Those vehicles may not be the ones we're looking for."

———— • ♦ • ————

Saturday, January 21, 2017
West of Rattlesnake Mountain
Terlingua, Texas

Bart stepped to where Franco was sleeping. He started to nudge him, and Franco said before he could touch him, "I'm awake. What is it?"

"You've done an excellent job helping me get into the US," Madison said. "But I need to cut down our signature. You and your men can return to Panama. With ten fewer men, that's a big step forward. The Zetas will take it from here. We'll rendezvous with Nassar tonight, and I'll cut five of the Zetas after they verify it's clear."

"That will only be you, Nassar, and two Zetas," Franco said. "Are you sure you don't need us to stay and help you?"

"No, we'll be fine. I want to transition to the vehicles and be out of the area as quick as possible. We'll travel faster after we have the vehicles. I'll contact you after I finish this. Keep it quiet as you leave so you don't wake the others. You know what to do."

"I understand. Is there time for a drink before we go?"

"Sure. The bottle is in my pack." Madison led him to where his pack sat by the rest of his gear.

Franco stood and donned his coat, then picked up his cup. He followed Bart.

"We've been together a long time," Bart said as he retrieved the whiskey from his pack.

Franco handed him his cup.

Bart poured two fingers of whiskey into it, then handed it to Franco. He picked up his cup and poured the whiskey into it. He set the bottle down, then held up his cup. "To old times, my friend."

Franco followed his lead and held up his cup. "And many new ones." He sipped it as Bart did.

"Looks like the rain is over," Bart said as he glanced to the sky. "We could do without the wind, though. Go as soon as you can, while you still have a couple hours of daylight left. You'll make good time. I doubt there'll be many people out, but keep alert."

"I'll be glad to get back to warmer climate," Franco said as he tugged on his coat. He then finished his whiskey.

"Good luck," Bart said as he extended his hand.

"You too," Franco said as he took Bart's hand, released it, then turned and stepped back to his gear. He set his cup down, then stepped to each of his men and gave them their instructions. Like soldiers everywhere, the words "we are going home" provided incentive for them to hurry.

Bart picked up his map, studied it for a moment, then looked over the terrain to the northwest. Carlos stepped next to Bart and asked, "Franco and his men are leaving?"

Bart picked up the bottle of Crown Royal Reserve and motioned with the bottle in his hand. "How about a drink?"

"Sí. I will get a cup." He stepped to his gear, picked up his cup, then returned to Bart. He stopped next to him, handing him his cup.

Bart poured two fingers into it, then handed it back. He picked up his cup and took a sip. Carlos did the same.

"Yes, Franco and his men are leaving," Bart said. "His agreement with me was to the US. I needed to reduce our signature, and now was as good a time as any for him to leave. When it's clear, I'll send all but you and one other home."

"You are not worried about the authorities?"

"I am." Bart sipped his whiskey. "That's why I am reducing our signature. The fewer of us there are, the better our chances of not being detected."

Carlos nodded, then sipped his drink.

"Nassar will meet us tonight," Bart said. "As soon as your scouts tell us it is clear, I want us to make the switch to the vehicles as fast as possible. Also, no lights tonight."

"The men know. You seem uneasy about something. What is bothering you?"

"Kenworth." Bart took another sip. "He was on our tail all the way from Panama. We haven't detected him in a while."

"Perhaps we lost him?"

"I don't think so," Bart replied. "He's out there, somewhere."

"Should we change plans and go to another location?" Carlos took another sip and held his gaze on him.

"I'll think about it. We'll leave after sundown."

"We will be ready." Carlos nodded, finished off his whiskey, and stepped away.

# CHAPTER 28

Saturday, January 21, 2017
Command Post
Terlingua, Texas

Danya and David had contacted all the car rental places within a 100-mile radius of Terlingua without success—none of the agencies had rented SUVs, other than the one they knew about in the last twenty-four hours. Andy received a callback from NSA. Unfortunately, they had not captured any traffic on the telephone numbers they had for Madison or Nassar. Andy and Max considered the possibility they had either changed phones or had begun communicating with alternative methods. Either was a possibility to be considered.

Gail, followed by Danya, approached Max and said, "We're ready to leave. I've coordinated with the Border Patrol, and they are expecting us. Here's where we'll be." She stepped to the map and pointed to a red tick mark on Highway 118, approximately twenty miles north of their position.

"The Border Patrol checkpoint has good visibility," Danya said. "We believe this is the most likely route Nassar will take."

"I hope you're right," Max replied. "Don't forget to check with the Rangers as you go out. Be careful and keep in touch. Remember, if you spot Nassar, do not apprehend him. Follow him and report in to David."

"Don't worry, Max," she replied. "We've done this many times before." She gave him a light embrace and kissed him.

Gail's phone rang, grabbing her attention.

"This's Gail."

"Hi, Gail!" came the chipper voice of Dawn Blakey.

"Hello, Dawn. Whatta you need?"

"I searched the area along the border from Laredo to Amistad Reservoir but didn't see anything."

"That's a shame. You're back in DC then. Right?"

"No, I'm still in Laredo. Where're you?"

"I'm traveling."

"What have you found out? *The secretary* suggested I link up with you."

"That won't happen. I'm on a case now." Gail was not opposed to lying to the nitwit, but anything to keep her away. Having her around would be a nightmare, and this was not the time for one.

"When will you return to the Texas border?"

Gail knew Dawn was fishing, and if she had the slightest hint of where Gail was, she would turn up.

"That's a good question. I've gotta go now."

"OK," Dawn said. "Please let me know when you find out anything. I need to let *the secretary* know."

"Sure thing, Dawn." Gail ended the call. *Fucking idiot!*

———— • ✦ • ————

Max paced inside the tent. He always hated the calm before the storm. He had checked with Captain Rowe and Lieutenant Barron to ensure all their men were in position and ready. The lieutenant reported that the two squads positioned to secure the road on either side of the town were concealed behind the ridgeline, and the squad south of FM 170 in the center of the low area was concealed in the dry riverbed. Communications with each position were checked.

Max looked at the map again. Andy had plotted Captain Rowe's positions. Lieutenant Barron verified that his soldiers had good commo with Captain Rowe, and he had their positions plotted. David acknowledged he had communications with Barron, Rowe, Gail, and the Highway Patrol assisting with the roadblocks, with their vehicles concealed nearby.

No one spoke as the tension rose. Max had chased Madison from Panama, trying to anticipate his next move. He had finally been able to set his trap, boxing Madison in where he couldn't escape. But in any operation, no matter how large or small, there is always a place for errors and accidents. The soldiers referred to that as Murphy's Law—*What can go wrong, will go wrong*. Max had planned for contingencies and was determined not to let Madison escape, but Madison was a formidable opponent—smart, cunning, and resourceful. He had managed to slip away several times in the past, and Max was not going to let it happen again.

Max motioned for Andy to join him at the map. "I'm going to Captain Rowe's position. You take charge here. Contact Rowe and let him know I'm coming. He knows the area. Find out the best route for me to get there so I won't be seen."

"Yes, sir. You're worried about friendly fire, aren't you?"

"I am, and I don't want Madison to escape. Madison might provide valuable intel. If possible, take him alive."

Max picked up a red pencil and connected locations of the OPs on the map—Lieutenant Barrion's position and Captain Rowe's—forming a rectangle. "I want Madison well into the kill box before we engage. He's not going to escape this time."

Fratricide or casualties from friendly fire are always a concern, and in this dangerous situation Max was doing everything possible to prevent them. But again, Murphy will be present. That was a big concern for Max. Preparations were complete, and all they could do now was wait. He anticipated Madison would make his move sometime after dark. Now as the sun began to set, the seconds on the clock seemed to tick off much more slowly.

———— ◆ ◆ ◆ ————

Saturday, January 21, 2017
West of Rattlesnake Mountain
Terlingua, Texas

Bart had prepared his equipment for the night's ride, then sat and waited. He studied the map again and scanned the terrain. He turned to see Carlos approaching and reached down and picked up his bottle of whiskey. When Carlos stopped in front of him, Bart said, "Let's have another drink."

"*Sí*. I will get my cup."

Bart watched him step away, then saw the others starting to get up. *So far, so good,* he thought. *I don't like being out in the open. Nassar has never let me down. Where the hell is Kenworth?*

Carlos sat down beside Bart and handed him his cup. "Is something the matter? You looked concerned."

"No, I was just thinking," he replied as he took the cup and splashed the whiskey into it. "Send your rider to check with the lookouts. If it's clear, tell him to return and bring one of the lookouts back with him. If there is trouble, call—but do not return. We'll wait here."

Carlos held his gaze on Bart, then took his cup and sipped. "I will send him on his way." He sat his cup down, stood, and walked away.

Bart watched him as he stepped to one of his men and gave him the instructions. While Carlos's back was to him, Bart looked in his own rucksack, checked his Sig Sauer pistol, and attached the suppressor. Closing the ruck, he then looked back to where Carlos stood, watched his man mount a horse, and start on his journey.

Carlos returned to Bart and sat beside him. "Now we wait."

———◆◆◆———

Saturday, January 21, 2017
Command Post
Terlingua, Texas

Max had relocated to Captain Rowe's position near the southern end of the kill box and notified David of his successful arrival. No one spoke inside the tent as they waited for reports from Lieutenant Barron and Captain Rowe. The only sound came from the wind rattling the fabric of the tent. David fidgeted and shifted in his seat. The radio crackled, bursting to life with Captain Rowe's voice. "Tango 96, this is Juliette 54, over."

Startled, David picked up the hand-mic and responded, "Tango 96, over."

"Tango 96, Juliette 54. We have visual of ten men with horses, dismounted, sixteen kilometers from you. They are heading southeast and appear to be setting up a position."

"Geez!" David said. "What the hell is going on?"

Andy stepped closer to David and took the hand-mic. "Juliette 54, this is 96. Say again your last transmission."

"96, this is 54. I say again, we have visual of ten men, with horses, dismounted, sixteen kilometers from your position. They are heading southeast. I am instructed not to apprehend the riders and will report their actions."

"54, this is 96. Roger, out."

David looked to Andy and said, "What's Madison up to? He's cut his force down."

"If the riders are heading southeast, they're going back across the border. They aren't a threat. We'll just keep an eye on 'em."

The radio crackled again, but this time it was Lieutenant Barron's voice, "Tango 96, this is Hotel 46, over."

David replied, "This is Tango 96, over."

"96, this is 46. Identified a two-man observation position. Standby for the grid."

"46, this is 96. Send it."

When he got the grid location, Andy plotted it on the map. "David," he said, "contact Max and let him know that's three kilometers south of the highway and very close to one of Barron's OPs. Does he want them apprehended?"

"Not yet," David relayed the instructions. "Madison is watching to ensure it's safe before he comes forward. Tell the lieutenant to keep eyes on the OP and report their actions. Madison'll contact them for confirmation, then move forward. We can expect his vehicles soon now."

David picked up the mic. "Hotel 46, this is Tango 96. Keep eyes on them and report."

"96, this is 46. Roger, out."

——— •✦• ———

Saturday, January 21, 2017
West of Rattlesnake Mountain
Terlingua, Texas

Only a few clouds lingered in the velvety black sky decorated with dazzling stars. A vivid band of milky-white stars, dust, and gas arched across the sky. The Milky Way is a beautiful sight many have never seen. The wind had calmed to a light breeze, making it a pleasant night. Bart, sitting against a large rock with his head back, looked to Carlos. "Have you ever just sat out and looked at the night sky?"

"I look up occasionally, but to stare at the sky, no. I do not have time for such things."

"You should, Carlos. It is beautiful." Bart pointed to the sky. "There is the Big Dipper, the Little Dipper, and there is Orion's Belt."

A rider entered their camp, followed by another, capturing their attention. "It is clear," he reported. "Our men have seen nothing. All is clear."

Carlos and Bart stood. "Good," Carlos said. He looked to Bart. "I told you I would get you here without being seen." He looked back to the riders. "Rest while the others get mounted."

They nudged their horses and moved away.

"Carlos," Bart said, "yes, you have done well. Thank you. You've done an excellent job leading us here and, like I told Franco, now I must reduce our signature. Send all of your men back to Mexico, except you and the lookout. Tell the remaining lookout to keep vigilant, and if he sees anything, use his phone. That's all I need. It'll take us about two hours to get from here to meet up with Nassar."

Carlos held his gaze on Bart. "There could be trouble ahead and you will need us. Are you sure you want my men to go?"

"Yes. We'll spend only a few minutes transferring to the vehicles and be on our way, as long as it's clear. Otherwise, we'll head to an alternate location. The fewer of us there are, the better our chances of not being detected. I think we can handle any situation from here on."

"Even Kenworth? You have been worried about him."

"We'll be fine. Send your men home. We'll leave in a little while."

Carlos picked up his cup and finished off the last few drops of the whiskey, then stepped away and disappeared into the darkness.

Bart looked at his watch, then returned to sit beside the large rock. He sloshed more whiskey into his cup. *If we leave in about forty-five minutes, we'll arrive about when Nassar should arrive,* he thought, then took a sip.

Within five minutes, Carlos returned. "The men are leaving now."

"OK, have a seat. Hand me your cup. We've got time for one more drink."

Handing his cup to Bart, he watched him slosh the whiskey into it. He sipped it, then nestled into a more comfortable position. Following Bart's lead, he looked up at the night sky. Although his appreciation of the sky was not the same as Bart's, he accepted the opportunity to relax before the final ride. The two sat in silence.

The alarm on Bart's watch vibrated against his wrist, waking him from the sleep that had overcome him. Noting the time, he turned off the alarm. Looking to Carlos, who also had dozed off, he touched his shoulder and said, "Time to go."

Both men stood, walked to their horses, made the last few preparations, then mounted. Bart looked around to Carlos. "You ready?"

"I am. Lead on."

Bart nudged his horse, and they stepped out. He checked his watch. *On time. Be on time, Nassar,* he thought.

— • ◆ • —

Saturday, January 21, 2017
Command Post
Terlingua, Texas

The radio beside David crackled again, breaking the tension. "Tango 96, this is Hotel 46, over."

Andy stared at the radio as David answered. "Hotel 46, this is 96. Go ahead, over."

"This is 46, I have five men on horseback heading southeast, over."

David looked up to Andy. "What the hell? By my count that's most of Madison's men. There can't be five of them left."

Andy took the hand-mic. "46, this is 96. Have your men been spotted?"

"This is 46, negative."

"This is 96, Roger. Keep an eye on 'em. Don't let them come up behind you. Stay down. Madison is about to make his move."

"Juliette 54, this is Tango 96, over," Andy said into the mic.

"Tango 96, this is Juliette 54, over."

"54 this is 96. Be advised Hotel 46 reports five men on horseback heading your way. Keep down and report their actions. Do not engage."

"This is 54, Roger out."

"Madison is reducing his force," Andy said. "That's why we could only find one SUV and car rented. I'll call Gail and Danya and let them know."

The radio fell silent again. The tension rose as they waited for the next radio call. The only sound was the fabric ruffling in the light wind. After about fifteen minutes of gut-wrenching silence, the radio came to life again.

"Tango 96, this is Julliette 54, over."

"This is 96, go ahead, over."

"96, this is 54. We see the five horsemen. We have also seen movement from the position the previous ten men occupied. We originally thought they were settling in for the rest of the night. It appears they are expecting these five men, over."

"54, this is 96, Roger. Have you been seen?"

"96, this is 54, negative, over."

"54, this is 96, Roger, out."

"Are they linking up to go back across the border together?" David asked as he looked to Andy.

"Good question. It is odd," he replied. "We'll get a better picture when Captain Rowe reports what he sees."

"Tango 96, this is Juliette 54, over."

"This is 96, over."

"This is 54, the ten men in position have just engaged the advancing five riders in an ambush. The five have dismounted and taken cover. The fighting is intense."

"This is 96, Roger. Keep eyes on them and report what you see."

"I don't understand what is going on," David said.

Andy replied, "You will soon. I have a pretty good idea."

# CHAPTER 29

Saturday, January 21, 2017
Command Post
Terlingua, Texas

D AVID HAD MADE another cup of hot chocolate and stepped next to Andy, who was studying the map. When his SAT phone rang, interrupting him, Andy shoved his hand to his pocket and retrieved it. "This is Johnston."

"This is Danya. We just picked up an SUV followed by a sedan. We are going to allow them to get a little farther ahead of us, then we will follow."

"Are you sure it's our targets?"

"We are confident they are. There have been no other cars on the road. The Border Patrol said there were two vehicles heading north about ten minutes before we arrived. That's it."

"OK, stay well behind. We don't want to spook them."

"See you soon." Danya ended the call.

Andy looked to David. "Notify Lieutenant Barron and the squads on either end of town that the targets are on their way. Tell Barron his OPs are to keep eyes on the target when they identify them. Stay concealed and let the vehicles pass. We'll notify him when to block the road."

David returned to his desk, set his hot chocolate on the table, and contacted Lieutenant Barron and the two squads. As soon as he ended the transmission, Andy said, "Notify Captain Rowe about the vehicles also. We'll notify him as soon as Barron's OPs identify them. Keep us posted on Madison's position."

David contacted Captain Rowe as instructed and relayed the message. Rowe replied, "I sent two men to check after the firefight ended. Everyone is dead. I say again, there are no survivors."

David replied, "Tango 96, Roger out."

Ten minutes passed, then David's phone rang again, breaking the silence. He answered and recognized Gail's voice. He waved, attracting Andy's attention. "David, we'll be there in about ten minutes," she said. "If that was Nassar we were following, he spotted us. Both the SUV and sedan turned off Highway 118 onto Dark Canyon Road, heading west. It's a dirt road, and we lost them. Watch for any indication Nassar alerted Madison."

"Will do, dahling," David replied. "Anything else?"

"See you in a few minutes." Gail ended the call.

David relayed Gail's message to Andy.

——— ✦✦✦ ———

Saturday, January 21, 2017
Dry Riverbed South of FM 170
Terlingua, Texas

The horses settled into their relaxed stride as they traversed the sandy landscape. Their hooves made a gentle crunch on the dry riverbed. Bart held the reins of the pack horse carrying the nuke. Carlos and his fighter followed. A light breeze found its way through the hills and into the valleys that rushing water had cut into the desert landscape.

Bart scanned the area ahead and the ridges on each side of them as they proceeded. Like a machine, repeating the process every few seconds, he lifted the night vision binoculars to his eyes to scan the terrain, then lowered them.

"Is there a problem?" Carlos asked in a low voice. "Do you see something?"

Bart looked over his shoulder, checked the pack horse, and said, "No, it's more of a feeling. Something isn't right."

"You are just worried," Carlos replied. "The horses are relaxed. If there was a threat such as a mountain lion or bear, they would be more nervous. Perhaps you are worried about the *policía*?"

"Perhaps." Bart checked his watch and noted the time. "Just stay alert."

Time seemed to pass more slowly than the horses moved, and Bart became more uneasy as they neared the rendezvous location. As he scrutinized the topography again, the desert appeared to be sleeping, but he knew it was alive. He just could not identify what was making him anxious.

He withdrew his map to check their location. *About two more kilometers*, he thought. He returned the map to his pocket and nudged his horse. Within a few minutes his phone signaled an incoming call. *Nassar*, he thought as he retrieved it.

Hearing Nassar's voice, Bart replied, "Have you arrived?"

"No, we might have a problem."

"What the fuck's the problem? I'm depending on you."

"I think we have a tail, they are hanging back, but we are being followed. There have been no other cars on this road."

"It's Kenworth. Don't take any chances. Don't go to the rendezvous location. Do as we discussed and I'll contact you when I can. You have about ninety minutes."

"Done, what about you?"

"I have plenty of sheltered low places to follow. I'll have the high ground to my back."

"Good luck."

"You too," Bart said and ended the call.

He pulled his horse to a stop, then looked over his shoulder again.

"What is it? Something wrong?" Carlos asked.

Bart dismounted his horse. "Change of plans. Nassar is being followed. I think Kenworth has set a trap."

Carlos turned to his man and relayed what Bart had said. While Carlos turned around to translate the changes, Bart retrieved his pistol from the rucksack on his horse.

Carlos got off his horse and stepped toward Bart.

Bart raised his weapon and fired, striking him in the chest before he had time to react. Then he fired again, hitting the confused, other man in the chest. His lifeless body tumbled from the horse like a sack of potatoes. Bart checked for life in Carlos's body. *Shit, still alive,* he thought.

Bart popped him again; the second shot blew a hole in his head. Certain he was dead, he turned his attention to the other man. Using the toe of his boot, he turned the body over and checked for a pulse. *Dead.*

For a moment Bart stood silent next to the man's horse and listened for any sound of movement to determine if anyone heard his suppressed shots. Hearing nothing, he removed the saddle and the bridle. Then he slapped the horse and watched it disappear into the darkness. He did the same with Carlos's horse, then stepped to the pack horse and untied the ropes securing the canvas cover on the nuke. As soon as the access door was exposed, Bart entered the time of ninety minutes, scrutinized the area, then held his gaze on the dry riverbed behind him. Satisfied no one was there, he pressed the *Enter* button, watched the counter begin the countdown, then stepped to the horse's head and removed the bridle. Keeping his hand on the horse, he slid it along as he moved to the rear, then slapped the horse's rump. As he wanted, the animal darted forward along the riverbed with the loose canvas flapping. *For you, Kenworth,* he thought. *By the time you figure out what is going on, you will cease to exist.*

Bart grabbed the reins of his horse, swung his body into the saddle, and kicked the horse. At a gallop, he raced southeast along the previously traveled route. He swatted the racing animal, trying to cover as much ground as fast as possible.

———— ✦✦✦ ————

Saturday, January 21, 2017
Captain Rowe's position
Terlingua, Texas

Max and Captain Rowe were watching Madison approach them just inside the kill box when they saw Madison stop his horses and dismount. Their view was interrupted by the shrubs and small trees growing on either side of the small crook in the dry river, and they could only see Madison when he emerged from the bushes shielding him. "I can't tell what he is doing," Max whispered. At that moment, the two men heard the three muffled shots pop in rapid succession.

"Jesus, he just shot the two men he was with!" Captain Rowe whispered.

Max lowered his night vision binoculars. "He's changing his plan. He was warned. Shit! He's not as far into the kill box as I had hoped. He's going to make a break for it."

He called David to report what he had just seen. "That's correct, Madison shot the two men with him. He's going to make a break for it. He sent the pack horse your way. I couldn't tell for sure what he did, but he may have armed the nuke. Stop the horse and get everyone to cover."

He ended the call without waiting for a response. Looking to Rowe, he said, "Quick, down to the riverbed and head off Madison. I want to take him alive if possible."

Rowe raised up as Max did, lifting his M4 carbine. Then he led the way out of sight of the riverbed and found a place to descend the ridge. Max followed right behind him. They moved as fast as they could down the slope. Rowe's footing slipped and he went down, sliding. He regained his footing and stood, darting out again.

Max also slid on the desert soil and rocks. A small tree limb slapped him, and he went down. In an instant, he got back to his feet and took after Rowe. The two of them pushed on, running, sliding, and stumbling. Dust swirled up behind them, and loose rocks seemed to race them down the slope. As they got lower and closer to the riverbed, the foliage became dense, and the two men jumped, increasing the distance of their stride as they descended.

Max pushed to get down to the riverbed as fast as he could. If Madison got there first, he would escape. No one would be between him and the border. Max looked over his shoulder and saw Madison approaching in the darkness. When they reached the bottom, Max said to Rowe as he huffed and puffed, "Take cover behind those rocks."

———— •••• ————

Saturday, January 21, 2017
Command Post
Terlingua, Texas

The radio beside David came to life again with Rowe's radio operator. "Tango 96, this is Juliette 54, over."

David picked up the mic and replied, "Juliette 54, this is Tango 96, over."

"This is Juliette 54, the target just shot the other two men with him and turned their horses loose. He accessed the load on the pack horse, but we couldn't tell what he did. He removed the horse's bridle and sent it your way. The target retreated to the southeast on his horse at a gallop."

Andy motioned to David and took the mic. "The target retreated to the southeast, correct? Do you still have eyes on him?"

"This is Juliette 54, Roger. The captain headed down the hill to intercept him, over."

"This is Tango 96, Roger, out."

David looked up to Andy. "What the hell is going on? Why's he killing his men? What is Madison doing?"

"My guess is he's not leaving any witnesses and sending the nuke to us armed. He's executing his escape plan and going to meet up with his Panamanian men. He probably doesn't know there are no survivors and he's on his own."

Lieutenant Barron reported in. "Tango 96, this is Hotel 46. I monitored the last transmission. I have eyes on the horse. It is moving toward you along the riverbed, heading northwest."

Andy replied, his voice cold and commanding. "This is Tango 96. Shoot the horse and try not to hit the load it's carrying. Make sure the horse goes down. Then have two men guard it until I can get someone there. Send the grid of the horse when it's done."

"This is Hotel 46. Understand kill the horse and report the grid. Out."

David's mouth gaped as he looked to Andy. "You want them to kill the horse?"

"Yes, David," he replied. "We can't have a horse wandering around with a nuke strapped on its back. I wish there was another way. Time is of the essence, and we don't know how much of it we have."

Gail entered the tent, followed by Danya. Andy looked to them and acknowledged their return.

"Where's Max?" Danya asked.

"He's with Captain Rowe," Andy replied.

Andy turned back to David and said, "Contact everyone and have them get their soldiers to low ground with a hill mass between them and the nuke as fast as possible. There's no telling how much time we have.

Make sure everyone gets the word and takes cover. We've got to get out of here. Grab the radio, and we'll head to the mountains to the north."

"Yes, sir."

"What's happened?" Danya asked as she stood next to Andy.

"I think Madison's armed the nuke and sent it our way on the horse."

Andy looked to Gail, "Get with the Highway Patrol and go after Nassar. Stay in touch with David. Take Danya with you."

The radio blared out again. "Tango 96, this is Hotel 46. The horse is down. Stand by for the grid."

"Hotel 46, this is Tango 96. Send it."

Lieutenant Barron replied with the grid. Andy, looking over David's shoulder, copied it down. David gave Barron the instructions to take cover.

Danya made a note of the grid and checked the coordinates on the map.

"David," Andy said as he started to take a step, "tell Barron to verify that the horse is dead. I don't want it to get up and wander off."

Overhearing the transmission, Danya walked to the corner of the tent. She picked up Max's small bag of tools and a flashlight, then started for the exit.

"Hold on, Danya," Andy said. Where are you going"?

"To disarm that fucking bomb!"

"Max wanted you to go with Gail."

"Who's going to disarm it then? You're busy here, Max is down-range, Gail is going after Nassar, and that leaves me. Save your breath, Andy. Call General Matherson and have him alert the nuclear bomb disposal team. Get me their phone number and have them stand by for my phone call."

Andy knew Danya well enough to know he was fighting a losing battle with her and there was no time for a debate. "Be careful," he said, "and good luck."

Danya exited the tent and went to an SUV. She opened the door, placed the tool bag and flashlight in the passenger seat, then got in.

"Shit, no keys." She started to get out and saw David coming toward her.

"Here's the keys," he said, handing them to her.

"Thank you." She took the keys and started the vehicle. The tires spun as she departed. Within five minutes the vehicle was bouncing along the dirt trail as she pushed to get to the location as fast as possible. The headlights penetrated the nightscape in front of her, their white beams illuminating the path ahead. The light skipped over numerous depressions until they were too close for Danya to avoid, jarring her. She worked the wheel and pedals for a little more than ten minutes when the headlights found two soldiers standing next to the carcass of a horse. She hit the brakes, and the SUV slid to a stop. She was greeted by Lieutenant Barron as soon as she got out of the vehicle. "Thank you, Lieutenant," she replied. "You and your sergeant clear out and take cover."

"Yes, ma'am. Good luck." Both soldiers turned and doubled-timed into the darkness.

Danya set the tool bag next to the horse and shined the light over the animal, examining the carcass and exterior of the load. She withdrew her knife and began cutting the remaining ropes to expose the nuke. Once the ropes were free, she inspected the canvas and cut the fabric to get it out of her way. The access door was exposed in front of her. *I need that number to the bomb, guys,* she thought. *Come on Andy.* She knelt beside the carcass, facing the cylinder. She examined the door to ensure there were no booby traps. Satisfied nothing was attached to the door, she opened it with the gentlest touch and leaned over. Her SAT phone rang, startling her. She raised up, retrieved the phone from her pocket, and said, "Yes."

"Here's the number," Andy said.

She copied the number, read it back to him, then ended the call. She punched in the numbers to the tech and waited.

A man's voice answered. "Hello, Danya. Are you ready to go to work?" His voice was calm, and he sounded pleasant.

Danya described the situation and told him what she had done so far.

"Do you have a light?"

"Yes."

"Shine it in the opening and inspect the inside."

The light beam moved to the opening. "The counter shows sixteen minutes and counting down."

"Can you send me a picture of what you see?" the technician asked.

"No, I'm on a SAT phone."

"Got it," he replied. "No problem. Remember, go slow and steady."

"Right. I'm putting you on speaker to free my hands." She placed the phone on top of the cylinder. Taking a deep breath, she exhaled slowly, leaned over and began describing every detail she saw inside. She was slow and methodical, painting a verbal picture for the tech. For almost five grueling minutes she portrayed what she saw—every detail, every component, the color of the wires, and where they were connected. Twice the technician asked her to clarify what she saw. Once Danya finished, the technician told her to look again to ensure no other wires were visible or if there was anything else she might have overlooked.

"No other wires, and I have covered everything," she said. "The counter shows eleven minutes."

Sensing tension in her voice, he said, "Sounds good. Let's pause for a moment, take a deep breath, and relax. We're doing fine."

She raised up and took in a deep breath of the cool night air. As she exhaled, she thought of Max and what he was doing. *I hope you are all right.*

"OK, I am ready," she said. Then she leaned over and shined the light into the opening. "There are nine minutes on the counter."

"We have lots of time," he replied. "Now we're going to cut the wires. Do you have a pair of wire cutters?"

"Yes, I have them."

"First thing, I want you to ground yourself. Rub both hands on the ground to get rid of any static electricity."

"OK, done. Next?"

"Now move to the metal surrounding the warhead. Without touching any of the components, place your cutters on the red wire and cut it."

Danya was in an odd and uncomfortable position, so she shifted her body and lay on her side. As she picked up the wire cutters, she saw the slight shake of her hand. "Just a minute," she said. Setting the tool down, she relaxed and stretched her arms. Taking a deep breath, then exhaling, she cleared her mind. A moment later she said, "OK, I'm ready." Picking up the cutters, and with the delicate touch of a surgeon, she grasped the red wire between the jaws, and held her breath. The wire came free with a slight snap. "OK, I've cut the wire. The counter is still ticking down."

"The blue wire goes to the counter, correct?"

"Correct."

"Place your cutters around the blue wire and cut it."

"Done. The counter is out."

"Good. I want you to inspect all around the inside for any concealed wires, then look on the outside."

Danya shined the light into the opening and did as he instructed. Then she examined the exterior. She reported back to the technician that no other wires were found.

The technician instructed Danya to remove two components she had identified earlier, then to cut two other wires.

"Well, Danya, that does it," he said. "It didn't go off, so I guess it's safe."

Danya rolled onto her back and sighed. She didn't hear his sigh. With a slight quiver in her voice, she said, "I take it that's a little bomb technician humor."

He laughed. "I guess it is."

"Thank you," she said. "Can you notify the courier officer to pick this thing up?"

"I will. I'll have him contact you at this number."

"Thank you again."

Danya ended the call, then punched in the number to Andy. When he answered, she said, "It's been disarmed and is safe. Can you get a couple of soldiers to guard this thing?"

"I'll see to it," he replied. "Stay there and guard it until I can get them to relieve you."

——— • ♦ • ———

Saturday, January 21, 2017
Dry River Bed South of FM 170
Terlingua, Texas

From behind the rocks, Max and Rowe tried to minimize their exposure as they remained motionless. Watching as the charging horse advanced, Max whispered, "Shoot the horse."

Rowe eased onto his M4 and took a good sight picture.

Madison was leaning forward on the mount, kicking and swatting it with the reins. The horse's nostrils flared, and the hot breath shot from its mouth in a cloud of mist in the cool air. The racing animal complied with all its might to obey the master. Then, all of a sudden, Madison raised up, pulled back on the reins, and tugged them to the right to turn the horse.

"He's seen us and is going around," Max said. "Fire!"

Just as the horse began to step up on the raised edge of the riverbed, Captain Rowe fired. The horse faltered and went down. Madison reacted and pulled the reins, but the animal would not respond and landed on its side. Madison fell from the horse, landing a few feet from his rucksack. The wounded steed was between him and the shooter. Using the animal as cover, he crawled to retrieve his pistol. He fished out the Sig Sauer and anticipated a confrontation with his nemesis.

Watching the mount go down, Max, with his pistol in his hand, was up and running toward it, with Rowe trailing a few feet behind. Just as Max got to the horse, it struggled to get up. "Give it up, Madison!" He said aloud, seeing him behind the animal. "Surrender."

A shot rang out. Captain Rowe fell to the ground, rolled, and took aim on Madison. Feeling the sting of the bullet in his left arm, Max took a quick aim and fired two shots in rapid succession. The first of the 230 grain, .45 caliber bullets hit Madison in the chest, and the second hit him in the head. His face plowed into the desert.

Captain Rowe stood, looked at Max, and asked, "Are you OK, sir?"

"I took one in the arm."

Looking at Max's bleeding arm, Rowe withdrew his field dressing and place it around the wound.

As soon as Captain Rowe finished with the bandage, Max retrieved his SAT phone and punched in the number to David. "Madison is dead," he said. "Where's the nuke?"

"It has been rendered safe," he replied.

Max let out a sigh of relief. "Did Lieutenant Barron disarm it?"

"No." David paused, then replied. "Danya did."

"Danya? Well, that's not a big surprise. Send me the grid of where it is. I'll stop there before I return to your location."

He ended the call as soon as he received the grid location.

—— • ◆ • ——

Saturday, January 21, 2017
Dark Canyon Road
Terlingua, Texas

Gail, leading the Highway Patrol, had turned onto Dark Canyon Road, which was blocked by other state troopers. They found the sedan one-and-a-half miles north on the old dirt road. It had rolled over on one of the curves. The Highway Patrol determined it was going too fast for the conditions and the driver lost control. There was blood in the vehicle, but no driver.

After a search of the area, the SUV was seen on a small trail a half mile north. After inspecting the vehicle, Gail saw some old ruins a hundred meters further up the road, and there were footprints leading to it. She directed the troopers to surround the remnants of the structure.

Lights were directed into the rubble, and Gail saw a man move. "This is the FBI," she called out. "Come out with your hands up." She waited in silence for a few moments, then repeated her demand. "This is the FBI. Come out with your hands up."

A Hispanic man made his way out of the ruins. He was holding his left shoulder, and blood streaked his head. "Don't shoot! I cannot raise my left arm." The small man raised his right arm. A shot sounded from within the ruins. Sensing that he was being shot at, the man crouched and began running. Gail and several of the policemen returned fire into the structure.

"Quick! Come down the path to the moving light," Gail said as one of the troopers moved his light in a circular motion. When he reached the light, a trooper took charge of him. The trooper determined the man had a broken collarbone. "Who was in there with you?" Gail asked.

"A man named Nassar," he replied.

"Is there anyone else?"

The man shook his head.

Gail looked back to the rubble. "Nassar, come out unarmed with your hands up." With her pistol raised, she watched where the first man emerged. Soon a figure appeared with his arms raised. In his right hand was a pistol.

A step past the ruins, he dropped his arm and began firing at the lights. Gail crouched, fired twice, and the man crumpled to the ground. "Shit! I wanted him alive. Dead men feel no pain." She retrieved her SAT phone and called David. "Yes, Sweet Pea, I am all right. Nassar is dead. The other man with him is in custody. What's the status there?"

"Oh, *dahling*," he replied, his voice gleeful. "Everything is fine. Danya disarmed the bomb and Max shot Madison. Max is wounded."

"Max was wounded! How bad is it?"

"He's OK. He was hit in the arm."

"That's good news. I will be heading back there in a little bit." Gail ended the call.

# CHAPTER 30

Sunday, January 22, 2017
Command Post
Terlingua, Texas

T HE SUN WAS just peeking over the mountains when everyone had been accounted for and had returned to the command post. Captain Rowe and his men returned to their bivouac site. Lieutenant Colonel Johnston invited them to his location, but they chose theirs instead. Getting as much sleep as possible was everyone's priority, as they knew they would only get a few hours.

Danya had insisted that Max be taken to the hospital for his gunshot wound. Big Bend Regional Medical Center in Alpine, eighty-five miles away, was the nearest one. The wound to his arm was determined to be a flesh wound, and he was admitted. The doctors wanted to keep him for several days to guard against infection and provide pain management, but he persuaded the doctors to allow him to return to Tampa and go to the base hospital at MacDill on Monday.

Lieutenant Colonel Johnston had directed that all the bodies and equipment be checked for possible intelligence. Although they were searched the night before, he wanted an additional search during the daylight. The soldiers recovered phones, maps, weapons, and miscellaneous identification. The most important items recovered were the phones from Bart Madison and Carlos, along with their maps. Very little else was found on them. All of the bodies were photographed, and DNA was collected.

Johnston made arrangements for the soldiers to return to their home station as soon as the courier officer took possession of the nuke. The officer was due to arrive by 1300 hours. All of the evidence recovered by the soldiers was collected at the command post for further processing by DIA. The Rangers were to meet their aircraft at the Alpine Airport.

After four hours of sleep, Gail was up, looking none the worse for wear. She ran her hand over her hair in a futile attempt to look somewhat alive and began making coffee. Her eyes landed on David, who was still asleep. *I hate sleeping on a cot,* she thought. *I think David can sleep anywhere.*

Lieutenant Colonel Johnston entered the tent carrying a thermos. Stopping in front of Gail, he motioned with the bottle in his hand and said, "Want some coffee?"

"God yes! I need some."

As he filled her cup, Johnston said, "I got it from the Rangers. It's probably a little stronger than your normal cup."

She sipped the hot brew. "Whew, that is a bit stout. I needed this." Her phone rang. She picked it up from the small table and looked at the number.

"Hello, Marion."

"What the hell is going on?" Captain Mackenzie said, his tone harsh. "I haven't heard from you in over a week. The Mayor and Chief are chewing on my ass. I need…"

"Marion, do you know how to say, good morning? How are you? What is going on in your world? Or something pleasant to start out with? Even, 'I miss you' would be something."

He took a deep breath before he replied. "OK, Summers. Good morning. How's your day going?"

"That didn't hurt, did it? Thank you for asking. I've been up about fifteen minutes and I'm just now having my first coffee. Colonel Johnston brought me a cup, and I think it'll eat the enamel off my teeth, but I need it."

"Where are you now?"

"I'm in Terlingua, Texas."

"Where the hell's that?"

"West Texas, Big Bend Country."

"What's the latest on your terrorist, Madison?"

"He and the Zetas guy with him were killed last night. Nassar, Madison's accomplice, was also killed. I'll send you a copy of my report."

"You've made my day. I got a bit of news for you."

Gail sipped her coffee. "What is it?"

"Jenny Gareth is dead. Her body was found yesterday floating in her pool. The coroner's report shows a high level of alcohol and fentanyl in her blood. The cause of death is listed as accidental. She was dead before she went into the water. We found a Scotch bottle with the drug in it, but no prints other than hers. The only thing I have to go on is her phone records show two calls from a burner phone. I don't believe it. Several things don't add up, but I can't prove it wasn't an accident."

"Thank you, Marion. Now I can really enjoy this coffee. I'm heading back to Tampa this afternoon. Talk to you later." Gail ended the call and sat at the desk.

Johnston stepped to where David was sleeping and started to wake him.

"Let him sleep," Gail said. Then she took another sip of her coffee.

# EPILOGUE

Saturday, February 18, 2017
Damaged House
Raqqa, Syria

A S A RESULT of the failed mission and death of Bart Madison and
Nassar, Dawud Al'alim called for a meeting with Abdal al-Ghazāli
and other top lieutenants of the Muslim Brotherhood. They were to meet
in the damaged city, located on the northeast bank of the Euphrates
River, 160 kilometers east of Aleppo, at the same house where they met
in December. ISIS declared Raqqa the capital of the Islamic State just
after it was captured in January 2014. The caliph of the Islamic State,
al-Baghdadi, was anticipated to be at the meeting. However, at the last
minute, al-Baghdadi sent word to Al'alim that he was delayed and would
not make it to the council.

Soon after the phones of Madison and Nassar were received by
DIA, phone numbers of the Muslim Brotherhood representatives were
discovered, and NSA targeted the numbers of the two men. Learning
of the meeting of the Brotherhood in Raqqa, a strike on the house was
planned. At 0200 hours a MQ-9 Reaper launched two AGM-114 Hellfire
missiles, destroying the house. An Elite Special Forces team entered
the rubble and confirmed all inhabitants were killed. They identified the
remains and photographed and took DNA samples of the bodies. It was
confirmed that Dawud Al'alim and Abdal al-Ghazāli were among the
casualties.

Lieutenant Colonel Johnston, through his contacts at DIA, learned
that the CIA was looking into the background of Stew Gareth right after
he died. Henry Colby was not nominated for the director of CIA position

and was under investigation for his involvement with Stew Gareth and Nassar, the Muslim Brotherhood representative.

———— ∙ ♦ ∙ ————

Friday, April 28, 2017
Siesta Key
Sarasota, Florida

Max and Danya sat in lounge chairs beneath a colorful umbrella on the beach. The midmorning sun was high in the clear blue sky, promising a beautiful day. The temperature was forecast to be eighty-eight degrees. Three sailboats cruised in the distance, and a couple of powerboats bounced across the water as they raced along. The popular beach was filling with people. Some were stretched out soaking up the sun; several strolled along the beach; others played in the seventy-seven-degree water; and many others lounged under umbrellas. Danya dug her feet into the quartz sand and grasped Max's hand.

"We made the right decision," she said. "I could spend the rest of my life right here."

While Max was recovering in the hospital, he and Danya planned for a future together. If they were to be together, they had to retire. Danya had returned to Panama soon after Max was released from the hospital and filed her reports on the terrorists. Then she submitted her retirement paperwork. Max completed his retirement paperwork soon after.

They planned a retirement party at the beach. Their friends from their offices, with guests, were invited. Those who had arrived with their guests the afternoon before included Thaddeus Nussbaum, Danya's boss from Panama; a couple of her colleagues from Panama and one from Israel; Lieutenant Colonel Johnston; Helen; David; Gail; and Captain M. Taner Mackenzie. Major General Matheson and his wife were expected that morning.

Gail, dragging two lounge chairs, was followed by Captain Mackenzie, who was pulling an ice chest and umbrella across the sand. Arriving next to Max, Gail placed her chairs next to him while Mackenzie placed the umbrella in the sand. "That's a hell of a walk across the beach," Gail said, stretching out her shapely legs and adjusting her wide-brimmed hat.

Max nodded as he listened to the turquoise water lap the powdery white sand. Both he and Danya were immersed in the tropical beauty.

"Did you see this article in *Newsweek*?" Gail asked, offering the magazine to Max.

"No, what's it about?"

"It's an article about the Gareth Foundation and the great man who died much too early. It goes on to talk about his wonderful wife, Jenny, and how her life was cut short by a tragic accident."

"Not interested. We've put that world behind us."

"I haven't seen David," she said as she dropped the magazine into her bag. "Have you?"

"He and the young lady with him went with Andy and his wife parasailing. That's probably them out there." He pointed to a boat in the distance pulling two parasailers.

Gail turned her head toward Mackenzie. "I think it's time for a drink, Marion."

He opened the cooler, scooped ice into two cups, and handed them to her. "Hold these," he said. Then he withdrew a thermos and filled the cups.

Danya leaned over and said, "Don't forget your sunscreen."

Gail held up her cup to Danya in acknowledgment. "Marion will take care of that."

# DID YOU ENJOY READING *WRATH AND RECKONING?*

Please take a quick moment to let everyone know by posting a review at your favorite online bookstore. Your feedback will mean the world to me, and I will be forever grateful.

Best Regards,

Patrick Parker

# ABOUT THE AUTHOR

Patrick Parker received his bachelor's degree in management and his master's degree in international relations. Patrick was commissioned in the Field Artillery and served in assignments in the United States, Europe, and Panama. After retiring from the military, he spent an additional fifteen years working in the defense industry. Now retired again, Patrick enjoys writing, astronomy, traveling, and going to the gun range. He lives in Texas.

# ACKNOWLEDGMENTS

A big thank you to my wife and best friend, Carole, for your confidence and support. You have been my best critic and provided invaluable input.

New Braunfels Writers Guild—Deborah Ellison, Don Burquest, Dr. Lefter Baklas, James Whelpley, and Lewis Sarkozi. You are a great group and helped me to bring my story to life. Through the many writings, critiques, edits and rewrites, thank you. I appreciate your candor, support and confidence.

Scott Kotowski—F-16 pilot with over 1600 hours in Iraq and other locations overseas and currently a pilot for FedEx Express. Thank you for your input and attention to detail of the F-16 Viper and Air Force. My go-to person on the Air Force and the F-16. Harrumph!! Thank you.

Bob Sabasteanski, a big thank you for your critique, suggestions, and attention to detail. You have provided a reality check and you are a great weapons expert.

Debra L. Hartmann, a superb editor! Your professionalism and dedication on this story took it to the next level. You are a great person to work with and you kept me straight.

Thank you, all!

# BOOKS BY PATRICK PARKER

www.ingramcontent.com/pod-product-compliance
Lightning Source LLC
Chambersburg PA
CBHW020823260626
47169CB00003B/810